Before becoming a novelist **Tatiana March** tried various occupations—including being a chambermaid and an accountant. Now she loves writing Western historical romance. In the course of her research Tatiana has been detained by the US border guards, had a skirmish with the Mexican army, and stumbled upon a rattlesnake. This has not diminished her determination to create authentic settings for her stories.

THE OUTLAW
AND THE RUNAWAY

Tatiana March

This book is produced from independently certified FSC™ paper
to ensure responsible forest management.

For more information visit www.harpercollins.co.uk/green.

Printed and bound in Spain
by CPI, Barcelona

MILLS & BOON

First Published in Great Britain 2018
by Mills & Boon, an imprint of HarperCollins*Publishers*
1 London Bridge Street, London, SE1 9GF

© 2018 Tatiana March

ISBN: 978-0-263-93286-7

Chapter One

Arizona Territory, 1882

Rock Springs was no different from other Western towns Roy Hagan had seen. Perhaps the single thoroughfare was shabbier than most, the signs over the stores a little more faded. The bank stood at the northern end, just before the boardwalk started. A square building of adobe brick, it had three tall windows that glinted in the midday sun, however the frosted glass prevented prying eyes from seeing inside.

Roy rode past the bank, reined his buckskin to a halt outside the mercantile and dismounted. The two men with him, Zeke Davies and Joe Saldana, also got off their horses.

After tying their mounts to the hitching rail, all three men stepped up to the boardwalk, boots thudding in an unhurried cadence. Saldana wore

Mexican spurs with big rowels that made an arrogant jangle as he walked. All three wore their hats pulled low and long dusters that covered their gun belts.

"You stay here," Roy ordered, talking in a guarded voice that carried no more than a whisper. "Roll a smoke, light up. Keep your eyes on the street. Count the number of people you see—men, women, children. Pay extra attention to anyone who goes into the bank."

The other two nodded. Neither of them spoke.

"I'll check out the store," Roy went on. "Then I'll come back outside and we'll sit down over there." He gestured at a timber bench near the saloon entrance. "I'll go into the saloon, buy three glasses of beer and bring them out. For an hour, we laugh and joke while we survey the town. We don't get drunk. We don't get into arguments. If anyone approaches us, we'll be friendly and polite. Is that clear?"

His associates nodded again. Saldana was tall and thin, with a droopy mustache and a long, pointed chin. Davies was compact and muscular, with a square face that gave him the belligerent air of a bulldog. Roy hardly knew either of the pair. All but one of his former associates had been shot to pieces while robbing a train in New Mexico a few months ago. Roy and the only other survivor, Dale Hunter, had taken refuge in the maze of canyons between Utah and Arizona, where they had drifted into joining the Red Bluff Gang.

Most of the outlaws in the gang had a bounty on their head and only left their remote hideout to do a job. Roy had no wanted poster out on him, for despite his distinctive looks he'd never been identified in the course of a robbery. The lack of notoriety served him well, for it allowed him to ride from town to town, scouting out potential targets.

Alert and tense, Roy cast another glance along the somnolent street. A stray dog lay panting in the shade of the water trough by the hitching rail. A tall man in a leather apron had stepped out of the barbershop and stood on the boardwalk, drinking coffee from a china mug. Somewhere in the distance, a woman's voice was calling for a child to come inside and eat.

Satisfied everything remained peaceful, Roy turned around and strode in through the open doorway of the mercantile. As he stepped up to the counter, he kept his hands pressed against the unbuttoned edges of his duster to stop the garment from flaring wide and exposing his pair of Smith & Wesson revolvers.

Inside the store, homely scents—coffee, peppermint, lamp oil—tugged at some distant corners of his memory. Roy crushed the sudden yearning for a normal, peaceful life. He would enjoy the few moments he could glimpse into that long-forgotten world and discard any pointless dreams of making it his again.

Behind the store counter, the elderly clerk climbed down from the ladder he'd used to stack bolts of calico on the higher shelves. He jumped down the last step, turned toward Roy and greeted him with a polite nod. "Good afternoon, sir. How can I help you?"

Alert and nimble despite his advanced years, the clerk appeared prosperous. His white shirt was pristine, his sparse hair neatly combed, the lenses of his steel wire spectacles sparkling. A man who took pride in himself and his profession. Roy felt another stab of regret, accompanied by some vague emotion that might have been shame.

"Matches," he said. "In a waterproof tin."

"Certainly, sir."

While the clerk bustled about, taking a small metal box from a drawer and filling it with wooden phosphorus matches, Roy felt a prickle at the back of his neck. Slowly, he shifted on his feet. His right hand eased to the pistol hidden beneath his duster, while his left hand went to the brim of his hat, making the twisting motion appear natural as he turned sideways to survey the store.

Between the aisles of merchandise, a young woman had paused in her task of sweeping the floor, and now she stood still, fingers clasped around the long handle of the broom. Medium height, middle twenties, she wore a faded green dress that revealed a full figure with feminine curves. Her hair was light brown, with a touch of gold where it had been exposed to the sun. From the few strands that fluttered free from her up-sweep, Roy could tell her hair would pull into a riot of curls if left unconfined.

He tugged at the brim of his hat. "Ma'am."

Still and silent, the girl stared at him from the corner of her eye, not facing him squarely. Roy's posture stiffened. He was used to women staring at him, but there was something different in this girl's perusal.

Usually, women stared at him with a mix of pity and curiosity, wondering what damage he might be hiding beneath the black patch that covered his left eye. Some studied him with un-disguised feminine interest, drawn by the thick waves of golden hair and the vivid blue of his single eye, fascinated by the contrast they made with the air of danger that surrounded him, hinting at his outlaw status, even while his pair of guns remained out of sight.

A fallen angel, a saloon girl had once called him.

But he could detect no pity in this girl's expression, and neither did he sense the invitation some women conveyed through their bold inspection. She was contemplating him with a hopeful, earnest look, as if in him she might have recognized a missing relation, or perhaps some long-lost friend.

But it could not be.

Roy knew it couldn't. He had no family, and no friends, except perhaps Dale Hunter. Could he have met her before? It was uncommon for a sporting girl to reform, but even that possibility Roy was able to rule out, for he could remember each one of the few women he had ever followed into an upstairs room.

Silently cursing in his mind, Roy returned his attention to the elderly store clerk and paid for his tin of matches. It might be a problem about the girl. Someone who had stared at him with such intensity might remember his features, could furnish a lawman with a description.

Too bad, Roy thought as he strolled back out to the boardwalk, however it was bound to happen one day. He couldn't expect to remain unknown forever—not since he had joined the Red Bluff Gang and was forced to take an active part in the raids. Earlier, before his former outfit got wiped out, his role had been limited to training horses for the robbers, but now both he and Dale Hunter had sunk one notch deeper into the outlaw life.

* * *

During the week that followed, twice more Roy rode into town and stopped at the mercantile. The first time the girl was nowhere to be seen, but from behind the aisles Roy could hear the rustle of skirts and the soft clatter of feminine footsteps.

A few moments later, while he was loitering outside on the boardwalk with his associates, Roy noticed the girl staring at him through the big plate glass window of the mercantile. Again, she kept her face averted, slanting a sideways look at him.

Roy couldn't figure out what bothered him about the girl so much. It was not just the allure of a pretty female with the kind of figure that could send a man's blood boiling in his veins. Neither was it the danger she posed, in terms of recognizing him.

It was those strange looks she was sending him.

As if they knew each other.

As if they had something in common.

The second time Roy returned to the store, the elderly clerk was alone, with no other customers to overhear the conversation. Roy bought a bag of Arbuckle's roasted coffee beans. As he dug in his pocket for coins, he spoke in a casual tone.

"The girl who works here, she your daughter?"

The clerk snapped to attention. "Celia Court-wood?"

"The girl with light brown hair."

"That's Miss Courtwood," the clerk replied. "No kin to me. I employ her a few hours a week to tidy up the shelves." The old man took down his glasses and pretended to polish them with a cloth he tugged out of his breast pocket. Intent on the task, he spoke with a mixture of embarrassment and eagerness. "She needs a husband, in case you might be interested. Her pa is poorly. Between you and me, I think that's why they came out West. Hoped it would be easier for her to find a husband out here."

"I'm a drifter," Roy pointed out. "I have no use for a wife."

"Every man has at least one use for a wife." The clerk took the silver dollar Roy handed out and made change, ill at ease, but something—the urge to help the girl, Roy suspected—kept him talking. "She's a lady, Miss Courtwood, mark my words. Don't let the people in town tell you any different. They're just a bunch of narrow-minded fools."

Puzzled, Roy picked up his purchase and walked out of the store. He had to fight the temptation to find out more, to discover what circumstances could give rise to such bold hints and veiled comments about the girl's reputation in the community. However, it wouldn't do to ask too many questions, attract unnecessary attention.

And yet, as Roy stood on the boardwalk, pretending to be engaged in conversation with his associates while they surveyed the bank, the old man's comments kept turning over in his mind. Why would a pretty girl like Miss Courtwood struggle to find a husband? And what could the townsfolk possibly have against her? Most of all, what could be the reason why she kept stealing those secretive, somehow hopeful looks at him?

Her heart racing, her face flushed with excitement, Celia hurried home to the small frame house along a dusty side street. He'd come back again, that man with a patch over his left eye. She'd assumed he was just passing through, but perhaps he was planning to settle in the area, and she'd have a chance to get to know him.

Even as the prospect formed in her thoughts, Celia knew it to be a false hope. The man bore the stamp of lawlessness, guns concealed beneath his long duster, his single eye sweeping his surroundings with the alert tension of a hunted animal. Deep down, Celia had an inkling why he'd come into town, but she refused to accept the idea.

Unconsciously, she lifted a hand to the scar on her cheek. Despite his disability, the young man seemed so confident, so—so *whole*. How did he do it? How did he find the inner strength to ignore the curious stares, to shrug off the pitying glances? She longed to learn his secret, to discover the key that might allow her to tell everyone in town to go to hell, which was where they deserved to be.

Letting the heels of her half boots ring out her anger at the citizens of Rock Springs, Celia clattered up the porch steps and let herself in. The front door opened directly to a parlor furnished with sagging armchairs and crammed bookcases they had purchased with the house. The books had turned out to be a treasure trove, one of the few things that gave her pleasure in this place that had wrecked her hopes.

In the kitchen, Celia stirred the embers in the big cast-iron stove and got a meal started, oatmeal gruel with tinned milk. The bland fare was one of the few things her father could eat without retching, the tumor in his belly having ruined his appetite.

By the time Papa came home, Celia had the table set, with a posy of wildflowers decorating the center. Long walks in the desert were another source of pleasure, something that allowed her to leave her worries behind for a few hours at a time.

As Celia watched her father shuffle into the kitchen and take his seat, a shaft of despair pierced her carefully maintained shield of courage. All his vitality was gone, leaving a thin husk of a man, with sparse brown curls and ashen skin.

For as long as she could remember, sickness had been part of her life, first seeing her frail mother succumb to one ailment after another, and now witnessing her father slowly fade away.

But even in his weakened state, Papa managed an encouraging smile at her. "Celia girl, are you all set for the church social on Sunday?"

Celia curled her nervous fingers into the cotton apron she wore to protect her threadbare gown. "Papa, it's no use…"

"Make your fried chicken," her father prompted. "Nobody makes it better."

The reproach in his tone caused Celia's sense of helplessness to flare into frustration, and she spoke more sharply than she had intended. "Papa, at a box lunch, men don't pay to eat. They pay to court a girl."

"You've got to keep trying, Celia girl."

There was such anguish in her father's eyes, such fear for her future in his manner, it added to Celia's list of woes. She wanted to tell him their only solution was to go away—to leave Rock Springs and move into some other town—but no business would employ a man in her father's state of health. The bank manager was only keeping him on because dismissing a dying man might be seen as a callous act that could cost him the goodwill of his customers.

Moreover, Celia knew Papa lacked the strength

for a new start. He loved the house, the books, the quiet town and the few friends who had yet to desert him on her account. Ever since Papa had learned his days were numbered, he'd been looking for a place to die in peace, and she could not wrench him away from what he had found in Rock Springs.

Celia sighed in resignation and straightened her spine. She'd not been to a church social since she fell out of grace with the town, but how bad could it be? So far, their only weapon against her had been rejection and ugly whispers. *Sticks and stones will break my bones, but words will never harm me*, she reminded herself—a gem of wisdom gleaned from one of the old issues of the *Christian Recorder* she'd found in the bookcase.

"I'll try, Papa," Celia promised, and made an effort to sound positive. "I'll make my fried chicken, and I'll wear my blue dress and put rouge over my scar."

Camped by a creek a mile outside town, Roy Hagan stood beneath the morning sun and dictated a message to Zeke Davies, to be delivered to Lom Curtis, the leader of the outlaw gang. It would be too risky to put the information in writing, in case Davies caught the attention of a lawman and the note was discovered.

"We'll need six men," Roy repeated, drilling

in the information. "Three in the bank and three outside. We'll hit at noon. The ranchers come into town in the morning, the miners in the evening for the saloon. Midday is the quietest, and the bank does not close for lunch."

Bulldog features furrowed in concentration, Davies memorized the details. After a week of constant companionship, Roy had learned to know his associates. Davies was slow-witted and liked to follow orders, grateful that some other man had done the thinking.

"Saldana and I will ride over to Prescott and wait there," Roy went on. "Tell Curtis to telegraph me at the Western Union office there, to let us know when he plans to arrive."

Lom Curtis, the leader of the Red Bluff Gang, had an inside contact, someone who would let him know when Wells Fargo was due to collect the gold the miners in the region deposited at the bank. The gang would time their raid just before the next collection, when the amount of gold in the bank's vault would be at its greatest.

Davies rehearsed the message a few more times, got on his sorrel and trotted off. Roy kept an eye on the man until the trail took him out of sight behind a rise. Then he turned to Saldana. The lanky Mexican was crouching beside the dying campfire, trimming his droopy mustache and admiring the result in the small mirror he carried in his vest pocket.

"We'll ride into town," Roy told him. "I want to see how many people come to the Sunday service. It'll give us an idea of how big a posse they might be able to put together."

Saldana gave his reflection one final perusal and put the mirror away. Roy had learned that the tall, lithe outlaw came from a good family in Tucson. After a secret tryst with a judge's daughter, trumped-up charges of rape had forced Saldana to choose between the hangman's rope and a life on the wrong side of the law. To Roy's surprise, Saldana showed no bitterness and had not been cured of his womanizing ways.

They broke camp, carefully sweeping the ground and burying the coals to hide the signs of their stay before getting on their horses. Roy rode a buckskin, a color that blended in with the desert scenery. Saldana put vanity before safety and rode a gleaming black stallion, useful for a night raid but easy to spot during a daylight getaway.

In town, a collection of buggies and carts and saddle horses stood outside the small, unpainted lumber church. Roy signaled to Saldana and they drew their mounts to a halt. People were streaming out of the church and congregating on a flat piece of ground where a few women were already bustling around a pair of trestle tables laden with food and stacked with baskets decorated with ribbons and bows.

"It's a church social," Saldana said, an eager glint in his dark eyes. He smoothed the ends of his mustache. "There'll be women. Dancing."

"No," Roy told him. "It's too dangerous."

"Even more dangerous to keep away," Saldana countered. "Men ride a hundred miles for a church social. It will look suspicious if we turn away."

Saldana was right, Roy had to concede. To reassure the town about their presence, they had put out a rumor that they'd been employed as security guards for a freight line out of Denver and were now drifting south, enjoying their leisure time until their money ran out. Those kinds of men—honest men—would feel entitled to take part in the festivities.

While Roy mulled over the dilemma, his attention fell on a girl in a blue dress. It was a different dress, and she wore a wide-brimmed bonnet to match, but no dress could hide those feminine curves, and no bonnet could confine that riot of curls.

Celia Courtwood. Her image had filled his thoughts at night, while he lay awake listening to the ripple of the creek by the camp. Why this particular female had stuck in his mind like a burr might stick to the shaggy winter coat of a horse, Roy could not figure out. He tried to tell himself it was the danger she posed, in terms of recognizing him, but he knew it to be a lie.

Watching the girl through his uncovered blue eye, Roy fought the conflicting impulses to ride away as fast as he could and to stay, to seek an opportunity to talk to her.

"All right," he finally said with a glance at Saldana. "But don't draw attention to yourself. Keep your guns hidden."

They dismounted and adjusted their heavy canvas dusters to make sure their pistols remained out of sight. Instead of tying their horses to the hitching rail outside the church, they picketed them at the edge of the grassy meadow beyond the clearing and walked over to join the crowd.

A few people darted curious looks in their direction as they came to stand on the outskirts of the throng, but most had their attention on a portly man with muttonchop sideburns and a bowler hat, who had taken up position behind one of the trestle tables.

The man banged a gavel against the timber top to demand silence. "Welcome all, friends and strangers alike," he boomed. "I'll just remind you of the rules. Each lady will hold up her luncheon basket and describe the contents. Gentlemen will bid, and the winner gets to share the luncheon with the lady. Bidding starts at twenty-five cents.

No bidding over five dollars. All funds go to the church maintenance fund."

A box lunch.

Roy had heard of those, but he'd never attended one. Another wave of regret washed over him. Living in the isolation of an outlaw camp since the age of fourteen, he'd never had a chance to court a girl. Apart from prostitutes, the only females he knew were Big Kate and Miss Gabriela who belonged to the men in the Red Bluff Gang.

Curious, Roy watched as the portly gentleman behind the trestle table gestured toward a gaggle of blushing young females who stood behind him, fluttering like a flock of brightly colored birds. A slender blonde in a frilly pink dress stepped forward, picked up a basket from the table and held it up. "Meat and potato pie and raspberry crumble."

A short man in a brown suit instantly bid five dollars. Beaming with pride, the girl moved aside and another one took her place. Mostly, the picnic baskets went for a couple of dollars. An odd restlessness settled over Roy as he watched Celia Courtwood. She was standing slightly apart from the others, looking increasingly fraught as the auction progressed and the group of girls thinned out.

Finally, only one basket remained on the table. The auctioneer glanced around, preparing to wrap up the proceedings and put his gavel down, but a gaunt man with pale skin called for him to wait and hurried over to Celia. With an agitated whisper, he ushered the girl toward the trestle table.

Attempting a smile, she picked up the last remaining basket and held it up. "Fried chicken and apple pie."

The man with muttonchop sideburns squirmed. Like water rippling across a pond, the entire crowd turned to stare at a tall man dressed in black. The preacher, Roy assumed, and for whatever reason the reverend ignored the questioning glances of his congregation. Silence fell, so thick Roy could hear the crunching of gravel beneath two dozen pairs of boots and shoes as people shifted nervously on their feet.

At the front of the crowd, Celia stood forlorn, her head turned aside. Beneath the brim of her bonnet Roy could see a smear of rouge on her cheeks, evidence of a clumsy effort to appear more attractive. She blinked to hold back the tears but Roy feared they would soon start falling. A slow burn of anger flickered into flame in his gut.

What was wrong with everyone? Why didn't anyone bid?

He craned his neck, peering over the forest of hats and bonnets in front of him for a better view, planning to call out twenty-five cents to get the bidding started. Surely, someone would follow his lead? Surely, one of the others would be gentlemanly enough to put the poor girl out of her misery?

Roy raised his hand, opened his mouth. "Five dollars!"

It came out of nowhere, through no conscious thought. Beside him, Saldana muttered a curse. A hush went through the crowd. Celia looked up from beneath the brim of her bonnet. Her eyes were tear-bright, but she straightened her spine and lifted her chin.

"Sir, do not seek amusement at my expense."

"I'm not seeking amusement," Roy replied calmly. "I'm seeking to eat, and I'm partial to fried chicken and apple pie."

"Stranger, what's your name?" the auctioneer called out.

"That's for the lady to know," Roy replied. He shouldered his way through the throng, came to a halt in front of Celia and held out his hand. After a moment of hesitation, she lowered the wicker basket to the crook of her elbow to free one hand and slipped her fingers into his. Roy could tell her hand was shaking. He tightened his hold, seeking to reassure her as he escorted her to the grassy meadow where the other girls and their suitors had already spread out their picnic blankets.

"Wait here," he told her.

He strode off, waving for Saldana to follow. The tall Mexican was grinning and shaking his head, making *tut-tut* noises, like an old woman. When they reached their horses, Roy gave his buckskin, Dagur, a reassuring pat on the neck and took down a blanket from his bedroll.

"Don't draw attention," Saldana complained.

"All right," Roy admitted. "It was a stupid mistake."

And yet he couldn't regret what he had done. The girl was a puzzle he wanted to solve. And witnessing her misery had tugged at something inside him, some faint remnant of sentimentality and compassion. He knew what it felt like to be ostracized, to be treated like an outcast. Whatever transgressions the girl might have committed, she didn't deserve such a public humiliation.

"What do you want me to do?" Saldana asked.

Roy hesitated. The sensible thing would be to escort the girl home and ride away before the townspeople had a chance to get a closer look at him, but doing the sensible thing seemed to be eluding him today. "Take the horses to the water trough by the saloon and make sure they drink their fill. I won't be long. Half an hour at the most. Then we'll leave, head north toward Prescott."

Saldana's narrow face puckered in dismay. "No dancing?"

"No dancing," Roy replied, and tried to mollify the Mexican by appealing to his vanity. "You're too handsome. The ladies would remember you."

Saldana smirked, tapped his eyebrow to indicate the black patch Roy wore over his left eye—a feature far more memorable than a neatly trimmed moustache or a seductive smile.

"My eye patch don't matter," Roy told him. "You'll understand later."

He left Saldana to deal with the horses and returned to the girl. She was sitting on the ground, arms wrapped around her upraised knees, watching him stride over. Roy spread out the blanket beside her, gestured for the girl to move onto it and settled opposite her, one leg stretched out, the other bent at the knee, the hems of his long duster flaring about him.

"Thank you," the girl said. She started to unpack the contents of her basket. "It was a gallant thing to do, to rescue me from standing out there like a convict in front of a firing squad." She kept her face averted, the words spoken barely loud enough for Roy to hear.

Not wasting any time, he got on with solving the puzzle she presented. "Why didn't anyone else bid? What do the townsfolk have against you?"

The girl didn't reply. She merely handed him a piece of fried chicken wrapped in a linen napkin and refused to meet his gaze. At her reticence, Roy let his irritation show. "Wipe that red muck from your face," he told her curtly. "You don't need it."

Still she didn't speak. Not acting insulted or angry, she pulled a handkerchief from a pocket in her skirt, uncapped the bottle of lemonade she had lifted out of the basket and tilted the bottle to dampen the scrap of cotton. With movements that were slow and deliberate, she lifted the handkerchief to her face and rubbed her cheek clean of the rouge, finally turning to face him squarely.

Roy stared. It hadn't occurred to him that every time he'd seen the girl, she'd presented him with the same side of her face. Now he understood the reason. The other side of her face bore a scar. Not a great blemish by any means, but an unusual one. Two lines of pale, slightly puckered skin that formed a cross, and beneath it an incomplete circle, as if someone had drawn some kind of a symbol on her cheek.

"That's why they didn't bid?" Roy frowned at the idea. "But the scar on your face is hardly noticeable. It certainly is not unsightly."

When the girl showed no reaction, when she merely contemplated him with a pinched, forlorn expression on her pretty features, Roy decided not to press the topic for now. Lowering his attention to the piece of chicken in his hand, he took a bite and spoke around the mouthful.

"This is good, very good."

After a moment of enjoying the food, he glanced up at the girl. Appearing more in control of herself now, she was studying him—his eye patch, to be more accurate. *So that was it.* That's why she had stared at him with such intensity—in him she had identified a fellow sufferer of some physical deformity.

"How did you get the scar?" Roy asked gently.

"I fell against a stove when I was small. The hatch had a decorative pattern. A cross, like a plus sign, and a circle at the end of each spoke. Part of the pattern burned to my skin."

"It's very faint. Hardly worth worrying about."

"I know." Her voice was low. "When I grew up, the scar faded. The skin is a bit puckered, but the blemish isn't terribly obvious. Not enough to ruin my appearance. But out here in the West the sun is stronger. The scar doesn't tan, and I like taking walks in the desert. As my face got browner and browner from the sun, the scar stood out more and more…and then the bishop came…"

The girl fell silent and darted a glance toward the crowd, where a teenage boy was playing "Oh! Susanna" on a violin and the others were singing along.

"The bishop?" Roy prompted. "Is he the tall man dressed in black?"

"That's the preacher, Reverend Fergus. The bishop is his superior." Abandoning any pretense of eating, the girl folded her legs to her chest again and wrapped her arms around her knees. "Have you ever heard of a satanic cross?"

Roy met her gaze, unease stirring within him. "Can't say that I have."

"It's a cross with an upside-down question mark at the base." The girl touched her fingertips to her cheek. "Like the open circle at the end of my scar. The bishop came out to bless the new church a few months ago. He is a fanatic, and he told people that I bear the mark of the Devil on my face."

Startled, Roy lifted his brows. "And they believe him?"

The girl's lips twisted into a disparaging smirk. "I don't think they really do. I think they want the reverend to tell them it is all complete nonsense, but he is a weak, spineless man, and he doesn't have the courage to contradict his bishop."

Roy swallowed. The chicken had lost its flavor. Now he could understand those questioning glances the townsfolk had been sending to the preacher while Celia stood holding up her lunch basket, and why the reverend had been pretending not to notice them.

"I wish I could help you," he told her quietly. "But I can't."

"I know. I am grateful for this." The girl released one arm from around her knees to gesture to the lunch basket. "I'm supposed to collect your five dollars and hand it in, but I won't do it. I'll tell them I forgot. I know it's petty, but it will make me feel better."

"If you like, you can tell them I refused to pay."

She let out a bleak gust of laughter. "If I do that, they'll say it's because I served you a lousy meal, so it will end up being my fault anyway."

"Don't..." Roy shook his head. *Don't beat yourself up so.*

"It's the same everywhere," the girl went on bitterly, the words flooding out on a wave of anguish. It seemed to Roy that the hurt had festered, and now it was gushing forth like a boil that needed lancing. "Back in Baltimore, no man would marry me, because my mother was sickly. They feared I'd be the same, and they'd be lumbered with a useless wife and a stack of doctor's bills. Then my mother died..."

Pausing to draw a breath, the girl dashed the back of her hand across her eyes. "My father has a growth in his stomach, a cancer, and he worries about me being left on my own, so he brought me out here, where women are scarce. To start with, everything went well. I had two suitors, Stuart Clifton from one of the ranches, and Horton Tanner, who works for the stage line and comes by twice a week. No knights on a white stallion but good, decent men...and then that blasted bishop comes along and ruins it all..."

Memories of being shunned flooded over Roy, bringing with them a wave of pain, even now, after half a lifetime. He swept a glance around the picnic meadow to make sure no one was observing them and turned back to the girl. After tugging the brim of his hat lower for added protection, he reached for the patch that covered his brown eye and said, "You're not the only one who has suffered because some folks claim you bear the mark of the Devil."

Chapter Two

Celia wished she could stop babbling about her misfortunes but her tongue refused to be reined in. When she paused to fight the urge to weep, the stranger swept a careful look around them and tugged at the rawhide cord securing the patch over his left eye. She'd been wondering what damage he was hiding beneath, and now she felt ashamed for her curiosity. It was no business of hers. She steeled herself against the sight of his injury, and then gasped as she met the blinking gaze of a perfectly healthy brown eye.

"Your eyes," she breathed. "They're of different color."

"One pale blue, one dark brown." The man restored the patch over his brown eye. "It's supposed to be the sign of a witch. Or, the way a girl put it once, God and the Devil are fighting over me, with one half each. A fallen angel, she called me."

Fascinated, Celia studied his face. *Fallen angel.* The description fitted. The stranger had elegant, finely crafted features, with a straight nose and high cheekbones, and wide, well-defined lips. The tall, rangy body and the breadth of his shoulders added a stamp of rugged masculinity to looks that otherwise might have appeared too beautiful for a man.

Shamelessly, Celia let her gaze linger on the man's countenance, wishing he hadn't slipped the black cotton patch back in place. "Is that why you cover up your brown eye?" she asked. "As a protection from prejudice?"

"No." The stranger seemed to hesitate. "Having different-colored eyes is a distinctive mark. When a man rides the owl hoot trail—"

"What's that?" Celia broke in.

"Owl hoot trail. It means the outlaw trail."

"You're an outlaw?" She felt compelled to ask the question, even though she'd already guessed the answer. Even now, she could see the shape of the twin holsters beneath his long duster, knew he was wearing a double rig of pistols, and despite his handsome features there could be no mistaking the air of lawlessness about him.

It occurred to Celia he might know her father was the teller at the bank. Behind his kindness might lurk a plan to extract information out of her. However, so far the stranger hadn't mentioned the bank. Perhaps, after all, he had merely bid for her picnic basket as a caper, an amusing way to spend an hour while his partner was occupied with some errand.

Despite his criminal associations, Celia couldn't help but be drawn to the fair-haired outlaw. His kindness appeared genuine, not calculated. Moreover, there seemed to be an air of decency about him, a sense of honor. With a sudden lurch of her heart, Celia accepted that the outlaw had made himself vulnerable by confiding in her. By revealing his secret, he had offered her a weapon she could use against him.

"Why are you telling me this?" she asked quietly. "If such a distinctive feature might give you away, are you not worried that I might go to the marshal and enlighten him?"

"Rock Springs has no marshal and the county sheriff is fifty miles away."

The answer came swiftly, the tone cool and confident. For a week now, the outlaws had been hanging around the town, and the man's reaction solidified Celia's suspicions. *Are you planning to rob the bank?* The question sprang to her tongue but she left it unsaid. As long as her father wasn't placed in danger, she didn't care if the outlaws took every ounce of gold in the vault. Her bitterness toward the town had grown so fierce it overruled her sense of right and wrong.

For a moment, they sat in silence, each absorbed in their own private thoughts, yet with a sense of camaraderie flowing like a current between them. Celia let her eyes roam over the stranger, drinking in his masculine beauty while she searched for something to say, some opening gambit that would trigger a conversation so interesting he would find it impossible to walk away, but she came up with nothing.

The man rolled up to his feet, adjusted the brim of his hat and slipped one hand beneath his duster. For a few crazy seconds, Celia thought he was going to pull out a gun and shoot her, like one might shoot a lame horse to put it out of its misery, but instead he produced a ten-dollar gold piece out of his pocket.

"I don't have five dollars and I expect you don't have change." He dropped the coin to the blanket, where it landed with a soft thud. "If you don't want to give it to the church, hold on to it for me."

Celia darted out a hand and clasped the coin in her fist before anyone could see it, gripping it so hard the edges dug into her palm. She'd cherish the gold piece as a keepsake. A talisman, to bring her luck. "Hold on to it for you?" She arched her brows, her attention riveted on the stranger. "Does that mean you intend one day to come back?"

The man said nothing, merely gave her a nod, the dip of his chin so faint it might have been in her imagination. When he took a step back, the edges of his duster flared wide, giving Celia a glimpse of the gun belt circling his lean hips. One of the pistols was holstered butt forward. Heavy and functional, they were the tools of his trade, like a hammer might be for a carpenter, or a shovel for a grave digger. The thought made her shiver.

"You can keep the blanket," the stranger told her.

Startled, Celia looked down at the gray wool blanket she was seated upon. She'd forgotten it was his. Another keepsake. Something stirred in her chest, a dangerous wave of warmth that could only lead to foolish dreams and pointless longings. She tried to quash the sensation but it refused to go away.

The man touched the brim of his hat in farewell. "Ma'am."

Celia watched him turn to leave, realizing they hadn't introduced themselves.

"Wait!" she called out. When the stranger turned back toward her, she spoke in a throaty whisper, making it clear she intended the information to remain a secret between them. "What is your name?"

The corners of his mouth lifted in the tiniest of smiles. Again, he offered no reply, only a slight shake of his head. "Goodbye, Miss Courtwood."

He knew her name! Desperately, Celia wanted to hold on to the moment, wanted to build on their conversation, add to the enchantment of shared confidences, the two of them against the world. A question popped into her head. "A moment ago, you said that God and the Devil are fighting for your soul. Which one do you think will win?"

That shadow of a smile she'd witnessed a moment ago vanished and instead something cold and hard settled over the man's handsome features. "Why, Miss Courtwood," he said softly. "Surely, you know the answer. The Devil has already won."

With that, the outlaw whirled around on his feet and walked over to the edge of the meadow, where his tall Mexican companion already stood waiting with their horses. They exchanged a few words, and then the man with mismatched eyes vaulted into the saddle and rode away without looking back.

Roy loitered outside the bank with an unlit cigarette dangling from his lips. The midday sun baked down from a clear blue sky, making his scalp itch beneath the black horsehair wig he always wore during a raid, with a tuft arranged to hang over his blue eye, leaving only the brown eye visible. His skin was darkened with a thick brew of tea. He wore denim trousers and battered boots and a dust-stained white tunic with a sash around his waist, and no gun. At a quick glance, he would pass for an Indian.

Ten yards up the street, Jimenez and Keeler stood with six horses, ready to bring them over at his signal. Curtis and Saldana and Davies were already inside the bank. Roy glanced at the fob watch hidden in the folds of his sash. Five minutes. It was taking too long. He put the watch away and dropped the cigarette to the ground—the signal to leave.

A bell jangled down the street. Alert, Roy surveyed the boardwalk. A jolt went through him. The girl, Celia Courtwood, had come out of the mercantile, as if conjured up by the thoughts of her that never seemed to be far from his mind. She began to clean the display window with a bucket of water and a rag. Apart from the girl, the street was quiet. Roy pivoted on his tattered boots and sauntered into the bank.

Inside, Curtis was holding the bank manager and the teller at gunpoint. Behind the wooden partition, Saldana and Davies were busy in front of the open vault. All three wore hats pulled low and neckerchiefs to hide their features. Roy avoided situations that required such a disguise, for it would draw attention to his unusual eyes.

"Time to go," he declared.

"We need a couple more minutes." Curtis

spoke without turning, keeping his gun aimed at the two hostages who sat huddled on the floor, their backs pressed against the wall. "The manager had trouble remembering the combination for the safe."

Saldana called out from behind the counter. "Take some of the load." He tossed a small canvas bag over the partition, then another. Roy caught them in the air. The bags were heavy with gold, the seams straining with the weight.

"Let's go," Roy said again. "Carry what you can and leave the rest."

Saldana and Davies came out through the open hatch and hurried past him, each loaded with bags of gold. Roy swept a look over the hostages. The manager was trim and dapper, in his sixties, dressed in a fine broadcloth suit. The expression on his face conveyed more anger than fear, and Roy suspected his inability to recall the combination had been a deliberate delaying tactic. The other man was gaunt and pale, with thinning brown hair that pulled into tight curls.

In that instant, recognition struck Roy. It was the man he'd seen talking to Celia Courtwood on the day of the box lunch. He must be her father, for there was a resemblance, and he bore the signs of a man suffering from terminal illness. Instinctively, Roy took a step closer. From the corner of his eye, he could see Curtis lift his arm and take aim, pointing at the teller's chest.

"What are you doing?" Roy blurted out and darted forward.

A gunshot boomed around the bank. Roy felt a slam at the back of his shoulder. The room dimmed in his eyes. He dropped the bags of gold. Stumbling forward, he braced his hands against the wall to remain upright. He could feel no pain. From experience he knew that the shock numbed the nerves. The pain would come later.

Behind him, Curtis swore. "You fool. Why did you get in the way?"

Keeping his right hand against the wall, Roy pivoted to face the outlaw boss. "What the hell are you doing?" he demanded to know.

Curtis lifted his gun, pointed the barrel at Roy. "Can't leave no loose ends."

With effort, Roy stood straight. He sucked in a deep breath to steady himself. "I'm fine," he said sharply. "I can ride." To prove his fitness, he bent down and picked up the two bags of gold from the floor.

Curtis gave him a quick perusal and nodded. He glanced at the hostages cowering against the wall and shrugged, as if to say it didn't really matter. Then he ushered Roy out of the building. Roy could tell Curtis was keeping an eye on him. The gang leader wanted no injured man left behind, for he did not trust any of his associates to keep their silence if captured by the law.

Out in the bright sunshine, Roy felt his head swim and his mouth go dry. He tossed the bags of gold to Keeler. Saldana and Davies were already cantering away. Roy gripped the pommel of the saddle, gathered his strength to climb up on Dagur. Spooked by the smell of blood, the buckskin took a frightened sidestep, causing Roy to stumble. The others got on their horses and thundered out of town, dust billowing in their wake.

From the boardwalk came the rapid clatter of footsteps. Roy turned to look. The girl was heading the formation of people charging toward the bank. The elderly clerk from the mercantile and the barber in a leather apron followed close behind. Still farther back, three men had burst out of the saloon. One had hurried to his mount at the hitching rail and was pulling a rifle out of a saddle scabbard.

Roy vaulted on his horse, pain throbbing in his shoulder. Once more, he glanced back, as much to look at Celia Courtwood as to assess the danger. The girl had jumped down at the end of the boardwalk, only a few paces away from him. Their gazes collided. From the way he saw her against the backdrop of the weather-beaten buildings and the dusty street, with a full depth perception instead of the flat vision of a one-eyed man,

Roy knew the protecting tuft of horsehair in his wig had shifted aside. And from the way the girl came to a halt, the shock of recognition stamped on her pretty features, he knew that she had noticed his mismatched eyes—had identified him despite the disguise.

For a moment, time stood still as they stared at each other, the air between them charged with unspoken questions and apologies and explanations. Then Roy turned to face forward, dug his heels into the flanks of the buckskin and shot down the street. Behind him came the girl's frightened scream. "Papa! Papa!"

Your father is fine, Roy thought with a trace of irony. *I took the bullet meant for him.*

He couldn't understand what had happened, why Curtis had fired at the teller, unless it was a random act of violence. Some men went crazy with the outlaw life, got into the habit of using gunplay as a means to demonstrate their power, or simply to alleviate the boredom of being shut away in the hideout for months on end, with little to amuse them apart from gambling and drinking and brawling.

A rifle shot cracked through the air. The rancher who'd burst out of the saloon must have fired, and soon others would fetch their hunting weapons and start shooting. Roy heard the bullet whizz by, chasing him. He squatted low in the saddle and urged Dagur on. One hole in his hide was enough.

As he left the town behind, the sun in the sky seemed to grow hotter and hotter. His vision wavered, making the landscape hazy. Pain rolled over him in waves that appeared to swallow him up. Sweat coated his skin, mixing with the stream of blood from his shoulder.

In the distance, he could see a cloud of dust where his associates were making their escape. He twisted awkwardly in the saddle to survey the trail behind him. A burning pain sliced through his side at the motion, but he saw no sign of anyone chasing him.

He slowed his pace, teetered in the saddle. He was losing too much blood. Unless he attended to his wound and got some rest, he'd never survive the long ride north, to the maze of canyons where the law didn't reach.

The gang had arranged to regroup at an abandoned mine, to inspect the haul and to retrieve the provisions they had stored there for the return journey to the hideout. However, Lom Curtis might feel that leaving behind an injured man posed too great a risk. He had a cast-iron rule that any man who joined the Red Bluff Gang could never walk away or be left behind, and in his weakened state Roy would be no match for the outlaw boss—not with fists, not with guns, nor in terms of outwitting him.

Taking a sharp turn into an outcrop of boulders, Roy pointed the buckskin toward the west, along a trail overgrown with sagebrush and creosote. Unlike Saldana and Davies, who'd spent their idle hours gambling, Roy had roamed the surrounding hills. He'd come across an abandoned homestead, with a log cabin and a spring.

If he could make it that far, the cabin would offer a place to hide, a refuge from both a posse and the outlaw leader who placed no value on loyalty.

Celia shook herself free from the trance she'd tumbled into when she'd recognized the man with mismatched eyes in his Indian disguise. She jumped up the front steps of the bank, shoved the door open with both hands and hurtled through.

"Papa! Papa!" She could hear the shrill ring of terror in her voice, could feel her heart hammering in the confines of her chest.

She raked a frantic glance around the room, divided by a polished oak counter and a glass partition above. Her father and the manager, Mr. Northfield, sat sprawled with their backs against the wall on the customer side. Celia rushed up to them, sank to her knees in front of her father.

"Papa! Are you all right? Are you all right?"

With searching hands, she patted his freshly laundered shirt and the suit coat that hung on his emaciated frame. No blood. No blood. But a glazed look filled her father's eyes and beneath her searching palms Celia could feel his frail body trembling with fear.

While she completed her examination, her father sucked in a calming breath and expelled it on a sigh. "I'm fine, Celia girl," he reassured her. "Just a bit shaken up."

She turned to the manager. From an affluent Baltimore family, Mr. Northfield had employed her father on a recommendation from shared acquaintances. In his sixties, cool in manner, trim in appearance, with neatly clipped graying hair and a pencil moustache, the manager kept himself aloof from his employees. Celia possessed no fondness for him, but she was grateful for the opportunity he had extended to her father.

"Mr. Northfield, are you all right?"

"I am unharmed, if that is what you mean." The manager sat upright on the floor and tugged at the lapels of his broadcloth suit. "But I am far from all right. They emptied the vault, all of it. Forty thousand dollars' worth of gold, the most we have ever held in the bank."

Her panic receding, Celia twisted on her knees to survey the disarray. A crack ran across the glass partition and ugly scratches marred the front of the oak counter. Behind the partition, the vault stood open, empty coin trays scattered about. Overturned chairs and papers strewn about completed the scene of destruction. In the air, the acrid smell of gunpowder mingled with the familiar scents of beeswax polish and lemon cleaner.

Anger flared in Celia, the edge of it dulled by a sense of guilt and shame. In her bitterness toward the townspeople, she had secretly welcomed the disaster, had gloated over having figured out what no one else seemed to have the brains to suspect.

Now, regret flooded her conscience. Her father loved his job. It gave him dignity, a position in the community. During the robbery, his place of business, the citadel of finance in which he took such pride had been violated, equipment damaged, order and precision replaced with chaos and lawlessness.

She turned back to the men. "I heard a gunshot."

Her father swallowed, his thin throat rippling. "That's the damnedest thing, Celia girl. One of the outlaws, the gang leader, pointed his gun at me. I believe he was going to shoot me, but another one of the robbers got in the way. The Indian, with long black hair. I think he got hit."

Celia's thoughts reverted to the stranger with mismatched eyes. She'd been waiting for him to return, and for the briefest of instants out there in the midday sun, as she jumped down from the boardwalk and her eyes locked with one brown eye and one blue, the thrill of recognition had made her forget everything else.

Just as she had suspected, the stranger had come back to rob the bank. And he had protected her father. Why had he done it? Was it to rule out the prospect of being hanged for murder if the gang got caught? Or had he known the teller was her father? Had he done it for her, to protect her from the loss of a parent?

"He got hit?" she asked, urgency in her tone as a new worry seized her mind. Such concern for one of the robbers might appear unwarranted, but she had to know. "The man with long black hair who stepped between you and the gunman got hit?"

Her father nodded. "A bullet in the shoulder. He walked out on his own steam, but he was in pain. I could tell."

As her mental processes sprang back to their normal clarity, Celia recalled hearing rifle shots out in the street while she'd been kneeling to examine her father for injuries. In her mind, she played back the image of the man with different-colored eyes. He had struggled to get on his horse while his companions were already making their escape. The last one to get away, he'd have been the target for those rifle shots.

Fear closed around her, startling in its intensity. She jumped up to her feet and spoke in a breathless rush. "I need air. I have to go outside."

As she whirled about and darted toward the exit, she noticed Mr. Northfield studying her father with a sharp, assessing look. Perhaps the manager was concerned about her father's fragile health, the impact the frightening events might have on it.

Out in the street, the bright sunshine made Celia blink. Vaguely, she worried about not wearing a bonnet, an omission that would deepen the tan on her skin and cause her scar to stand out even more vividly.

"Did you shoot him?" she cried out to the cluster of men who stood staring into the distance. There was Mr. Selden, her boss at the store, and Mr. Grosser, who ran the barbershop, and three ranchers, one of them holding a rifle. A crowd was gathering around them, but no one was shooting or going to fetch their horses.

"Sorry, Miss Celia," Mr. Grosser replied. "He got away."

He got away.

Her hand went to her chest, where her fingers felt the round shape of the gold coin she'd hung around her neck in a tiny pouch sewn from a scrap of silk. The stranger with mismatched eyes had managed to escape. A sense of destiny, a sense of an inevitable crossing of paths, solidified inside Celia. Every instinct told her that their fates would be intertwined.

Chapter Three

Roy hung grimly in the saddle, pain burning in his shoulder, the blood-soaked shirt sticking to his back, cold shivers racking him. He ought to have packed his wound to stem the bleeding, but he daren't stop, not even to take off the itchy black wig and put his hat on.

He'd slipped the cotton patch back in its place, to protect his brown eye, unused to daylight, from the glare of the sun. Already, his body was shutting down, making him light-headed and giving him a tunnel vision that closed out everything except the trail ahead that led to a place of safety.

At last, the small log cabin, half dug into the hillside, with an earth roof over it, hovered in his sights. With one final burst of effort, Roy urged Dagur up the path, reined in and slid down from the saddle. He stumbled to the entrance and kicked the door open. Ducking his head, he stepped in through the low frame and pulled the buckskin inside after him, then kicked the door shut again.

Darkness filled the cramped space. The horse gave a frightened whinny. Leaning against the heavy flank of the animal to steady himself, Roy stroked the lathered coat.

"Easy, boy. Easy now, Dagur. We're safe."

He tugged aside the patch that covered his brown eye. Protected from light, the eye needed no time to adjust to the darkness, allowing Roy to survey his surroundings.

The place was just as he'd left it two weeks ago. Sturdy log walls, floor of hard-packed earth swept clean, the single window firmly shuttered. Some previous occupant must have burned any remaining furniture for firewood, but they had left the water barrel that stood in the corner next to the primitive stone chimney.

A standard-sized whiskey barrel, it held fifty-three gallons. During his earlier visits Roy had painstakingly cleaned the timber container and filled it from the spring outside, spending hours shuttling to and fro with nothing but a canteen to transport the water.

To complete his preparations, he'd gathered firewood into a tall stack along the rear wall, and with handfuls of desert sand and grit he had scrubbed away the layer of grease from the rusty iron pot that stood on tripod legs inside the stone hearth.

Now he turned to Dagur and pulled his hat from the folds of his bedroll where he had tucked it away, pushed the crown back into shape and sank to his knees beside the water barrel. Using a piece of firewood to knock loose the wooden plug, he lined his hat beneath the hole in the barrel and filled the hollow of the crown to the brim. After replacing the plug on the side of the barrel, Roy held up the hat for the buckskin to drink.

"Good boy," he murmured. "Rest now. Later, when it gets dark, I'll let you out to graze. There's a strip of grama beyond the spring, much better than the desert grass you've been eating recently."

The horse blew and snorted, as if to agree. Twice more, Roy filled his hat and let Dagur drink. Then he took out his canteen and quenched his own thirst. After allowing himself a moment of rest, he poured water into the iron pot in the hearth, arranged firewood beneath the tripod legs and took out his tin of matches to start a fire.

The pain closed around him, burning like a hot poker in his shoulder and streaking down his side with every move he made. He needed to get the wound cleaned and dressed before he passed out. The bullet wouldn't kill him, but the fever that followed might, if he didn't manage to stem the bleeding and prevent an infection.

As the flames caught in the hearth, a warm yellow glow danced over the log walls. The reassuring scents of wood smoke and pine resin, familiar from a thousand campfires, filled the cabin. Roy imagined primitive man, living in caves, hunting and gathering. For him, a bonfire must have meant life, just as much as water and food did, and more—a fire must have been the first step toward civilization, mastering the elements of nature.

Sitting cross-legged in front of the stone chimney, Roy pulled a knife from the scabbard in his boot and sliced away his shirt. Easier than trying to lift his arms overhead to undress. The coarse white cotton was matted with blood but the bleeding had slowed to a trickle.

Gently, Roy felt the wound in his shoulder with his fingertips. There was no exit hole, but high up on the front he could feel a small lump beneath the skin. The surge of relief nearly made him faint. From the way he'd been able to move his arm, he'd known the bone remained intact, but had the bullet lodged deeper inside his shoulder, it might have been impossible for him to remove.

Leaning toward the fire, Roy enjoyed the comfort of heat while he held the tip of his knife to the flames to purify it. When he was satisfied the blade was clean, he made a small incision at the front of his shoulder, in the fleshy part where the muscle sloped toward the neck, to create an exit wound. With pressure from his fingertips, the bullet slid out.

It was a .36 caliber homemade lead ball. Despite the small size, had the bullet struck lower, it would have shattered the bone, most likely leaving too many fragments to remove. And even if Roy hadn't already known, the small lead ball would have revealed the shooter to be Lom Curtis. Short and slight, the leader of the outlaw gang liked his pair of lightweight Navy Colts and had never switched to more powerful weapons or jacketed ammunition.

Roy tossed the bullet into the fire and inspected the remains of his shirt, assembling the back panel like a jigsaw puzzle. A small circular piece was missing. He swore. During his years on the outlaw trail, he'd seen plenty of doctoring for gunshot wounds, both by qualified surgeons and by anyone with a knife and a steady hand, and he understood that a piece of fabric left inside the wound could kill as effectively as a vial of poison.

Behind him, Dagur was snoring, asleep on his feet. Roy twisted around and raised his voice. "Dagur, sit down."

The horse blinked his eyes open, gave a protesting whinny but folded his legs and sank to the earth floor. Roy reached over and tugged his saddlebags free. Summoning all his strength, he loosened the cinch on the saddle girth and pulled the weight off the horse, letting the saddle tumble to the ground.

"It's okay, boy," Roy said. "Go to sleep." With another whinny, Dagur rolled over to his side and extended his legs, filling half the cabin, and resumed his snoring.

Roy tore a section from the clean part of his shirt and spread the piece of fabric on the earth floor. From his saddlebags, he took out a piece of rawhide string, a flask of whiskey and a bottle of kerosene, and a needle. Moving stiffly, fighting the pain, he arranged the objects on the cloth. Last, he snatched the black wig from his head, used his knife to snap away a couple of the horsehairs and dropped them into the iron cauldron on the fire to boil.

Using the rest of his shirt for rags, it only took him a minute to wash away the dried blood. When he was finished, Roy soaked the rawhide string in the bottle of kerosene, took a gulp of whiskey and then he pushed the string into the exit wound he had made, feeding the rawhide through his shoulder with his fingers until he could reach over to his back and pull the cord through. Stoically, he closed his mind to the fiery pain and lifted the rawhide string to inspect it in the light of the fire crackling in the hearth.

No scrap of cotton clung to the cord.

Fighting a dizzy spell, Roy soaked the rawhide

string in kerosene again, tied a knot to one end and repeated the process. On the fourth pass, a piece of fabric clung to the knot. His body shaking with exhaustion, his movements clumsy, Roy lined the scrap of cotton with the hole in the back panel of his shirt. It fit. Relief cut through the haze of pain that dulled his brain. He'd gotten all the cotton fibers out. He had a good chance now.

Three more times, Roy dragged the kerosene-soaked string through the wound, sipping whiskey in between to revive himself. When a man had someone else to do the doctoring, he could escape the pain into unconsciousness. A man alone had no such luxury.

Satisfied the wound was clean, Roy compared how much kerosene and whiskey he had left. About the same, a couple of inches. But there was no lamp, so he kept the whiskey for drinking and poured the kerosene over the wound, front and back.

Once more, he held the blade of his knife to the fire, keeping the steel in the flames until it glowed white-hot. Gritting his teeth, he pressed the tip of the blade to the exit wound to cauterize the skin and did the same to the entry wound, awkwardly reaching around to the back of his shoulder. Finally, he fished the horsehairs out of the boiling water. After checking they had softened enough, he cleaned the needle with a drop of whiskey, threaded it with a strand of horsehair and closed the holes in his flesh with a few crude sutures.

He longed for a cup of coffee, but his strength gave out. Barely able to muster up enough energy to rummage in his saddlebags, he took out his tin cup, scooped it full of boiling water, tossed in a few lumps of sugar, added a dollop of whiskey and drank the mixture as soon as it had cooled enough not to scald. Then he yanked his bedroll free from the straps behind the saddle, rolled into the single remaining blanket, laid his head down and let unconsciousness slide over him.

When darkness fell over the surrounding hills and filtered in through the closed shutters, Roy roused himself long enough to strip the bridle from Dagur and shove the door open. The horse wouldn't stray far from the spring.

The fever came on the second day, drenching Roy in sweat and sending icy shivers through his battered frame. Days and nights blurred together in the shadowed interior of the dugout cabin. He ate nothing but drank plenty of water, boiling it first, in case it had gone stale inside the oak barrel. At all times, he kept his pair of loaded guns within an easy reach.

In dime novels, when an injured outlaw came to, there would be a pretty girl standing by his bedside, smiling down at him and patting his brow with a cool cloth. There was no girl with a cool cloth for him, and no soft bed, only the hard earth floor, but when Roy's mind grew hazy, he imagined Celia Courtwood leaning over him, her gold-streaked curls tumbling down to his naked chest, a smile brightening her features. Then reality would intrude, and he realized it was only a dream—could never be anything but a dream.

Celia squatted on her heels by the oak counter of the bank, rubbing furniture polish into the ugly scratches the outlaws had made with the rowels of their spurs. She'd already scrubbed every inch of the floor, as if the violence had left behind a layer of filth she must remove. On the polished timber planks, a few drops of blood had painted a trail toward the exit.

His blood. The man who had protected her father. Before scrubbing away the dark stains, Celia had pressed her fingertips to them, relishing that small connection to the stranger whose memory filled her with a flurry of mixed emotions—from gratitude to disapproval, from resentment to fascination, and beneath all those other emotions a strange longing that felt almost like a physical ache in her chest.

With increased vigor, as if to banish the handsome outlaw from her thoughts, Celia smeared more polish into the wood. For two days now, she had worked—unpaid—helping her father and Mr. Northfield to restore order in the bank. In truth, her father wasn't contributing much. Mostly, he was sitting down, gasping for breath, his hands clasped together in front of him, palms pressed to his belly.

Every now and then Celia noticed the bank manager casting a hostile glance in her father's direction. She suspected Mr. Northfield was ready to overcome his scruples about dismissing a sick man, which would leave them to survive on whatever little she could earn in her part-time position at the mercantile.

Refusing to give in to despair, Celia straightened on her feet. She dropped the turpentine-soaked rag into the steel bucket on the floor, wiped her hands on a piece of clean linen cloth and raised her voice to carry across the cracked glass partition.

"That's the best I can get it."

Before Mr. Northfield had a chance to come around and pass judgment on her efforts, footsteps thudded by the entrance. All day, curious visitors had crowded into the bank. Celia moved aside. It was up to the manager to deal with anxious inquiries from customers who might be worried about the safety of their deposits.

The man who strode in was thin and wiry, with a walrus mustache and a piercing blue gaze beneath an expensive tan-colored Stetson hat. Celia noted the pistol at his hip, then homed in on the tin star pinned to the man's rawhide vest. He must be the county sheriff from Prescott, fetched by one of the saloon keeper's sons.

Mr. Northfield ushered Celia away with a flap of his hand. "You can leave now, Miss Court-wood." The dismissive gesture conveyed no gratitude for her unpaid labor.

"Perhaps my father could leave, too?" Celia suggested, her brows lifted in a tentative appeal. "He is still very shaken up after the ordeal and could do with a rest."

"No," the manager replied, his tone sharper than the request warranted.

"It's all right, Celia girl," her father cut in. "I am needed here. I shall have to make a statement, tell the sheriff what happened."

Celia glanced from her father to the bank manager. There was something going on between those two, some undertone of hostility she failed to comprehend. Since the robbery, Mr. Northfield had been looking at her father with a dislike that bordered on disgust, even though the two of them had always been on cordial terms before.

"All right." Celia attempted a bright tone. "I'll get supper started. I'll expect you home shortly, Papa." She nodded to the men and walked out past the wiry sheriff. At the hitching rail outside, a bay gelding stood basking in the afternoon sun. Iron shackles and a coil of sturdy rope hung from the saddle, in readiness for a prisoner.

Tools of a man's trade, Celia recalled thinking two weeks ago when she'd caught a glimpse of the pair of guns the outlaw with mismatched eyes wore beneath his long duster. And just like on that other occasion, a shiver of apprehension rippled over her.

Her hand crept up to her chest, to touch the small silk pouch where she wore the stranger's gold coin on a string around her neck, like a keepsake to make sure they would meet again. But why dream of such an encounter, when an outlaw was like a hunted animal and any romantic interest in such a man could only bring a woman grief?

Footsteps thundered across the porch. Even before she hurried to the door, Celia knew it could not be her father, for a tired shuffle would announce his arrival. It was the barber, Mr. Grosser, a tall, rawboned man whose body always seemed to be listing to one side.

"Come quick, Miss Celia," he said, even in his haste polite enough to snatch his hat down from his head. "I have your father at the back of my shop."

Startled, she stared at the gangly barber. *At the back of my shop*. Rock Springs had no jail, and no marshal since Todd Lindstrom had been gunned down by rustlers a year ago. When someone needed to be detained, he was locked up in the small, windowless storeroom at the back of the barbershop, and kept there until he sobered up or, in the case of more serious crimes, until the county sheriff from Prescott arrived to fetch him.

"But why?" Celia implored. "Why?"

"Well, Miss Celia..." The barber turned his hat over in his hands. "They say he was in on the robbery. That he tipped off the gang of outlaws about all that gold in the bank and advised them how to go about stealing it."

"W...what...?" After she'd overcome her startled reaction, indignation flared within Celia, like a flame licking at her insides. Her poor, sick father, to be bothered with such crazy accusations. "That is nonsense. Complete, utter nonsense." She squared her shoulders, bracing for a confrontation. "Where is the sheriff?"

"He's in the saloon, having his supper. When he's finished, he'll take your father to Prescott for a trial. It is a full moon tonight, light enough to travel after sunset." Mr. Grosser replaced his hat on his head and turned to go. "Miss Celia, you'll need to come quick if you want to see your father. I'm here against the sheriff's orders. He does not want you to talk to your father, in case he might use you to pass a message to his accomplices."

"Use me?" Her voice grew shrill at the incongruity of it. "To pass a message? To his *accomplices*?" Never had she heard such utter balderdash. Could this be some kind of a practical joke at her expense? Yes, that's what it had to be. She'd play along, act her part as the hapless victim of the warped sense of humor of the citizens of Rock Springs.

Celia snatched her bonnet from a peg by the door, flung it over her upsweep and marched out, tying the laces beneath the chin as she tried to keep up with the barber's long strides. On the normally quiet Main Street, a dozen people were loitering about in artificially casual poses, men flicking dust from their coat lapels, women pretending to be inspecting the displays in the store windows, while their true purpose was to steal covert glances at her.

Not looking left or right, Celia clattered up the steps to the boardwalk in her leather half boots. For an instant, she was forced to stand still while the barber bent his head to unlock his premises. The force of all those curious stares bombarded her in the back, like a flurry of Indian arrows landing between her shoulder blades.

Finally, the lock clicked open and the barber held the door wide while Celia stepped through. The pungent smells of cologne and shaving soap filled her nostrils. She'd never been to Mr. Grosser's premises before. In normal circumstances, she would have enjoyed the opportunity to inspect such a bastion of masculine grooming, but today she paid scant attention to her surroundings.

The barber ushered her past the big leather chair to the rear of the shop and slid open the crudely made hatch in a thick, iron-studded oak door. Equipped with heavy steel hinges and twin bolts, the storeroom had been specifically reinforced to act as a place of detention.

"I want to go inside and talk to him," Celia said.

"Sorry, Miss Celia. You must talk to him through the hatch." The barber retreated to the front of the premises and busied himself by arranging the jars and bottles lined up on the mahogany cabinet behind his chair. He turned his back on her, offering an illusion of privacy, but Celia could tell he was keeping an eye on her through the big gilt-framed mirror mounted on the wall.

She pivoted on her feet to face the jail room and rose on tiptoe to peer through the hatch, positioned for a man's height. Her father was sitting on the edge of a narrow cot. The room had no other furniture, only the cot, and beside it no more than two feet of empty space. Should a prisoner feel restless, he might take three steps toward the far wall, turn around and take three steps in the opposite direction, while trying not to trip up on the slop bucket in the corner.

"Papa!"

Her father glanced up. For an instant, Celia could see despair etched on his gaunt features. Then his lips curved into a shaky smile. Moving slowly, he got up and eased over to her. The hatch in the door framed his face, making him appear like the portrait of a dying man.

"Papa, what is this all about?"

"Well, Celia girl, they think I had something to do with this robbery. The bandit leader tried to shoot me, and the sheriff claims it is typical behavior for these outlaw gangs. They get a man inside to help them with the robbery, and then they kill him, so he can't talk and give them away."

"But that is nonsense! Anyway, the robbers didn't kill you. The theory does not fit the facts."

"The sheriff says there are often internal feuds in these gangs. Maybe the leader wanted to shoot this other man, too, but he ran out of time and couldn't kill either of us."

"Ran out of time?" Celia said tartly. "Just how slowly does a bullet fly?" She gave her head a determined shake. "We'll have to put a stop to this foolishness. I'll speak to the sheriff. If that fails, we'll get a lawyer. Someone competent, from Prescott or Flagstaff."

"Celia girl, listen to me."

There was an odd shine in her father's eyes, a strange fervor in his expression. Celia held her breath. A terrible fear unfurled in her belly. Surely, the accusations could have no merit? Surely, there was no possibility that her father had actually been involved in the crime?

"Yes, Papa?" she prompted him, her body rigid with tension. "I'm listening."

Her father spoke with a breathless eagerness. "This is the solution I've been looking for. Soon I'll be too weak to work. You'll be left to support me, with little money coming in. You spent your young years nursing your mother, and I don't want you to bear the burden of nursing me, too. If I go along with what they claim, the authorities will have to take care of me. And you'll be free. The house is in your name, and I've got a bit of money put aside, not in the bank but elsewhere, and I'll get it sent out to you."

"No, Papa, no! We'll fight them. Prove your innocence."

"No, Celia." Her father frowned, looking pained. "I'll not hear a word from you against this plan." His expression softened. "Don't you understand, Celia girl, I want you to have a chance. I'll send you the money. You can sell the house and go away, start over in some other town."

"I'd rather nurse you than move to a place full of strangers."

A smile eased her father's gaunt features and he spoke tenderly. "Come closer."

Celia flattened her palms against the reinforced oak panel and hovered on her toes, her face lined up with the hatch. Her father pressed a gentle kiss on her forehead. "I love you, Celia girl. And I understand that you want to look after me, give me comfort in my final days. But the greatest comfort you could give me is to write to me in Yuma prison and tell me that you've settled safely in some other town where people have no prejudice against you. Then I'll be able to die in peace."

"Papa…" Her voice caught in her throat. It was an unreasonable demand for him to make, and yet how could she ignore it? How could she deny her father what he was asking for? And in some horrible, practical way, she understood the logic in his thinking. With only her meager earnings to rely upon, they might not have enough money for doctor's bills and other expenses. This way, the territorial government would have to take care of him, feed him and eventually bury him.

"All right," Celia replied, anguish tightening her chest. "I won't try to reason with the sheriff. But promise me this—when they question you, you'll tell no lies. And if they end up releasing you, you'll come home to me, and let me nurse you, like I nursed Mama."

"I promise you that, Celia girl."

Voices erupted on the boardwalk outside. The barber hurried over to Celia. He shoved her aside and slammed shut the hatch in the oak door. Speaking with a nervous agitation, he grabbed her by the elbow and bundled her toward the rear exit. "Go out the back way."

Celia wrenched herself free. "I'll go out the way I came in." Holding her head high, she marched out of the shop. In the street, she could see the lean, wiry sheriff with the expensive tan Stetson hat leading over two horses, his bay and a dun gelding she recognized as rental stock from the livery stable.

The sheriff came to a halt by the boardwalk and turned to detach the shackles from his horse. Carrying the clinking chains in one hand, he climbed up the steps to the boardwalk. Celia stood still, her wide skirts blocking the entrance to the barbershop. When the sheriff came toe-to-toe with her, she held her position for a moment, then shifted aside to let him through. There was no point in resisting. If the sheriff knew his job, he'd get her father to reveal the truth and send him home to her where he belonged.

Chapter Four

Even after Roy had conquered the bout of fever and set about restoring his strength, he couldn't shake Celia Courtwood from his thoughts. She'd recognized him, and she knew his secret. Was there a wanted poster circulating for a no-name bandit with one blue eye and one brown? If he came across a lawman, would they demand that he lift the patch over his left eye and let them take a peek beneath?

He had to know. Not only whether it was safe for him to go out in public. He had to see Celia Courtwood again, find out if the bond of attraction he'd felt between them had been real and she had protected him by keeping her silence, or if she had betrayed the confidence and given his secret away.

I like taking walks in the desert, the girl had said. When fit enough to leave the safety of the cabin, Roy spent a week keeping an eye on the trails in the vicinity of Rock Springs, carefully remaining out of sight. He saw no trace of Celia Courtwood. As the days went by, his impatience grew.

If his part in the robbery was known, what could they do to him in town? Nothing, Roy decided. They had no marshal, and none of the citizens could match him with gunplay. Unless someone bushwhacked him, he'd be safe, and he doubted the townspeople in Rock Springs had an appetite for murder.

A cool gust of wind swept along the dusty Main Street on the morning Roy rode in and dismounted outside the mercantile. Two matronly women strolled along the boardwalk, heads bent together in conversation. They gave him a curious glance but quickly averted their faces, classifying him as someone not meriting a greeting.

Roy pushed the mercantile door open, sending the bell jangling above. The neatly dressed elderly clerk stood behind the counter, straightening the line of candy jars. At the sight of Roy, his expression brightened but quickly faded into a look of disappointment.

"Welcome back, stranger," he said, but his tone conveyed no delight.

"Howdy," Roy replied. He shifted on his feet, uncertain how to start the conversation, but then the pristine man across the polished timber counter took care of the problem.

"It's a shame about Miss Courtwood," the storekeeper said, shaking his head. "I had hoped that, after you bid for her box lunch, you might have changed your mind about needing a wife and come back for her."

"I been laid up." Roy rolled his left shoulder. "Got into a saloon fight in Prescott and someone stuck a knife in me. Since I'm passing through again, I thought I'd drop in on Miss Courtwood and say hello, see if she remembers me."

"She's gone."

"Gone?" Roy frowned. "Where to?"

The storekeeper took down his spectacles and began polishing them with a cloth he pulled out of his breast pocket. Roy remembered the action from before and knew to expect some kind of an awkward revelation.

"It's not my habit to spread gossip, but since you'll hear it in town anyway, I might just as well be the one to tell you. About a month ago, the bank was robbed, and Miss Courtwood's father was in on it. He was the bank teller. He's doing five years in Yuma prison."

Roy managed to hide his surprise. "And Miss Courtwood?" he asked, keeping his tone even. "What happened to her?"

The clerk shifted his shoulders, a gesture of

uncertainty. "No one knows. She just vanished. She doesn't have a horse, and nobody saw her take the stage. She was friendly with Horton Tanner who works for the stage line. People think she got him to stop outside the town and let her climb on board without anybody looking on."

"I see," Roy replied. Everything fell into place in his mind. Now he understood why Lom Curtis had tried to shoot Celia's father. In a bank robbery, the inside man was often the weak link. Unaccustomed to a life of crime, feeling the pressure from the law, they could be tempted to betray their accomplices in exchange for a pardon. The leader of the outlaw gang trusted no one and might have wished to eliminate the risk of such an outcome.

The elderly clerk went on, "Of course, Miss Courtwood still owns the house, and she might come back one day. The property was in her name. Her father had an account at the bank, but the funds have been frozen." The clerk's expression grew pained. "She had no means to support herself here in Rock Springs. I could no longer employ her, for I couldn't afford to lose my customers." He gave a small, awkward shrug. "I expect she's gone back East, to live with relatives."

"I see," Roy said again. He spoke lightly. "Could you give me directions to her house? I might leave a note, in case she comes back."

"Sure." The clerk gestured, pointing at the

street outside. "Turn right onto the boardwalk, cross over and it will be the first street on your left. It's the white-painted house, maybe fourth or fifth along. It's the only one with a porch instead of a front yard with a picket fence."

Roy said his thanks, went out and untied his horse. Not mounting, he walked down the street, leading Dagur behind him. He identified the house easily enough. The windows were shuttered, the flowers in the hanging baskets on the front porch wilted.

He tied the buckskin to the porch railing and went to the door, letting his boots echo on the timbers to announce his arrival. Just to be polite, he pounded on the knocker. No reply, just as he had expected. He leaned closer, lined his face with the crack by the door frame and inhaled. A faint smell of wood smoke teased his nostrils.

He left the porch and walked around to the back. The garden plants looked remarkably healthy—a big apple tree laden with fruit on the left, neat rows of vegetables on the right, borders planted with flowers. In the center of the yard stood a well, and the rear section of the property housed a small stable and a woodshed.

Roy examined the well first. It had no pump, only a timber frame and a bucket on an iron chain. Dropping to his haunches, he tested the mud with his fingertips. The earth felt damp, and it hadn't rained in days. Moving along, he studied the ground. A trail of moisture led to the back door—no doubt water splashing from a heavy bucket someone was struggling to haul inside.

Straightening on his feet, Roy headed for the stable, a small timber construction with a sloping roof. He peered in through the open doorway. No smell of manure. The stable must have been unoccupied for some time, and yet from inside came the frantic buzzing of flies. Roy pulled his eye patch aside to see better in the dark and stepped into the cool shadows of the interior.

In the corner of a stall, he found a burlap sack that gave out rancid odors. He looked around, spotted an old broom and used the handle to poke at the sack. Flies dispersed with an angry buzz. Empty tin cans rolled out, metal waste that could not be burned in a stove. The labels were still clear enough to read, indicating that the tins couldn't have been there for long. Roy bent closer to study the labels.

Borden's Evaporated Milk
Van Camp's Pork and Beans
Winslow's Green Corn

Satisfied with the results of his search, Roy left the flies to their feast. Outside, he paused to survey the house. A curtain twitched in an upstairs window. Not letting on he'd noticed, Roy ambled back to the front, untied his horse and walked away, mulling over the situation.

Had the girl too been in on the robbery? Had she known all along, perhaps even persuaded her father to become involved? The current between them that he'd taken as an attraction between a man and a woman, had it been something else on the girl's part? Had it been a bond between two coconspirators in a crime?

Tension held Roy in its grip, new possibilities tumbling around in his mind. All his years on the outlaw trail, he'd dreamed of a home, of an honest life, of belonging in a place, of being equal to other men, able to hold his head high in public. But if he could not have that, could he have what Lom Curtis and Burt Halloran had—a woman who belonged to him, if for no other reason than she had little choice?

Once more, Roy tied his horse to the hitching rail outside the mercantile and went in. He found the clerk crouched between the aisles, refolding a stack of shirts a customer had left in disarray.

"I need a spare horse," Roy said, offering no explanation. "Where can I get one?"

The clerk pushed up to his feet. Something flickered in his eyes, perhaps relief. "Ike Romney, who owns the livery stable, has a few horses he rents out. There's a dapple-gray mare Miss

Courtwood rented occasionally, with a Mother Hubbard saddle. Romney has a sidesaddle for ladies but Miss Courtwood favored riding astride."

"That's interesting to know." Roy kept his tone bland. "I might need a bedroll and a couple of blankets, too, and an extra pair of saddlebags."

The clerk sauntered along the aisle, all business now. "Romney sells saddlebags, and we don't like to step on each other's toes, but I'll set you to rights on a bedroll and blankets. Give you a good price, too." He pulled out a pink blanket in soft wool. "How about this one?"

Roy took a step back, dismissing the question. "You choose. I'll go and see about a horse and come back."

He left the store, walked over to the livery stable on the edge of town where a few horses pranced around in a pole corral. After a quick negotiation, Roy bought the dapple-gray mare for forty dollars and the nearly new Mother Hubbard saddle for another fifty, with a bridle and a pair of saddlebags thrown in.

He led the mare back to the mercantile, tied her next to Dagur at the hitching rail and went inside the store. The clerk presented him with a neatly wrapped bedroll and two sturdy canvas bags with something packed inside them. "It's five dollars for the bedroll," the storekeeper informed Roy. "I put in two blankets, the expensive kind that don't itch so much." He held up the canvas bags. "These are useful to line the saddlebags. Easy to unpack, you can just lift out the contents." Looking awkward, the old man added, "I put in a few odds and ends that might come in useful. No charge. The contents are on the house."

Roy settled his bill. When he gathered up his purchases, the clerk spoke quietly. "Don't forget what I said, stranger. Every man has at least one use for a woman. If that is what you have in mind, do right by her. Make her into a wife."

Roy pretended not to hear. Outside, he paused to peer into the canvas bags, to see what doodahs the storekeeper had provided. Hairbrush. A cake of French milled soap. Small mirror. Hair ribbon in pink silk. Tooth powder. Toothbrush. A length of white muslin, something a woman might use to protect her face from dust while riding the desert trails.

With a sudden pang of nostalgia, Roy realized he'd not come across such feminine items since he was ten years old and his mother died. Closing his mind to the past, he loaded the goods on the dapple-gray mare, mounted Dagur and rode out of town at a slow walk, leading the mare by the bridle. He'd wait until dark. The girl must have a reason why she wanted to hide, and he would respect her desire to remain unseen.

* * *

Celia eased the back door ajar and slipped out into the cool darkness of the September night. The scents of lavender and yellow sweet clover and blue passionflower surrounded her. In the bleakness of her life, her precious garden remained the only source of comfort. Soon the apples would be ripe enough to eat and the potatoes and carrots ready to harvest, and she could supplement her unappetizing diet of tinned goods and oatmeal porridge.

"Good evening, Miss Courtwood."

Nothing had alerted her to the man's presence—no snap of a twig beneath the sole of a boot, no clatter of hooves on the street outside, no nervous whinny of a horse tied to the porch railing. Why had he searched her out? And why had he come back now? Earlier, when he'd knocked on her door and toured the garden, Celia had longed to hurry downstairs and stop him from leaving, but the battle of conflicting emotions within her had kept her frozen by the bedroom window, where she had watched him from behind the lace curtains.

"Why did you come?" she asked, staring into the shadows beneath the apple tree.

"The name's Roy Hagan, Miss Courtwood. Sorry I didn't tell you before."

"What are you doing here?" Her voice quivered, revealing her agitation. She battled the urge to hurl herself against his chest, to scream out her loneliness and confusion and rage. If she did, he might pull her into his arms and she could lay her head upon his shoulder and let the tears locked inside her flood out in a purifying stream that might ease her misery.

But she did none of it. Years of tiptoeing around her mother's sickbed and a lifetime of trying not to add to her father's woes had taught Celia to contain her emotions, to act with a serene dignity. Right now, the silent clenching and unclenching of her fists at her sides was the only sign of the turmoil that went on inside her head.

Beneath the huge, gnarled apple tree, the shadows shifted, separated and became a man. Standing in the moonlight, dressed in black trousers and a dark shirt, the brim of his hat tugged low, the man looked part of the night. He had uncovered his left eye, leaving the padded cotton patch dangling around his neck by its rawhide strap.

"Can we talk inside?" he asked. Without waiting for an answer, he closed the distance between them, took her by the elbow and ushered her back into the house.

It was barely a touch, his fingers resting lightly against her arm, but even through the fabric of her dress, Celia could feel the warmth of his skin, could feel the strength in him. It sent an odd shiver through her, that physical contact. It was the first human closeness she had experienced since the sheriff hauled her father away, and it made her feel as if a glass wall around her was shattering, exposing her to life again.

At the rear door, the man fell back, allowing Celia to enter first. The kitchen was small, with a row of white-painted cabinets beneath the window and a square table with a pair of chairs along the opposite wall. She'd opened the shutters to let in the moonlight, but she had not yet lit the stove. To cook her supper, she preferred to wait until past midnight, when the thin column of smoke through the chimney had a better chance to remain unnoticed.

Celia waited for Roy Hagan to step across the threshold and close the door behind him. Then she faced him, making no effort to hide her scar by turning to one side. Her fingers fisted into her calico dress—she'd abandoned her rustling skirts and layers of petticoats—and for the third time she asked, "Why are you here?"

"I came to see if you are all right, Miss Celia."

Just like that, he had taken the liberty of calling her by her given name. Even though no one called her Miss Courtwood, apart from Mr. Northfield and Mr. Selden, both sticklers for formality, the sound of her name on the stranger's lips and his intrusion into the safety of her kitchen put another crack into Celia's rigid self-control.

"I wish you hadn't come," she blurted out.

"No, you don't, Miss Celia," he replied. "You're glad I'm here."

There was no arrogance in the man's tone, only understanding and compassion. Knowing that he had spoken the truth caused the gates of restraint to fling wide-open inside Celia.

"How can I be glad that you're here?" The words poured out of her, but despite her agitation, her voice didn't rise from its even pitch. "You may have protected my father, saved him from a bullet, but had you not robbed the bank in the first place he would not have been put in danger. You were the danger and the rescue, the peril and the protection. I owe you no gratitude for saving him from a danger you brought upon him yourself."

She paused to draw a breath, then went on with a burst of anguish. "What eats me up inside is that I knew what you were planning to do. Secretly, I gloated over my cleverness, having figured out that you'd come to rob the bank, and I did nothing to stop you. Nothing." She stared at him, a plea in her eyes. "Do you understand how that makes me feel? I could have stopped it, but I didn't, because I wanted to pay back the town for ostracizing me."

"Don't beat yourself up so, Miss Celia."

"Beat myself up?" A bitter groan wrung from

her. "You haven't heard the half of it. The bank manager, Mr. Northfield, got it into his head that my father had been in cahoots with the robbers, and he shared his suspicions with the sheriff. My father refused to defend himself, and now he is serving five years in Yuma prison. He'll die in prison, alone and neglected, for nothing but the noble misconception that by accepting the blame he'll set me free, relieve me of the burden of supporting him while he grows too weak to work."

Tears burned in Celia's eyes but she refused to let them fall, just as she had refused to let them fall during the long years of her mother's illness, or when every birthday trapped her deeper into spinsterhood, with no prospect of love, no prospect of a family and home, nothing but loneliness and the struggle to earn her living looming in the future.

"And you know what, Mr. Hagan?" Celia let the words form on her tongue, admitting to the guilt that pressed like a vise against her chest. "Deep down inside me there is this awful feeling of relief." She lifted her chin in a gesture of defiance. "So don't tell me that I must not beat myself up. I contributed to placing my father in danger, and when he takes on the blame for a crime he didn't commit, I feel relief because it spares me the trouble of nursing another dying parent and leaves me with only my own mouth to feed."

* * *

Always on guard, Roy observed his surroundings while he listened to the girl unburden her mind. Again, the long-forgotten smells tugged at his memory—crisp, clean laundry, flowers in a vase on the table, the lingering scents of home cooking.

Celia's last words pulled him back to the present. Earlier, he'd wondered if she had been in on the crime, but it had never crossed his mind that she might believe her father to be innocent. Rapidly, he reviewed all the possibilities. No. It could not be. Everything pointed to the man's guilt, including what the girl had just explained. Roy opened his mouth to speak, closed it again. He didn't want to be the one to tell her the truth.

"Why are you hiding?" he asked.

Barely had his voice faded away when a thud echoed from the front of the house. In a flash, the heavy Smith & Wesson revolver appeared in Roy's hand. On soundless feet, he inched past the girl and opened the connecting door to the parlor.

"Don't." She reached out and tugged at his arm. "It's just youngsters. They throw clumps of manure at the house. It does no harm." When Roy glanced back at her, he could see a shadow of a smile hovering around her mouth. "Manure is good fertilizer for my garden. Saves me from sneaking out to the hitching rails on Main Street to collect some."

He returned his gun to the holster, eased back into the kitchen and closed the door to the parlor. Before he had a chance to collect his thoughts, the girl burst into speech again.

"Does that answer your question about why I'm hiding in my house?" Bitterness sharpened her tone. "Before, the town was suspicious of me. Now they believe I'm evil. According to their thinking, I drove my father into betraying them. Nobody lost anything in the robbery, the gold was fully insured, but they hate me all the same, as if they were facing financial ruin."

"No," Roy said. "That does not answer my question."

Her lips pursed as she considered his comment. Then her chin lifted in the proud tilt he was beginning to recognize. "You think I'm a coward? That I should have the courage to ignore them and sashay down the street as if nothing was wrong?" She flapped a hand to indicate his guns. "It's easy for someone like you to shake off the weight of public disgrace. I haven't quite gotten used to being an outcast. It still hurts."

It never stops hurting, Roy wanted to tell her. *You just learn to accept it.*

"What are you going to do?" he asked. "Your food will eventually run out."

"I have a gun. A Winchester rifle. I can hunt game."

"In the darkness? On foot? You'll have to go a long way out of town to find game."

"I…" She hung her head, darted a glance at him from beneath her brows. "My father said he has some money put aside and he'll arrange to have it sent to me. I've been waiting for it to arrive. Without the money, I can't leave."

There it was. The final proof. Her father must have been talking about his cut from the take. And if Roy knew anything about Lom Curtis, a prior agreement bore no weight with the outlaw leader. If a man could not make a demand in person, he had little chance of collecting his cut. The only way Celia could get her father's share was to ride up to the outlaw camp and ask for it.

"I doubt your father can send instructions from Yuma prison." Roy glanced out through the window. A cloud had drifted across the moon, deepening the darkness. They needed to get going while they could rely on some moonlight. "I've come to take you with me," he told the girl. "Pack what you can carry on a horse. You've got fifteen minutes. I want to be out of here before the clouds thicken."

"You expect me to go with you?"

"You can't stay here."

"At least I've got a roof over my head. A place of safety."

"What will you do when your food runs out?"

She didn't reply right away. Roy let his gaze rest on her. In the shadows he could not see her scar. Her hair, loosely gathered at the nape of her neck, was pulling into ringlets. Her lips were moist and full, her gray eyes luminous, full of feminine allure. As he studied her, he could hear her quick intake of breath and knew she, too, had felt the attraction flare up between them, hot and swift, like a spark from a bonfire.

When Celia finally spoke, her tone was strained. "You may have been right to think I was glad to see you, but that doesn't mean I'm willing to throw away the last of my dignity. If there is only a shred of my good reputation left, I'll cling to it with all the more ferocity."

"I didn't mean—" Roy broke off abruptly. Just what did he mean? He'd not thought beyond rescuing her from her self-made prison. But how exactly was he going to help her? Now that he knew she'd not been involved in the crime, he couldn't expect her to make the sacrifice of becoming an outlaw's woman. He did not regret that her honesty put her out of his reach. Dreaming of something pure might be better than a tarnished reality.

He spoke slowly, formulating the plan as he put it into words. "I have money coming to me from the bank job. Five percent of the take. I don't know how much it is—"

"They took forty thousand, six hundred and thirty-five dollars in gold and cash. Five percent is close to two thousand dollars."

He nodded. "I'll take you with me, and we'll go and collect the money. You can have it. The amount ought to be enough to buy you a new start somewhere."

"I'll not accept your ill-gotten gains."

Roy shrugged. Once the girl learned the truth about her father, she'd have to take that stiff pride down a peg or two, and now was as good a time to start as any. His tone was blunt. "You have little choice but to come with me. If you stay here, you'll end up a whore."

"A whore?" Her eyes narrowed. "Certainly not." She took a deep breath and squared her shoulders, like a soldier launching into battle. "I shall become a financier. A speculator on the stock exchange. Perhaps not in New York, but at the new one opened up in Chicago earlier this year. I've got it all planned out. I have a good brain, and the ticker tape does not care about your gender. A woman's money works just the same as a man's."

Startled, Roy studied Celia's expression. He could see determination in the haughty tilt of her chin, faith in her abilities in how she met his scrutiny without a flinch.

"An investor needs capital," he pointed out. "What if your father's money never arrives?"

"Then I shall…" Her words petered into silence and her rigid posture slumped. Uncommonly intelligent, she could map out the gloomy prospects of her future without him spelling them out for her, but he did it anyway.

"An empty belly is a cruel master. You'll stick it out for a bit, until your stomach swells from nothing but water. You'll grow weak and dizzy, but the will to live is strong in humans. You'll be too proud to beg, so you'll leave the safety of this house and go knocking on doors, hunting for work. No one will hire you, but some man will be bold enough to sidle up to you and whisper a suggestion in your ear. You'll put your chin up and tell him to go to hell. Might even muster up the strength to slap him. But then a second man asks, and a third. By the time your body screams with pain from lack of nourishment, you'll find yourself saying yes to those men, and it will be you who has ended up in hell."

She contemplated him. "And if I come with you?"

"I promise not to hurt you, and I'll give you the money. If you feel bad about taking it, we can make it a business transaction. I'll finance your

stock speculation against a share in the profits."
He gave her a crooked smile. "It can be my retire-
ment fund. Every outlaw needs one."

"I…" She took another deep breath. "You
promise? You promise to give me the money and
ask for nothing in return? Even if I lose it all
through poor judgment? The markets can be un-
predictable."

"I promise." Roy reached past the girl to where
a water bucket stood on the counter. He filled the
steel dipper, lifted it to his lips and drank, watching her over the rim while the silence weighed
heavy in the air. When the dipper was empty he
hung it back in the bucket, pulled out one of the
chairs by the table and sat down in it. "It's up to
you," he said. "I'll leave in ten minutes. You can
come with me and collect the money, or you can
stay here and accept your fate, as you wish."

Chapter Five

Celia studied her reflection in the glow of the kerosene lamp burning on her dresser. She had changed into the elegant riding outfit she'd ordered before leaving Baltimore, a split skirt in blue velvet and a fitted jacket to match, with yellow piping along the edges and gleaming brass buttons at the front. She'd dreamed that one day she would be wearing the outfit as she rode out beside a man, ready to start a new life.

Be careful what you wish for, her mother used to say, and now Celia understood the meaning of the warning. She'd be riding out with a man. And she was headed for a new life. But instead of a husband and home, she was putting her trust in the promise of an outlaw and counting on her own ability to make her way in the world.

Refusing to dwell on shattered dreams, Celia took out a pair of dangling earrings and fastened

them into her earlobes. Her parents had consented
to the flamboyant jewelry because the flicker of
amethysts on gold wire drew attention away from
her scar. With her hair tumbling down in a flurry
of curls, she looked as wild as a gypsy. She added
a flat-crowned black hat and black gloves. Finished, she picked up the small carpetbag she'd
packed with a few personal possessions, blew out
the lamp and headed downstairs.

As she stepped into the moonlit kitchen, Celia
noticed how Roy Hagan's mismatched eyes widened at the sight of her. Like a gentleman, he rose
from his chair. Celia held her breath. At least one
aspect of reality lived up to her dreams, surpassed
them even. She was riding out with a man more
handsome than she could ever have imagined.

For a moment, their gazes locked. An odd tension knotted in Celia's belly, a tingling sensation
that seemed to radiate outward from her center.
Like before, she yearned to have Roy Hagan bundle her into his arms and hold her tight. Even if he
couldn't offer her the security she longed for, he
could give her an illusion of comfort, a moment
of forgetfulness, a distraction from the grim re-
alities that awaited her.

With a sigh, Celia forced her gaze to veer away
from those mesmerizing eyes. Feeling awkward,
she balanced on the balls of her feet and tried to
gather her composure. She didn't know what to

make of the pull of attraction between them, how to resist it, or if she even truly wanted to. Going away with a man would ruin her reputation anyway, and she was tired of being condemned for sins she hadn't committed. Perhaps she ought to enjoy the sinning rather than just pay the penance.

"Do you have a spare horse, or do we ride double?" she asked.

"I bought you a horse. The dapple-gray mare from the livery stable."

He'd bought her a horse. Celia felt a sinking sensation, like a swimmer caught in an undertow. Instinct told her she was heading for ruination, her moral boundaries already crumbling. But what choice did she really have, except perhaps one method of ruination over another, as the man had so bluntly spelled it out to her a few moments ago?

And yet, she knew she was not accepting the invitation to join him just because it was her only choice. Her blood was flowing swiftly in her veins, her skin tingling. If she had to give up the dream of a secure, happy future, she would seize the chance of an adventure and make the most of it.

She gestured toward the quiet street outside. "Where are the horses?"

"Left them on the edge of town."

Celia moved deeper into the kitchen, dumped

her carpetbag on the table. "Would you mind fetching them and riding up to the house?"

"I thought you were hiding from your neighbors."

"Some people may have figured out that I'm still here..." She paused, fidgeted with the clasp on her bag. How could she explain the vagaries of feminine pride? She spoke in a low voice, not meeting his gaze. "I want everyone in town to know that I'm gone. That I'm gone with you...a man who cared enough to come and fetch me."

Something flashed in his eyes, and Celia knew that Roy Hagan had understood, even without explanations. Curiosity stirred in her anew. What was in his past? What rejections had he suffered that made him so attuned to her plight, and how had he come through those hardships so strong?

"I'll only be a few minutes," he told her, and strode to the back door.

Celia watched the outlaw melt into the darkness, and then she lit the lamp on the table and carried it into the parlor. In the soft glow of the flame, her eyes traveled over the bookcases, the pictures on the walls. Despite everything, the house contained good memories, and she wished them to remain unsullied.

Quickly, she returned to the kitchen and packed a burlap sack with whatever foodstuffs she had left in the cupboards. The task completed, she lit another lamp, used it to illuminate her passage to the woodshed in the rear of the garden and carried over two heavy planks of timber. By the time the muted *clip-clop* of hooves came down the street, she had searched out a hammer and a handful of nails.

She unlocked the front door, stepped out onto the porch. Ragged clouds drifted across the sky, allowing the moon to play hide-and-seek. Celia stared into the shadows. The moment she could discern the outline of a rider and two horses, the clouds parted, and moonlight fell on the stranger. He had kept his eye patch pulled aside, but now he quickly restored it as he saw the glow from her lamp. He halted by the porch, dismounted and looped the bridle reins of both horses over the porch railing.

"Could you do something for me?" Celia asked. "I've bolted the back door from the inside but the lock on the front door is flimsy, easy to force open. I want you to nail these boards across the door frame to secure the entrance."

"A crowbar will pull them loose in no time."

"I know. But I want to send the message that this is still my home, not an abandoned dwelling, free for anyone to loot or vandalize." She held out the hammer and nails.

"The noise will wake up the town."

"That's the idea," Celia replied quietly.

Roy Hagan gave her a rueful smile and shook his head, but he took the hammer and nails and set to work, lining up the first board across the door and hammering the nails into the frame. The pounding echoed in the quiet of the night. A light came on in a window across the street, then in another one. By the time the man had finished, a dozen yellow squares cut into the darkness. He put the hammer and remaining nails away in the saddlebags and turned to Celia.

"What next?" he asked, amusement tugging at the corners of his mouth.

"Curtains are twitching up and down the street," Celia replied. "I want you to put your hands around my waist and lift me on the horse like I'm the most precious thing you've ever handled."

"All right." His fingers curled around her waist and she sailed into the air. For a second, he held her high, as if to boast about his strength. Then he gave what sounded like a groan of pain and settled her in the saddle. After releasing his hold at her waist, he clasped her ankle and fitted the toe of her boot into the stirrup. "Anything else?" he asked in a tone that held a hint of laughter.

Speechless, Celia shook her head. A sense of humor was the last thing she would have expected from the outlaw, but he seemed to possess an endless capacity to surprise her. "I'm ready," she told him. "Just lift up my carpetbag and the burlap sack with provisions and fasten them behind the saddle."

He did as she'd asked, and then he untied the horses, mounted and set off at a slow walk. Celia lined her dapple-gray beside his buckskin and rode out of town with Roy Hagan, her head high in defiant pride, as if it was Prince Charming himself who'd come for her.

When they reached the end of the street, the man pulled ahead and Celia fell into line behind him. Moonlight threw eerie shadows, making the desert landscape appear strange and mysterious. There was no sound except the steady clip of the horses' hooves and the occasional hoot of an owl. The night air was cool and fresh.

After perhaps three miles, Roy Hagan pulled to a halt. The clouds had thickened, obscuring the moon. For the last mile, they had ridden in near darkness, relying on the keener eyesight of the horses. Celia could hear the rippling of water, could smell the rich scents of damp earth, and she figured out they had skirted around the town, heading north, and were now at the bend of the stream where the water tumbled over rocks to form a small pond.

The creak of saddle leather and the scrape of a boot made her aware the outlaw had dismounted. An instant later, she felt a pair of strong hands curl about her waist. "This is as far as we'll go tonight," Roy Hagan told her. He lifted her down and settled her on her feet, but he did not remove his hands from around her waist.

When he spoke again, his voice sounded very near. "During the robbery, did anyone in Rock Springs recognize the two men who came to scout out the bank with me?" She could hear the urgency in his tone. "If someone did recognize them, could they remember having seen me in their company earlier and connect me to the robbery?"

"I don't know," Celia replied. "I haven't heard anyone mention anything, but with my father accused of involvement I'm the last person people would have confided in."

The hands around her waist slipped away and the voice drifting through the impenetrable darkness grew more distant. "Just in case, I'd prefer not lighting a fire. And we'll need to get going again at the first glimmer of dawn. I'll put your bedroll down and you can go to sleep. I'll take care of the horses."

Boots thudded against the hard earth. Dead leaves rustled, pebbles scattered. Celia could picture the man stomping about, making sure no snakes or other critters had taken refuge in the lee of the rocks.

"Do we need to post a guard?" she asked. "I'll take my turn."

The outlaw's soft laughter rippled in the darkness, a strangely carefree sound from a man in his dangerous profession. "Celia, you're dead on your feet. You'll be sound asleep the second your head hits the bedroll. Anyway," he went on, "there'll be no need to stand on guard. Dagur is a good watchdog."

A frisson of awareness skittered along her skin. By not calling her Miss Celia, the outlaw had taken the intimacy one step further. She had expected to call him Mr. Hagan, but his boldness made her change her mind. She would take similar liberties and call him by his given name.

"Is Dagur your horse?" she asked.

"Yeah."

"Does the name mean anything?"

"It's one of the Norse gods, from the old legends. My ma's family was from Norway. Dagur is the god of daylight. I named him to remind me that even after the darkest night the dawn always comes."

From the somber tone of his voice, Celia knew he was not talking just about the sun rising and falling in the sky. He meant that even after the deepest moment of despair a ray of hope would eventually cut through the gloom.

"Can we give the mare a name?" she asked.

"The owner of the livery stable just refers to his stock by the color. The gray mare, he called her."

"If you don't mind, I'd like to call her Baldur. It's another Norse god."

"Baldur." Celia tried out the name. "I like that. What is Baldur the god of?"

"Beauty. And love and forgiveness and peace."

Again, Celia felt an unfamiliar warm feeling spreading in her chest. How could the stranger convey so much emotion, so many dreams and hopes and possibilities in a few simple words? Or was it just her imagination? Was she crediting him with poetry and the knightly chivalry of paying homage to a lady's beauty, when he was merely passing on a piece of ancient folklore?

"Baldur," she said softly once more, and made no further comment. Standing still, so she wouldn't get in his way or stumble on the uneven ground, Celia listened to Roy Hagan go about his chores. Saddle leather creaked, bedrolls rustled. A horse gave a quiet whinny, and then the outlaw was by her side, his fingers curled about her elbow to guide her.

He directed her a few steps away from the sound of rippling water. With a gentle pressure, he tugged her downward. Celia sank to her haunches and fumbled about. Her searching hands met the folds of a wool blanket—the fine, expensive kind.

"Lie down here," he told her. "There's a boulder

behind you, to give you shelter in case the wind picks up during the night."

"Where will you be?"

"Right nearby."

Celia stretched out on the bedroll and Roy Hagan arranged the blankets around her, like a parent tucking in a child. Something formed a pillow beneath her head. Celia examined it with her fingers and discovered it was his canvas duster, folded into a bundle.

"How can you see in the darkness?" she asked. "I can see nothing."

"It's my brown eye. Because I keep it covered most of the time, it has grown more sensitive to light. Like a cat, I can see in the night. But bright light hurts it now, so I prefer to keep my brown eye covered during the day, even when there's no one around to notice the mismatched colors."

As Celia listened to the mellow, deep cadence of his voice, her limbs grew heavy and her eyelids refused to stay open. The outlaw had been right about her inability to stand guard. Exhaustion rolled over her, as unstoppable as a flash flood after a burst of rain. His words faded into a distant murmur and then she fell into a deep, dreamless sleep.

Roy awoke to a faint gray light on the eastern horizon. For a moment, he kept still, watching from between half-closed lids, listening to every sound around him—the ripple of the creek, the early-morning call of a desert sparrow, the soft rustle of some small rodent in the sagebrush.

Satisfied his surroundings posed no immediate threat, he lifted his blanket aside and eased up to his feet. The cold night air closed around him. He rubbed his hands together to warm his fingers, then put on his hat and strapped on his pair of guns.

Moving without a sound, he walked over to the creek to check up on Dagur and Baldur, picketed by the water. By the time he came back to the sleeping girl, the first pink hues of sunrise streaked the horizon. Soon, they'd have to get going, but he was reluctant to disturb Celia's sleep.

While he formulated a plan for what lay ahead, Roy let his attention linger on the girl, admiring her beauty. Her face was flushed from sleep, her hair a riot of curls, the color more golden than brown in the soft morning light. She must be dreaming, for her lips were moving, as if in silent speech, and he could see a rapid flickering beneath her eyelids.

What would it be like, to have a woman like that belong to him? To have her share his nights and days, his failures and successes, his sorrows and joys? With a woman like that by his side, a man would want to build something, to make a home. There would be no need to strive for riches, for she would be enough.

But it was not for him ever to have the chance to find out how it would feel to have a woman like that for his own—or any kind of woman, for that matter. The thought flashed across Roy's mind, as sharp and painful as the blade of a knife. For a moment longer, he watched the girl, and then he turned away, reluctant to intrude on her privacy.

Squatting on his heels, Roy held his hand to the hard, night-chilled ground, to check for any vibration caused by horses thundering along the trail. He could feel nothing. Moreover, Dagur remained calm. It seemed unlikely that anyone in town had made the connection between him and the robbery and set off in pursuit. He could let the girl sleep.

That decided, Roy walked off to collect firewood and water, never straying far enough to let the girl out of his sight. He had breakfast ready by the time she finally stirred. Instead of puffy and disheveled, she awoke bright-eyed, looking as fresh as morning dew.

"Good morning," he called out.

"Good morning." Her voice was husky from sleep. She shook off the blankets, smoothed her hair and adjusted her elegant riding costume. Then she got to her feet, came to crouch by the fire and held her hands out to the heat of the flames. Watching him from beneath her brows in the shy manner Roy had noticed before, she spoke quietly. "I thought you said we would have to leave at first light. Why didn't you wake me up?"

"Thought you'd like some breakfast before we ride out." He picked up the soot-blackened pot. "Coffee?"

"Yes, please."

He poured into a cup and held it out to her. "Be careful," he warned her. "The cup gets hot to hold."

Gingerly, she cradled the battered tin cup between her fingertips, took a small sip and nodded her approval. "Very good," she said, appearing surprised. "I thought cowboys brewed coffee thick enough for a spoon to stand up in it."

Roy smiled, a flash of humor mingled with pleasure over the occasion. He'd never sat down for breakfast with a pretty girl before, with the rising sun gilding the sky and a campfire crackling and nature awakening around them.

"Outlaws do things to their own liking. I prefer my coffee hot and not too strong." He pulled a cast-iron skillet from the flames, shook a flat, circular bread onto a tin plate and took out his knife to cut the bread into quarters. "I usually make this for breakfast," he explained as he ran the blade across the plate. "Something between bread and pancake. Learned it from a feller who came from a place called Persia."

"It's a country, between Africa and Asia, near Turkey. They had a severe famine there a few years ago. Two million people starved to death. I guess some of the survivors might have come over to America and brought their customs with them."

Surprised, Roy glanced up at the girl. He'd given little thought to her background. He knew she was an Easterner and appeared to be all alone in the world, but was she a high-born lady fallen on hard times?

"You must have had some schooling, to know such things," he commented.

Celia nodded with a hint of pride. "I went to school in Baltimore until I was sixteen. I had hoped to go on to Normal School and become a teacher, but I had to give it up, so I could look after my sick mother." Her shoulders rose and fell in a casual shrug. "Mostly, I've educated myself from books. One of my father's friends owned a bookstore and he let me take books home provided I was careful to keep them looking like new." Her lips curved into a rueful smile. "I still get an urge to put on a pair of cotton gloves every time I touch a book."

Roy held the pan bread out to her. She took a quarter, nibbled at it for a taste, then devoured the rest, taking sips of coffee between mouthfuls.

"Did you not go to school?" she asked when she was finished.

"For a couple of years, until I was ten and my ma died."

"How did you come to be an outlaw?"

"Not a sensible career choice, huh?"

Her smile blossomed fully now, a lovely smile that lit up her features and made her look carefree and young. Roy wanted to see that smile again, so he put extra effort into telling his sorry tale, embellishing the details for a more comic effect.

"I became an outlaw because I was riding a half-broke horse."

"Half-broke horse?" Celia lifted her brows. "You mean a lame one?"

"A part-wild one." Roy peered inside the coffeepot. "There's a drop left. You want any more?"

When she shook her head, Roy put out his hand. "Can I have the cup? I didn't think to buy another, so we'll have to share this one until we get to a store."

"Oh?" A blush flared up on Celia's cheeks. It was something Roy had noticed—despite the honey tan on her face, flashes of color gave away her emotions—pink for embarrassment, pale for fear and bright flags of crimson when she fought to suppress an outburst of anger.

Roy took the tin cup from her. He felt her watching him as he tipped the last of the thickened brew from the pot into the cup and drank it in a few gulps, his lips pressed against the rim where hers had just been, like a transferred kiss of sorts.

Between bites of pan bread, he talked, trying to coax one of those smiles out of her again. "I was riding along the trail, minding my own business. I had just left the homestead where I grew up, and I was riding a mustang I'd caught only the week before, a black stallion. He was a devil, but he was a magnificent horse, and he was the one I wanted to take with me.

"The ground beneath us started shaking, and I could hear the thunder of hooves behind me. I twisted around in the saddle to look back along the trail, and I saw a group of men charging toward me at full gallop. I tried to control the stallion, but he was thrilled by the stampeding horses, and when the riders passed me, the stallion joined the herd, racing along.

"Eventually, I regained control of my half-wild mount and fell back from the crowd. But by then another group of riders was emerging from the cloud of dust behind me, and these men had their rifles pointed at me.

"It was a posse, I realized, and the first group of riders must have been bandits trying to outrun them. It dawned on me that should I fall behind, I might be taken for a straggler, one of the outlaws.

The posse would shoot first and ask questions later, by which time I might no longer be alive to answer them. So I kicked my heels into the flanks of the black stallion. Magnificent beast that he was, he shot forward and caught up with the escaping bandits. I joined the group and rode with them, all the way to their secret canyon hideout. It was only after we'd pulled to a halt that the outlaws noticed they'd picked up an extra man."

Celia gave a wry smile. "And just like that, you became one of them?"

Feeling awkward, the gloomy memories stirring in his mind, Roy busied himself rinsing the empty cup with a drop of water from his canteen. "They were not going to let me ride out after I'd learned the route to their camp."

He could have added that when boy of fourteen who'd been treated no better than a stray dog finally had people acknowledging his existence, talking to him, treating him like a person, it had been all too easy to mistake the basic human interaction for friendship. By the time he'd learned that many of the outlaws felt no loyalty and could shoot each other over a minor dispute, he had drifted too far outside the law to break away from the gang and go back to being an honest man again.

Head tilted to one side in question, the girl contemplated him. "Do you like the outlaw life?"

"Did you enjoy hiding in your house?" Roy countered.

Her gray eyes widened, then narrowed in dismay as she figured out his comment. A man—or a woman—did what they had to do to survive, whether they liked it or not.

When she opened her mouth to speak, Roy held up a hand to silence her. "Save your breath," he told her. "It's too late for me. This is my life, and one day I'll go at the end of a rope, or from a bullet, or in some remote canyon when my ammunition runs out and my canteen is empty. There's nothing I can do about it, and I no longer even bother to worry about it."

Shocked by his blunt statement, the girl blinked. She turned toward the dying breakfast fire and stared at the smoldering coals for a long moment. Then she looked up at him again, an oddly compassionate expression on her face. When she spoke, her voice was very soft. "But does it not occur to you that someone else might care if you live or die?"

Roy's earlier thoughts rushed back to fill his mind. What would it be like, to have a woman like Celia Courtwood belong to him? An uneasy sensation, dangerously close to yearning, flooded over him. To start with, having a woman of his own might mean that there would be someone in the world who put a greater value on his life than he put on it himself.

Every muscle in Celia's body ached from the day's riding and she'd never been so tired in her entire life. If she hadn't been so ravenous, she would have simply closed her eyes and tumbled into sleep right there, seated on the hard ground with her legs tucked under her, a fire crackling in front of her, the scents of bacon and beans from the pan Roy was stirring over the flames surrounding her.

But despite the hardships of the day, for the first time in as long as she could remember she did not feel afraid of the future. Perhaps, when the worst had already happened, there was nothing left to fear. Moreover, being on the trail had given her a sense of freedom, an illusion of having left past troubles behind.

"This stock exchange dealing, do you have any experience of it?"

The question took her by surprise. She'd been covertly watching Roy, letting her eyes skim over his broad shoulders, the slope of his back, the slim hips circled by the gun belt, the muscular legs that held him in graceful balance as he crouched by the fire.

"I'm just trying to figure out if my investment is safe," Roy went on, glancing at her over his shoulder. The firelight turned his hair into a curtain of gold and his uncovered blue eye twinkled at Celia with the humor she found so appealing.

Flustered, she gathered her wits. "Oh, yes. Yes. I know how to do it."

"Care to tell me how you gained the skill?"

Celia wanted to wrap her arms around her knees and curl into what Papa used to call her hedgehog roll, but she resisted the temptation and merely shifted on the ground to stop a pebble from biting into her backside.

"When we lived in Baltimore, my father would bring home old ticker tapes with the stock quotes. I would study the newspapers, learn about different corporations and pick stocks. Just for my own amusement, I entered my investments into an old exercise book and kept accounts. I was very successful at it."

Her cheeks colored, and she felt compelled to add, "Of course, it is easy to make millions when it is all in theory. With imaginary money there is no need to worry about losses, so an investor can afford to take greater risks."

Roy lifted the pan from the flames. "Why take chances with the money? If you lose it, you'll be right back where you started. Why not find another job in a store, or in a boardinghouse? Or even become a teacher? You told me that's what you planned once."

"I want to be independent. Not at the mercy of an employer."

"Be honest, Celia." She could hear laughter in Roy's voice. "I bet you want to make millions so you can sashay back into Rock Springs and queen it over all those people who were unkind to you."

Despite her fatigue, her back stiffened. "And if I did, what's wrong with that?"

"Nothing. If you believe revenge is worth the risk."

Celia felt her hands curl into fists. *Revenge.* Perhaps, deep down, she ached to triumph over all those people who had turned against her. But more than that, she wanted never to be exposed to a rejection by a man again. Rejection from cowardly suitors. Rejection from men too lacking in chivalry to spare twenty-five cents to ease her humiliation during a box lunch. Rejection from employers too worried about public opinion. And if independence would save her from rejection, she would bury the dream of a husband and home and put her energies into earning her livelihood in a way that relied on no man's favor or permission.

Chapter Six

After two days on the trail, Roy accepted he'd acted on impulse when he took the girl with him. He'd wanted to rescue her, but he had not fully considered the havoc the constant proximity of Celia Courtwood would wreak on his peace of mind.

And now he was paying the price. Every moment of night or day, he was aware of her presence, never quite able to concentrate on anything else. At night, he would lie awake in the darkness while she slept only a short distance away. During breakfast and suppertime, his eyes drew to her, lingering on her feminine shape, desire building up in his blood.

Unaccustomed to long days in the saddle, Celia suffered from sore muscles and needed his assistance to mount and dismount. Every time he touched her, his hands curled about her waist, the edge of his thumbs butting against the underside of her breasts while he supported her weight, Roy had to battle against a physical reaction to her nearness.

In the evenings, they shared the camp chores, and while they sat down to eat they would talk. Little by little, he was making progress in solving the puzzle of Celia Courtwood. She worked hard, never complaining. She had a keen mind and a love of the rugged landscape. Her feelings ran deep and strong, but she hid her emotional reactions behind a wall of restraint that seemed as suffocating as an iron harness.

On their third morning together, Roy walked up to the breakfast fire to find Celia staring at the blackened, hissing coals. The coffeepot had toppled over, pouring its contents onto the flames. Next to the pot, the skillet stood askew, the half-baked pan bread spilled out, covered in ashes and scorched beyond rescue. Celia was staring at the dying fire, hands fisted by her sides. A few paces behind her, Dagur stood still, looking contrite.

"What happened?" Roy asked.

"Your horse butted me in the back and I knocked over the coffeepot and the frying pan."

"He likes to do that—butt my shoulder—to get attention." Roy put down the firewood he'd collected and edged closer to the dying flames. He could see Celia's fraught expression, could feel the pent-up anger and frustration sizzling within her like a lighted fuse wire.

"You're doing that thing with your hands," he said calmly.

She shot him a glare from the corner of her eye. "What thing?"

"Clenching and unclenching your fists, like you want to strangle somebody."

Her voice came out low and strained. "I dropped the skillet and knocked over the coffee-pot because your stupid horse butted me in the back."

Roy grinned. "I can see how you can't strangle a horse."

Celia's expression softened and a tiny twist of humor tugged at the corners of her mouth. "I don't want to strangle—"

"Why don't you let the anger out?" Roy cut in. "Yell at Dagur, or swear."

"A lady does not yell. Or use swear words."

"Try it. Say *damn*."

Celia remained silent, standing still, her face impassive, her posture rigid.

"Say it," Roy prompted again. "*Damn*. Or, if your starched-up lady manners can't handle that, how about 'gnats'? My ma used to say that. When my grandparents caught her doing it, she'd flap her hands about her head, pretending insects had been bothering her."

Celia frowned at him, then uttered the word in a placid, conversational tone.

"That's no good," Roy told her. "Why do you bottle up your reactions? When you get angry, you choke up like you've swallowed a porcupine. Even when you're happy, you put a lid on it. I've never heard you laugh properly, or whoop with joy. You never shout or yell. You don't even raise your voice in an argument. You just keep it all buttoned up inside."

Except when it all gets too much for you. Roy could have added. *Then it pours out.*

But even at the height of her distress, when she had shared her suffering with a complete stranger on the day of the church social, Celia had revealed her grief in a low, tear-muffled voice.

"I learned to do it when I was growing up," Celia explained, talking in that too-placid manner of hers. "While my sickly mother was alive, I had to curb any childish exuberance, in order not to disturb her. And it was the same with my father. He liked peace and quiet, and I did my best to provide him with a tranquil, serene environment at home."

"Well, they ain't here now, are they?" Roy said with a calculated harshness. Only now did he realize how much Celia's carefully maintained reticence had been bothering him. He wanted to break through it, to free her from the cage of artificially controlled behavior she had imprisoned herself within.

"Say it," he prompted her again. "Damn."

"Gnats." Celia bit her lip, then repeated the word with a greater effort behind it. "Gnats. Gnats!" She tipped her head back and yelled it up to the heavens. *"Gnaaatss!"*

Falling silent once more, she lowered her chin and returned her attention to him. Her eyes sparkled with humor and her features were animated, alive in a way that drew the eye away from her scar far more effectively than the dangling pair of earrings she'd worn on the night they rode out of Rock Springs.

As Roy watched her, he felt an ache in his chest. He wanted to give her a life where she could feel safe and happy, but there was little he could offer her beyond the money he'd already promised her. But perhaps he could show her the healing power of laughter.

The morning sun was low, the air cool and crisp. Celia was wearing her blue velvet riding costume piped with yellow, almost like a cavalry uniform, but she had yet to put on her hat, and her hair was piled in a loose knot on top of her head. Even from three feet away, Roy could see a hairpin sticking out from the mass of dark-gold curls.

Without warning, he lurched forward and reached out to tug the hairpin free. A flurry of ringlets tumbled down. Just for good measure, Roy burrowed his fingers into the remaining knot of golden-brown tresses, found another hairpin and pulled it away.

"Don't," Celia protested, lifting her hands to her unraveling upsweep.

"You've got to do better than that." Roy took a step closer. He caught one of the cascading curls between his thumb and forefinger and tugged at it.

Celia gave a little squeak of indignation and jerked her head aside.

"That's it," he told her. "Shout at me. Tell me what a lout I am, to tease a lady."

Each arm darting out in turn, he kept tugging at her curls, all the while making sure to keep the pressure gentle, not to hurt her. Celia attempted to retreat, shuffling backward on her feet, but he followed, as relentless as a bee buzzing around a crock of honey.

A frown battled against a smile on Celia's face. Her hands flapped at his, trying to stop him. "Gnats!" she shouted. "Gnats! Damn!" And then, when her upsweep collapsed completely, curls tumbling over her eyes, obscuring her vision, she gave up the battle, lowered her arms to her sides and yelled, "You lout!"

"That's good," Roy said, like a teacher praising a student. He closed the single step between them, wrapped his arms around her waist and lifted her high and spun her in a wild circle, sending the desert scenery sweeping in a flurry around them.

"Don't," she cried out. Breathless, oscillating between delight and annoyance, she clung to him, her hands curled over his shoulders, and let delight win. Her head tipped back, her hair streaming like a river of molten gold behind her, and she laughed out loud, a deep, husky sound that made her body vibrate beneath his hold. For the first time since they met, Roy saw a truly carefree expression on her face.

He ceased his spinning and lowered her back to the ground. Unsteady on her feet, she clung to his shirtfront and continued to rock with laughter—a rollicking, joyful laughter, not the strained chuckle he'd heard from her once or twice before.

"That's better, isn't it?" Roy said, smiling down at her. She'd recovered her balance now, and without any conscious thought he released his hold from around her waist and lifted his hands to her face, brushing back the mass of unruly curls.

All of a sudden, he could feel her body tense, could sense her hold her breath in anticipation. Her hands remained on his shoulders, her fingers clinging to the fabric of his wool shirt, and she looked up at him, the heat of passion evident in her clear gray eyes.

Desire rippled through him. Every instinct he possessed urged him to kiss her, and he knew she would allow it. The fine, educated lady that she was, she would allow it, welcome it even. The realization hit Roy like a spark from a fire. He wanted to do it, more than anything, but it wouldn't be right. If he started, he wouldn't know how to stop, and his aim was to give her a better life, not to add to her problems.

He cupped her cheek, felt the softness of her skin, breathed in the scent of flowers and vanilla from the soap the storekeeper in Rock Springs had packed for her. Summoning every trace of chivalry, every ounce of decency he possessed, Roy forced himself to put a stop to something that had not truly even started.

"I can't give you much," he told her, a rough edge to his tone that served as a warning. "Beyond the money I've promised you, the only thing I can offer you is a sense of yourself as a beautiful woman. A woman who is capable of laughter and happiness. Who deserves better than anything I could give you." He paused to study her expression. "You understand that, don't you, Celia?"

For a long moment, her eyes held his. Finally, her lashes came down to shield her emotions. "Yes," she replied. Drawing away from him, she added, "Of course, I understand. A woman would be a fool to think otherwise, and I'm not a fool."

Roy felt worry knot up inside him as he watched Celia crouch down to deal with the messy remains of their ruined breakfast. *I'm not a fool.* He gave a rueful shake of his head. He didn't know much about women, but he knew enough to understand that when it came to matters of the heart, every woman, even one as clever as Celia Courtwood, could be a fool.

The heat of the midday sun baking down on her, Celia rode on her gray mare behind Roy on the narrow mountain trail. The ground was rising steeply now, not a blade of grass in sight, only dust that clogged her lungs. Around them, red cliffs formed jagged walls, like a maze luring them into its depths.

Lulled by the monotonous clip of the horses' hooves, Celia found herself absorbed by the memory of the interlude at breakfast, when Roy had teased her into losing her ladylike decorum. The incident had only taken a few minutes, but she suspected those brief moments might have a lasting impact on her life. She felt light-headed now, her body restless, as if eager to break out of the straitjacket of a dutiful daughter she had worn all her life.

A straitjacket that did her no good now. Papa was languishing in jail. Bound by her promise not to intervene, she could do little to ease his plight. Surely, now was the time to be selfish, to seize whatever joy might be available to a spinster of twenty-six, with a scar on her face and not two pennies to rub together.

Moreover, if she wanted to make a success of being an independent financier, she needed to learn boldness of action. Speculation on the stock exchange was not for the timid. She would need to make decisions without hesitation. Stand her ground. Argue with brashness. Be prepared to defy the rules of society and not feel ashamed for it.

As they climbed up another steep rise, Celia peered through the veil of muslin she wore to protect her face from the sun and the trail dust. She felt a jolt in her chest when Roy twisted around in the saddle to look back at her. Beneath the brim of his hat, his hair shone golden in the sun, and the black patch over his eye gave him a reckless, pirate look.

An outlaw. A criminal. A man who lived by his guns.

Celia let her thoughts drift back to Stuart Clifton and Horton Tanner, the two suitors she had only a few short months ago pinned her hopes upon. When she'd imagined kissing them, she'd wondered if Mr. Clifton's moustache would tickle, or if she could tolerate the taste of Mr. Horton's chewing tobacco.

But with Roy… When he touched her, when he looked at her, she could not think at all. She only felt, with every fiber of her being. It had seemed as if all reason had abandoned her, leaving nothing but a throbbing yearning that started somewhere deep inside her and spread and spread until it consumed all of her.

A woman would be foolish to give in to such a yearning. *I'm not a fool*, she had declared with a touch of haughty pride. But perhaps she was. Perhaps every woman had the right to be foolish, just once in her life.

By the time twilight fell, exhaustion dominated Celia's thoughts. They were in the canyon country now, a maze of plateaus and gorges with vertiginous drops down to the riverbeds. Controlling the horse on the precarious trail had taken all her concentration.

Ahead of her, the path widened and Roy reined to a halt. Baldur's hooves clinking on stone was the only sound as Celia caught up and halted alongside the buckskin. Some twenty paces up the trail, the glow of a bonfire danced among the evening shadows.

Roy leaned closer to her and spoke in a murmur. "There's a party already camped by the spring. We have no choice but to join them. It's the only place for miles around with water." He hesitated before adding, "They might be the rough type of men. Best tell them that you're my wife."

Not waiting for an answer, Roy urged Dagur into motion again. Celia followed, keeping close. If she hadn't been so tired, she might have laughed at the way life seemed to be taunting her. Now that she had discarded the dream of a husband and home, she was forced into pretending that she was some man's wife.

They emerged into a rocky clearing bordered by a circle of soaring cliffs. Darkness was thickening now. A pair of big, bearded men stepped forward to greet them, rifles firmly clasped in their hands.

"Looking to camp for the night," Roy called out.

"Just the two of you?" a deep voice called back.

"That's right. Only me and my wife."

One of the men gestured toward the fire. "You're welcome to join us. Supper's just about ready and there's plenty. No need for you to cook." Despite the friendly invitation, the man did not relax his grip on the rifle.

"Obliged," Roy replied, in the laconic manner of many Western men.

They dismounted and took care of the horses, letting them drink from an old iron bucket chained to a rock basin. Water coursed down the cliff in a narrow stream, so slow it made no sound as it gathered into the hollow depression. While she moved about, Celia could feel the eyes of the men following her, and she could hear them talking. In addition to the pair who had greeted them, there were two others, a man and a boy of no more than ten.

Finished with the chores, Roy led her to the light of the fire. One of the men jumped up from the big stone he'd been seated on. "You sit here, ma'am. It's nice and flat."

She managed a polite nod. "Thank you."

Roy gave her arm a tiny squeeze, as if to tell her that these men were not the rough kind, even though they carried guns. In silence, he settled her on the flat-topped stone, and then sank to sit cross-legged on the ground beside her.

The third man, the only clean-shaven one, lifted a blackened stew pot from the fire and began to ladle food onto tin plates. The boy darted about, handing out the portions, starting with Celia, with a curious look at her. Celia tensed, but she did not avert her face to hide the scar on her cheek.

"Name's Gus Osborn," the clean-shaven man said, not interrupting his serving of the stew. "This here lad is my son, Gus Junior, and the other two are my brothers, Ben and Walt."

One of the bearded men spoke up. "I'm Ben. And since there's a lady present, we might make it Augustus and Benton and Walter."

At the friendly introductions, Celia felt her anxiety ease. And yet there was a tension in the air, the rifles very much in evidence. Covertly, the men were keeping a careful eye on Roy, and Roy was sitting in a casually relaxed pose that did not hide his alertness.

"Gus and Ben and Walt is just fine with me," Celia said, forcing a lively tone. "Although Gus Junior might be quite a mouthful for a little boy."

"I'm not little," the boy protested. "I am seven. And three-quarters."

Walt burst into laughter. "No word is too big for that boy's mouth. He reads like a sponge and chatters like a magpie. He's not used having a woman about, is all. Soon he'll start jabbering again. We had a heck of a time keeping him silent while we waited for you to ride up, to see what kind of folks you were."

Celia could think of no reply to that, and Roy remained silent, so she hid her unease by tucking into the food. The stew was surprisingly tasty, rich with meat. Curious about their hosts, Celia observed the men while she ate. Stocky in build, all three had homely features, with a big nose and shaggy dark hair, alike enough for the family connection to be evident at first glance.

"Where you headed?" Roy asked.

"Place called Gold Crossing," Gus Osborn replied. Around forty, he was the oldest and clearly the spokesperson for the group. "Do you happen to know the place?" he went on. "There's been a big gold strike down there."

Roy shook his head. "Not my line of business."

"What's your line of business, mister?" the boy piped up.

Celia tensed. She'd learned it was not a question to ask in the West. There might be a grain of truth in Walt's comment that the boy was a chatterbox.

"This and that," Roy replied, with a careless shift of his shoulders. "Have been doing some gold transport, for banks and railroad companies. Don't know much about mining."

"Didn't get your name, stranger," Ben said.

"That's because I never gave it." Calmly, Roy scooped up another mouthful. Silence fell, the atmosphere suddenly charged with danger. Celia held her breath. The other men must have noticed the outline of Roy's pair of pistols beneath his duster, must have some inkling that he earned his living with his guns. Was she going to get her first glimpse at how an outlaw dealt with unwelcome questions?

After he'd chewed and swallowed the mouthful, Roy pointed his spoon at her. "The lady here, she's Celia Courtwood. And I'm Roy. It's not short for anything. Just Roy."

A sigh of relief whooshed out of Celia's chest. She'd noticed Walt's hand tighten around the rifle balanced upon his knee. Now his grip eased again. She resumed her eating and listened to the amicable talk between Roy and the men pick up once more.

"You planning to get rich with gold?" Roy asked.

Gus Osborn gave a dismissive snort. "Not me. I have a sensible head on my shoulders. I mean to set up a mercantile and sell supplies to the miners. These two foolish brothers of mine are keen to stake a claim and try their luck."

The boy, Gus Junior, had finished his supper and was standing up, giving Celia an intense perusal. She fought the urge to avert her face, or to lift a hand to cover her scar. Ill at ease, she lowered her head and scraped the last of the food from her plate into her mouth.

"Mrs. Courtwood, did you come from a catalog?"

"What?" Forgetting her good manners, Celia spoke with her mouth full. Was the boy asking her how she'd come into being—brought by a stork, or found under a gooseberry bush, or some other such fairy tale concocted to satisfy curious young minds.

The boy stared at her. "Are you—"

"Gus Junior," his father cut in. "Shut up."

"But Pa, Uncle Walt and Ben said—"

"Don't repeat everything you hear."

"But Pa, they were saying—"

One of the bearded men held up his hand. "I'm real sorry, Mrs. Courtwood. It's our fault. The boy don't mean to be nosy. It's just that me and Ben have been talking about sending off for a woman from a catalog." He gave an awkward shrug. "You know, a mail-order bride. When we saw you, we wondered if you knew anything about it. If you had any advice on how to go about it and avoid the pitfalls."

The other bearded brother, Ben, chimed in. "We don't want to end up with a woman who's so buttoned up she'll throw a fit if a man lets his eyes drift lower than her neckline. Or one so persnickety she won't let a man have a beer in a saloon. Or…"

Celia held up a hand to stem the flow of qualities to avoid in a wife. "I get the point," she said. "Perhaps the sensible approach would be to correspond with a prospective bride until you can ascertain that she is suitable."

"A woman could lie," Gus Junior pointed out. "Women do that."

"Gus Junior!" his father admonished.

The boy shot him a belligerent look. "You said—"

"Gus Junior!" his father bellowed.

The sharp tone did the trick and Gus Junior fell silent. Celia fought to suppress a smile. Sponge indeed. And not just what he read in books or newspapers. The boy must file away every comment he heard, every bit of gossip that reached his ears.

"It's all right," she said, her lips twitching. "Maybe it is a feminine quality to believe that occasionally a slight bending of the truth is allowed." She turned to the pair of bearded, homely-looking brothers. "If you want to see what you might be getting, my advice to you is to forget the matrimonial advertisements and look in places where unmarried women who need to earn a living might be employed—stores, cafés, restaurants. Roy found me behind a mercantile counter."

"Would not work for us," Ben said with an assessing glance at his brother. "A woman will run a mile when she sees our ugly mugs. We reckon a catalog woman is our only chance. And she won't get no photograph either, to scare her off before she starts the journey out."

Celia hesitated. It was indecorous for a woman to speak so boldly, but she felt empathy toward the brothers. "Don't make the mistake of thinking it is only a man's facial features that can make him attractive to a woman," she told them quietly, grateful for the night shadows that hid her embarrassment as she went on, "A strong, masculine body can send a feminine pulse racing."

The brothers bent their shaggy heads together and muttered something to each other. Celia couldn't quite hear, but it sounded as if they were plotting how a man could take off his shirt in front of a lady and let her have a proper look. Alarmed at the possibility, Celia cleared her throat and provided more detailed instructions.

"If you court a girl, seek an opportunity to help her up to a buggy, or on a horse, and while you are doing it hold her high to demonstrate your strength. I guarantee you it will impress her." Celia stole a glance at Roy, to see if he remembered how he had helped her into the saddle when they left Rock Springs. He was looking right back at her, and the glint of masculine satisfaction in his blue eye confirmed that he did.

By the time they had finished supper and were ready to settle down for the night, it seemed to Roy that the tension was thick enough to fall like a cloud of dust over the stone clearing and suffocate them all. Celia could sense it, too, he was sure of it. It would be impossible for anyone not to notice how the Osborn brothers were watching his every move, their rifles always within reach. More than once, two of them had moved several paces away from the fire and conferred in muffled tones, while the third remained seated, keeping a watchful eye on him.

"You and your wife can sleep over there." Gus Osborn pointed into the shadows where the cliffs formed a small alcove. "The ground is a mite softer there, with a layer of sand."

"What about posting a guard?" Roy asked.

"We've already agreed shifts," Gus Osborn replied. "You can sleep."

Roy pushed up to his feet, addressed his words to Celia. "I'll get the bedrolls."

He walked off into the darkness. When he was out of sight, he pushed his eye patch aside. Now would be the time. With his superior night vision he could take care of them, make them hand over their guns. But that would mean risking a gunfight, in case the brothers chose to make trouble.

He slipped his eye patch back on, collected the bedrolls, walked back into the firelight and went to Celia, who sat perched on the rock, her eyes darting nervously from one man to another. Roy dumped the bedrolls beside her. "Can you go and spread these out? I need to talk to Gus."

Alarmed, she looked up at him. "I'd rather wait here."

"It's all right," he told her in a gruff murmur. "I'll join you in a moment."

Celia gave a slow nod, but the fear did not leave her eyes. Roy hated to see her worrying, but there was nothing he could do to reassure her, apart from curling his hand over her arm and giving her a tiny squeeze, the way he'd done earlier. Again, it seemed to work, for she pushed away from the stone, picked up the bedrolls and withdrew into the shadows, the heels of her button-up boots clicking on the stony ground. One good thing about the design of women's shoes, Roy thought ruefully. He could always hear Celia moving in the darkness and knew exactly where she was.

Once she had vanished into the shadows, Roy turned to Gus Osborn. The man must have signaled to his brothers, for Ben was standing to one side of the fire, rifle cocked and pointed at Roy. Walt and the boy were nowhere in sight. Roy could hear the boy's angry protest and knew his father had ordered him to be ushered out of the way.

"I guess you've figured out what business I'm in," Roy said quietly.

"Gold transport, you said." Gus Osborn's tone was strained. "Only I reckon you didn't ask the bank's permission before you hauled away their gold."

"That's right." Roy held his hands away from his body, waist high, palms out. Not quite in surrender, but the gesture of a man seeking peace. "What do you plan to do about it?" he asked, only giving an impression of mild curiosity.

"Ever kill a man?"

"No. Never hit a woman either, or mistreated a horse."

For a moment, silence fell. Timber collapsed in

the bonfire, sending up a hissing spray of sparks. Roy could see Gus Osborn start at the sound. Roy himself had not moved a muscle.

Finally, Gus Osborn spoke. "You seem to think that hitting a woman or mistreating a horse is a worse crime than killing a man."

"Seen plenty of men who deserved killing. Never met a woman yet who deserved hitting, or a horse that deserved mistreating." Roy was talking quietly, making sure his voice didn't carry out to Celia. "I want no gunplay. Not with the lady around, and the boy. If you have a mind to haul me in, I'll give you no trouble. I'll come without a fight, but I need your word that you'll see the lady to rights. She has no family."

"Is there a wanted poster out on you?"

"No. Never caught the attention of the law."

"Well…" Gus Osborn's voice grew light with the rush of release that came from the ebbing of tension. "Seeing there's no reward for you, it seems a fool's errand to haul you off to a sheriff."

"'Preciate it," Roy said simply. He turned away and went to Celia. The skin on the back of his neck prickled. If Gus Osborn and his brothers were not the good, sincere men they appeared to be, he'd be dead by morning. There was no way on earth he could stay awake and alert throughout the night. Not against three men who could take turns to sleep.

Chapter Seven

Night settled over the clearing. His eye patch pulled aside, Roy kept watch on the Osborn brothers in the faint light of the crescent moon that had risen in the sky. Two of the brothers slept, with the boy sheltered between them, and the third sat by the fire, a curl of smoke rising from his cigarette, the acrid smell drifting over on the light breeze.

As the temperature plummeted, Roy's ears picked out a faint sound, like a series of muffled clicks. It was Celia, he realized. Her teeth were chattering. Torn with indecision, he listened. He'd settled as far away from her as possible within the confines of the horseshoe-shaped depression in the rock wall, to give her the maximum of safety in case the brothers did something unexpected.

He'd learned not to trust anyone, but now he would have to trust these strangers, just as they had trusted him to share their campfire. Without a sound, Roy eased into a crouching position and moved over to Celia. She lay huddled against the rocks, curled up into a ball, the cocoon of blankets quivering as her body trembled within.

"Are you cold?" he whispered.

She looked up at him, her eyes wide in a pale, pinched face. "Freezing."

"It's colder at high altitude, and the fire is small." He reached for his gray blanket, pulled it along the ground and spread it on top of her pair of fluffy pink ones. "This will help."

"You can't—"

"Hush!" Roy cut in, but it was too late. Behind him came the click of a hammer on a pistol. Barely pausing to slip his eye patch back in place, Roy lifted his hands in the air and pivoted on his heels to face whichever of the Osborn brothers was holding him at gunpoint.

"Everything all right?" the man asked.

With his brown eye covered, Roy had lost the advantage of night vision, but the man's raspy voice revealed it was Ben Osborn. "My wife is cold," Roy replied. "She's not used to sleeping outdoors. Could you add more wood to the fire?"

"Sorry, friend. We have to ration the firewood, to make it last until morning." The voice grew light with humor. "If I had the good fortune to have me a wife, I'd think of better ways to keep her warm."

There was another click as the pistol hammer fell, and Ben Osborn turned away and went back to the fire. Roy hadn't seen him carry a handgun before. Most men possessed a rifle for hunting but pistols were less common. He guessed the brothers shared one between them and passed it to whichever of them was taking his turn to stand guard.

On the edge of his vision, Roy caught the flare of fabric and returned his attention to Celia. Without a word, she had lifted the edge of the blankets, inviting him to lie down beside her. Roy felt his gut tighten. Why was it that when a man did his best to act with honor, the circumstances conspired to tempt him in the opposite direction?

For a few endless seconds, he remained crouched beside her, irresolute. Then he said, "Move over. I'll go behind you, with my back against the rocks. That way I can see what's going on around us, and you'll get whatever heat there is from the fire."

Celia inched forward to make space for him, but she did not move far enough, and Roy had to wedge his big body into the narrow gap between her and the cliffs. Easing down on his side, he draped one arm across her waist beneath the blankets. He could feel the underside of her breasts pressing against his forearm, and when she curled up tighter, her rear end butted into his groin, drawing an instant response.

Blood pounding in his veins, Roy lay as still as a stone statue. His brain seized up, empty of any thought except the feel of the woman in his arms. For days, he had let his eyes slide over her feminine shape, building up a hunger that clamored to be satisfied. If he cast aside all propriety, he could let his hand roam over those endlessly fascinating peaks and valleys, for Celia would not dare to protest. After all, they were meant to be man and wife.

Just when Roy's resistance was about to break, Celia shifted against him. Wriggling inside the blankets, she turned to face him and arched her back, her eyes searching his in the dim glow of the fire. Roy clamped down on the need and spoke the words that weighed on his conscience.

"Those two men are looking for wives. You could..."

"No," Celia whispered back. "It's no longer what I want. I've set my heart on becoming an independent woman, beholden to no man. And anyway, it's too late. We've already told them that I'm married to you."

Roy nodded. Men, even those who thought as little of their prospects as the two bearded brothers did, would be suspicious of the lie and would not accept a woman they assumed lacked virtue. It was best to stick to their story, pretend to be husband and wife.

"Sorry," he whispered, and wondered if his relief showed.

Even in the darkness, he could see her smile. "Were you hoping to save your money?"

It took him a moment to understand. She was talking about the money he had promised her. Humor lurked in her eyes, and it served to break Roy's resolve. He had wanted to ease her out of her starched-up lady manners, and seeing her relax, knowing it was his doing, acted like a shot of good whiskey, heating the blood in his veins.

Slowly, he tightened his arms around Celia. With a sigh, she let her body mold against his as they lay together on the hard ground. He could feel how she fit against his hips, could feel her narrow waist beneath his hands, her breasts pressing against his chest.

He wanted to slip his eye patch aside to see her better but he was too afraid to release his arm from around her, in case she might pull back, or perhaps tuck her head against his shoulder, instead of craning her neck to look at him, the way she was doing now. He leaned forward and brushed his lips against hers, gently, giving her every chance to protest.

She made a small sound of acquiescence and Roy deepened the kiss, his mouth settling upon hers, tasting, teasing. Safe in the knowledge that the presence of others would stop things from getting out of hand, Roy let himself do what he had dreamed of doing for days on end.

Celia, Celia. Her name whispered through his mind. He could feel the softness of her skin, could smell the vanilla and flowers from her soap, and Roy knew that he would forever associate that scent with her, with tonight. For long minutes, he kissed her, but even as the pleasure throbbed in every beat of his pulse, he knew there would be a price to pay.

He had never been attached to a woman, could not predict how quickly and how strongly the ties of love could bind a man, cut into his heart. But he understood that with closeness came the pain of separation, the pain of saying goodbye, and the greater the closeness, the deeper the pain. With reluctance, Roy ended the kiss.

"All right?" he asked, studying Celia's expression in the darkness.

She didn't say anything, merely stared up at him with wonder in her eyes. Her lips were parted, her breathing swift. A blush radiated on her cheeks, and she looked up at him like no human being had ever looked at him—with acceptance and longing.

Finding the surge of emotion too much to handle, Roy bundled her against his chest. As Celia nuzzled up against him, warm and supple and yielding, he knew that each day she remained with him the pleasure of having her around would grow, and so would the depth of his solitude when the time came to part.

Dawn had broken by the time they said goodbye to the Osborn party but the low eastern sun didn't reach down into the stone clearing. The tension of the night hummed in Celia, and she was glad to be alone with Roy again.

As she clung to Baldur's back on the steep descent down to the river gorge, her mood changed to one of exultation. Perhaps deep down she had dreamed of Roy kissing her ever since the day of the box lunch, but she had not realized how good it would feel. Not just the kiss—although it had been everything she'd imagined—but wishing for something and getting her wish come true. It was a rare event in her bleak life.

Once they reached the bottom of the gully, the ground leveled along a shallow stream that meandered over pebbles, breaking into ribbons of water and gathering into pools. On the opposite side, a cliff soared vertical, the red rock surface as smooth as a mirror.

"There's an echo here," Roy told her when they dismounted for a lunch stop. "The legend says it will call back if you're telling the truth but keep silent if you call out a lie."

Celia unwrapped the muslin veil that protected her face. "You're making that up."

Roy replied with a boyish, carefree grin. "All right," he admitted. "I read it in a book, and maybe it was about some other place. But it could have been here. Try it out."

One hand on top of her hat to hold it secure, Celia faced the cliffs opposite. Tilting her head back, she filled her lungs and yelled at the top of her voice. "My name is Celia!"

"Celia... Celia... Celia..." the echo bounced back.

The corner of Roy's blue eye crinkled in a smile. "See?" he said. "Now try a lie."

Laughing, Celia shook her head. She took a step closer to the edge of the rippling water and shouted, "I am a good person!"

"Good person...person...person..." the cliffs replied.

She glanced back at Roy. He was frowning now, his eyes intent somewhere around her mouth. Celia felt her pulse quicken, but instead of taking a step closer to him, she lifted her chin once more and shouted out another claim. "I deserve to be happy!"

"Happy...happy...happy..."

Only after the echo had fully faded did she turn to Roy again. She had expected he would tease her, demand that she try an untrue statement next, but instead he reached out one hand and touched her face, a light brush of his fingertips. "What's wrong with your skin?" he asked. "It's all pink and angry. Like burned, but you've been protecting your face from the sun."

Heat flared up to her cheeks, and she knew the color of her skin had deepened from pink to scarlet. "It's you." She made a small, awkward gesture to indicate his jaw. "From last night...your beard stubble..."

Comprehension flashed in Roy's eyes. He stroked her delicate skin with the back of his fingers, his expression troubled. "I'm sorry," he said quietly. "I shouldn't have..."

"Don't you dare," Celia said in a voice sharp with emotion—emotion she might have kept carefully locked away before Roy encouraged her to embrace her feelings. "Don't you dare to try to take it back, make it undone."

Roy withdrew his hand and dropped his arm down his side. Turning away, he occupied himself with the horses. When it became clear that he did not wish to continue the conversation, Celia got on with setting out the food and they ate lunch in an uneasy silence, the previous night and what it might mean unresolved between them.

Afterward, they mounted their horses and resumed the trail that followed the river, skirting around boulders and weaving between stunted trees. To Celia's surprise, that evening Roy called for a halt early, before dusk had fallen. In the scrub along the banks of the pebbled riverbed, birds were hopping around, singing their evening chorus.

"Why don't you collect some driftwood for a fire?" Roy suggested, his manner easy now, as if he had conquered whatever had troubled him before. "I'll take care of the horses."

Her leather half boots crunching on pebbles, Celia strode off along the dry edges of the riverbed and collected an armful of driftwood. Her nerves thrummed as she thought of the nightfall. Tonight, they would be alone, without the constraint of others around them. Would they resume the intimacy they had started the night before, perhaps even take it further?

She came back to find Roy standing awkwardly beside Dagur. Hatless, shirtless, knees slightly bent, he had his hands lifted to his face. His eye patch dangled on its leather cord around his neck. When Celia got closer, she discovered he was shaving, with the aid of a mirror balanced against the pommel of the saddle.

After she'd dumped the firewood on the dry bank where Roy had set out their bedrolls, she edged over to him. "Why are you shaving like that?" she asked. "Why don't you prop the mirror against something that doesn't move."

"That's the whole point," Roy mumbled, the blade scraping across his cheek. "Dagur is an outlaw's horse. When I command him to stand still, he needs to obey. This is how we practice."

"Does the horse always follow orders?" Celia asked, intrigued.

"Like clockwork."

For a moment, she stood in silence, watching Roy shave. She liked seeing him without the black patch covering his left eye. It made him look younger, took away some of the aura of violence about him. As she studied his features, now softened by the suds of shaving soap, an intense longing seized her, as powerful as a vice around her chest.

An echo reverberated in her head.

I deserve to be happy...happy...happy...

Perhaps happiness was not a constant state. Perhaps happiness was a collection of fleeting moments, and one had to seek them, like panning for nuggets of gold in the dull gravel of everyday life. And now Celia sensed one such moment within reach.

"Want to bet the horse stays still?" she asked.

The blade scraping against Roy's jaw ceased its motion. "Bet you..." Roy paused to consider. "Bet you the breakfast chores for the rest of the trip."

"Wager accepted," Celia replied with a mischievous grin. She hurried over to the burlap sack that contained their provisions and searched out the oats she'd packed from her kitchen to make morning porridge. She shook a small quantity onto her palm, stuffed a few sugar lumps in her skirt pocket as insurance and went to stand a few feet in front of Dagur.

"Here, boy. See what I have for you," she crooned, extending her cupped hand toward the horse. When Dagur failed to respond, Celia stepped closer, making sure the horse caught a whiff of the oats. She could see the buckskin's nostrils flare, could see his ears prick up with interest. "It is *soooo* good." Celia made munching sounds. "Come and take it."

The horse craned forward but did not lift his feet from the ground. Celia extended her hand close enough to let Dagur almost take a nibble of the oats, almost to reach the offered treat, and then she eased back a step again.

"You've got to come and get it. I'm right here."

Dagur's muscles bunched and rippled, but the horse remained still. Watching Roy from the corner of her eye, Celia could tell he was rushing the shave. The blade rasped along his soap-lathered jaw with a frantic speed now. His eyes, one so clear blue, one warm chocolate brown, kept flickering in her direction. In his hurry, he nicked his skin and drew a drop of blood. He muttered a curse but did not slow down.

By now, one cheek and most of his jaw were clean. Time to collect on the insurance. Celia dipped a hand in her skirt pocket and pulled out the sugar lumps. "See what I have for you here, Dagur? Sugar and oats. Just for you."

She reached out and let the horse take a single lump of sugar from her palm before pulling her hand away again. With a whinny that sounded like a complaint, the horse lurched forward. After snatching the remaining sugar lumps from Celia's palm, Dagur hurried back to his previous position, as if hoping Roy might not have noticed the temporary absence.

With an exaggerated precision, Roy scraped away the last of the stubble on his jaw. He took down the small towel draped over the saddle horn, wiped the blade clean and put the mirror and razor away in his saddlebags. Slowly, he lifted the towel to his face and wiped off the few clinging soap-suds, and then, in a sudden motion, he flung the towel on top of the saddle and charged toward Celia.

"That was cheating," he said, humor in his tone.

Celia pivoted on her boots and darted to the other side of the horse. "That was a fair bet," she called back. Frantically, she searched for an escape route and chose the rocky ground on the left, where agility might give an advantage over strength and speed. "I'm going to enjoy the lie-in while you cook breakfast," she yelled as she jumped from stone to stone. "And the snooze while you wash the pots and pans."

No reply came from behind her, only the quick cadence of masculine footsteps. She leaped down from the rocks, took a path into the clump of creosote bushes. The footsteps chasing her lost their hurried pace. Either the thicket was too dense for Roy to push through and he was getting snagged by the thorns, or he was slowing down on purpose, to keep up the fun of the chase.

Emerging on the other side of the thicket, Celia glanced back over her shoulder. He was through and gaining on her, only a few steps behind. She burst forward, swung around a boulder, stormed past a deadfall. Her foot snagged on a buried root and she toppled forward. The hard desert ground hurtled toward her. She braced herself for the impact, but at the last fraction of a second, a strong hand gripped her arm, breaking her fall.

Spinning in the air, she landed on her back with a muted slam, a coarse clump of grass pricking at her skin through her clothing. Roy sank over her, straddling her, his hands braced on either side of her head, his face looming above hers. He was grinning with merriment, his eyes crinkling at the corners.

"That was girl cheating," he said.

"It was a reckless bet. Masculine overconfidence."

"What's the punishment for cheating?"

Celia held her breath. Her heart was beating swiftly from the chase, her body thrumming from the exertion, but now another kind of tension took hold of her. Slowly, slowly, Roy bent his arms at the elbows, lowering his shoulders, dipping his head toward hers. His gaze flickered over her features and finally settled on her mouth.

He was going to kiss her again. Maybe do more than kissing. Dusk had fallen, and in the low light Celia could see his blue eye shining bright, his brown eye dark and shadowed. She could smell the scent of the shaving soap on him, could feel the warm puff of his breath against her skin. An acute awareness of his weight on top of her overwhelmed her senses.

When his lips were only inches away from hers, Roy stopped moving. She could feel his body grow rigid, could see a muscle tugging on the side of his jaw. Something pressed against her belly, a swelling in his groin, the meaning of which should have raised alarm bells in her mind, but instead it caused a hot throbbing in her veins.

"Celia…" Roy spoke her name on a harsh intake of breath. She understood he was fighting with himself, torn between taking what he wanted and staying true to his promise not to harm her. A promise from which she could release him.

"Yes," she said.

Again, his gaze roamed her features. "What are you saying yes to, Celia?" he asked in a voice that was low and rough. "A kiss? Or more? To me stripping you naked and sliding inside you? What exactly are you saying yes to, Celia?"

"I don't know," she whispered.

Roy's expression grew shuttered. "Don't say yes to a man unless you know what you are saying yes to." With a quick shove of his arms, he straightened on his knees. For a moment, he remained there, poised above her, his mismatched eyes holding hers, the internal battle evident in the stony set of his features. Then he gave a deep, shuddering sigh, stood and reached down a hand to haul her up to her feet.

"I think it is time to cook supper."

He helped her up, and then he released her hand and walked away, his movements unsteady, lacking their usual grace. Celia watched him go, saw his golden hair reflect the last of the evening light before he vanished into the shadows. Echoes of past rejections crowded her senses, like mocking shadows. A few seconds ago, she had wanted something more. But in her turbulent mind she could not define what that more might be, only feel the sharp edge of disappointment and the hollow ache of being unwanted, just like she had always been.

They ate supper in silence, the weight of emotions between them too great to allow for a casual conversation. Roy had slipped his eye patch back on, and it added an edge of mystery to his masculine good looks. Celia stole glances at him in the flickering firelight, a mix of old and new dreams churning around in her head.

When she could no longer tolerate the silence only broken by the cool desert breeze that stirred the stunted cottonwoods along the river, making them whisper in the darkness like a reflection of her confused mind, she blurted out one of her tangled thoughts.

"Could an outlaw reform?"

Roy took a sip of his coffee. Beneath the brim of his hat, Celia could see a wary glint enter his blue eye.

"Drop it, Celia," he said. "I already told you. It's too late for me."

"Please," she said quietly. "Can't we at least talk about it?"

For a moment, she thought Roy might ignore her. When he finally spoke, his voice was casual. Too casual. The way he sat on the ground, hunched forward, his attention on the flames that crackled in the darkness, revealed his indifference to be feigned. It seemed evident to Celia that an escape from the lawless life had very much been in his thoughts.

"Twenty years ago it was easy," Roy said. "When the War Between the States broke out, you signed up for the fighting and stayed on until the end. If you came out alive, you could start with a clean slate."

"But now?"

"Sometimes the law might turn a blind eye, pretend not to recognize you if you change your name, but that doesn't make a man into an honest citizen. For that you'll need a full pardon from the territorial governor, or even from the president."

"Is there no other way?"

"A judge might make it known he is prepared to be lenient if an outlaw turns himself in. You can serve your time at the territorial penitentiary and come out a free man." Roy's mouth twisted into a grim smile. "And a much older one."

"You protected my father…took the bullet intended for him…that ought to help…" Celia's mind leaped ahead. In her eagerness to make sense of the jumble of ideas in her mind, she forged on, not pausing to consider the impact of her words. "You could turn yourself in. The authorities wouldn't hang you. You'd get five years in prison, perhaps ten. And you might get paroled much sooner than that…perhaps in just a few years…"

A scowl settled over Roy's features, but Celia paid no mind to it. She craned closer to him, the heat of the fire enveloping her as her words poured out in a breathless stream. "And then… once you've turned yourself in…you could tell them about my father, that he is innocent, and we could—"

Like a lash from a whip, Roy's voice silenced her. "Is that what this has been all about?" His expression grew harsh. "Is this what your kisses were leading up to? You want me to trade places with your father? Sacrifice my liberty so he can gain his?"

"What I meant—"

Roy cut her off with an angry gesture of his hand. "And of course, a man needs an incentive to throw his freedom away. Is that why you were so eager to say 'yes' to me a moment ago, Celia? Were you trying to seduce me into turning myself in, so you can use me as a bartering chip to get your father released?"

"I didn't mean it like that."

"There is no other way to mean it."

"Please," she said. "Let me explain."

Roy tossed the remains of his coffee into the flames and pushed up to his feet. For a moment, he stood there, staring at the hissing cloud of steam, the empty cup clutched in his fingers. The impassive mask that usually hid his emotions slipped, and on his features Celia could see hurt—hurt and a sense of hopelessness.

She wanted to jump up, wrap her arms around him and comfort him, but the stillness about him warned her to stay away. How thoughtless she'd been! In her eagerness to clear up her own tangled mind, she had put her ideas all wrong. She longed to undo the damage, but the words she had so thoughtlessly spoken could not be taken back.

She saw a shudder travel down Roy's powerful frame, as if releasing him from his frozen state. He hauled in a deep breath, then another. When he finally spoke, his voice was raspy and harsh, like rusty nails rattling in his throat, but the words were casual enough. "I need to check on the horses. I'll take care not to disturb your sleep when I get back."

Roy pulled the patch from his brown eye and strode away into the darkness. He could feel his body shaking. He'd known from the start there would be a price to pay for taking Celia with him, but each day that went by the cost seemed to escalate.

How could he have been so careless and let her stir his emotions? He should have guessed she might be manipulating him for her own aims. What else could be the reason for her sultry looks and her tempting smiles? Women like Celia Courtwood were not for the Roy Hagans of this world, and he'd be a fool to think otherwise.

Boots splashing through a puddle, Roy headed to the edge of the riverbed, where a grassy spot provided grazing for the horses. Dagur lay asleep on his side, legs stuck out like an obstacle to trip up a careless man. Roy circled around the horse and squatted on his haunches beside the buckskin's head.

Rubbing the horse's nose, Roy muttered to himself as much as to the animal. "Don't ever trust a filly, Dagur. You might have lost the urge when they cut off your male bits, but that hasn't stopped you from making a fool of yourself over Baldur. Mark my words, though, a stallion prances along and the mare won't give you another glance."

Dagur neighed and shook his head.

"Are you telling me I'm wrong, boy?"

The horse did not reply. Roy kept up his gentle stroking, the repetitive motion soothing his troubled mind. Had he reacted too swiftly? Could it be that the memory of a thousand childhood rejections had clouded his thinking? Surely, there could be no deviousness in Celia—she had made her suggestion out of love for her father. If he had any experience of the bond of parental love himself, perhaps he would understand her reasoning and not resent her for it.

Slowly, Roy felt his bitter anger fade away. The cool night air stirred his hair, helping his heated mind to calm. Humid scents drifted over from the stagnant ponds in the shallow stream, easing his throat after days of breathing the desert dust. Above him, a million stars dotted the sky. In the distance, a hyena barked, no doubt fighting for a carcass.

The inevitability of death and the vastness of the landscape around him filled Roy with an acute sense of loneliness. He thought of Celia, how she had flinched at his cutting words. He ought to go back to her, explain about his past. For the rest of the trip, he had to find the strength to resist the temptation she presented, but there was no reason why they couldn't be friends.

After saying good-night to the horses, Roy walked back to the campfire. Celia had not settled down to sleep but remained seated by the fireside, arms wrapped around her upraised knees. When she heard his footsteps, she looked up. The glow of the flames illuminated her face, and the anguish Roy could read in her expression cut like a knife.

Pulling his eye patch back on, he stepped out of the shadows. "It doesn't work like that," he said quietly, and crouched to add another piece of driftwood into the flames.

"I'm sorry... I didn't mean...not the way it sounded..."

He held up a hand, an easy gesture that brushed away the need for apologies. Celia fell silent, but instead of lowering her chin to rest on her knees again, she contemplated him, her gaze flickering over his features. Feeling suddenly self-conscious, Roy toyed with a piece of firewood, searching for the right words to make amends. Sticking to the facts was best, he decided. Emotions were too treacherous a ground for a man to tread.

"The law wouldn't simply believe an outlaw's word and let your father go free. And they wouldn't just pat me on the back for having surrendered peacefully. They'd put pressure on me to testify against the rest of the gang. Perhaps threaten me with a hanging. Might even go through with it, if I got them riled enough. And if they decided to let me live, I'd have to watch my back in prison, for my former associates would rather see me dead than risk me changing my mind about testifying against them."

Celia hugged her knees, drew tighter into herself. "I didn't consider..."

Roy fought the urge to reach out and bundle her into his arms. He wanted to banish her anxieties, to soothe her fears, and what better way to do it than to hold her close, let her feel the warmth and strength of a man's embrace. However, a moment ago, he'd resolved not to allow any more intimacies between them, and he needed to stick to the promise he had given himself.

"It's all right," he said, and forced a ghost of a smile. "You meant well, even if your ideas were not fully thought through. Best we forget the whole conversation."

She put her hand up, like a pupil in a schoolroom. "Just one more question. Why is it not possible to simply leave the outlaw life behind? Ride away, take on a new identity, start over in some place far away?"

Roy sighed. He didn't want to have the conversation, but he owed it to her to reply. "It's not that simple. Lom Curtis, the man who controls the Red Bluff Gang, has sworn never to let anyone leave after they have thrown in with him. He is not the true leader, though. There's a power behind him, some man in Prescott who is all respectable on the surface. Anyone who tries to break away, he'll put a bounty on. With my unusual eyes, I'll never be able to hide behind a new name. I'll always be recognized, wherever I go. I'd have the law as well as bounty hunters and Lom Curtis coming after me."

Celia's mouth tightened as she digested the information. Then, appearing to accept his suggestion to abandon the topic, she spoke in a carefully neutral tone. "Why do you cover your brown eye even when it is dark? I prefer it when I can see your face."

Roy replied with the same air of detachment. "With a fire burning, it is tempting to stare into the flames, and that blinds a man for a few seconds when he looks away from the bright light. If I keep my brown eye covered, I can pull the cloth patch aside and instantly see in the darkness. It gives me an advantage against another man sitting by the fire, and puts me on even footing with a man hiding in the shadows."

"I should have thought of that." Celia gave a slow shake of her head, her gaze veering away. "I guess there is a lot I don't know about the outlaw life."

Amen to that, Roy thought. *And let's hope you'll never have to learn.*

Aloud, he said, "Time to turn in for the night. I'll sleep over there by those big boulders. You can stay here and enjoy the heat of the fire." And with that, he walked away, the boundary between them as clearly marked as a barbed wire fence dividing the range.

Chapter Eight

The following morning, the trail dipped down farther and took them to a shady gorge beside a rushing river. The air was cool and moist, filled with rich scents of damp earth. The roaring of the water drowned out all other sounds, making conversation difficult.

Instead of enjoying the dramatic scenery, Celia dwelled on her troubled mind. Last night, she had allowed herself to be swept along with the new sensations Roy stirred up in her, but then her discarded dreams of a husband and home had clouded her thinking. She had talked about an outlaw's redemption, seeking for ways to turn Roy into a man who could fit into such a life. But she was following a different course now, that of an independent woman capable of forging her own fate. And such a woman could afford to have a liaison without the bond of marriage—the rules of society no longer mattered, for she was already beyond them.

But she had behaved as if her kisses came with a price tag, and even though they had made up their argument, a strain remained between them —a strain she had caused by her misguided comments.

As the sun began to sink in the sky, the gorge opened up to form a narrow valley. The river widened, rippling quietly over shallows between the low banks. From the trail of hoofprints that led to the water's edge, Celia could tell they had reached the river crossing.

Roy drew his horse to a halt and dismounted. His back was rigid, and he did not look at her as he spoke. "We'll cross tonight. There's enough daylight left."

Celia's mood sank. From what Roy had told her, she understood it was only one day's ride from the river crossing to the maze of canyons where the outlaws had their hideout. Soon, their time together would come to an end. Before that happened, she wanted to heal the rift between them, make sure their parting would not be marred by resentment.

Instead of pausing to help her down from the saddle, Roy strode to the edge of the river and studied the swirls of the current. Celia remained on her horse. After several days of riding, her muscles were no longer sore. She could feel a new strength and suppleness in her body. A similar, newfound strength flexed in her mind now. Somehow, before they reached their destination, she would find a way to remedy her mistake.

Roy came back up the slope from the water's edge. "I'll cross on Dagur first. He's been over many times. Then I'll come back for you and guide Baldur across."

"Baldur and I can follow you."

"No, you must wait for me. I don't know how the mare will react to water."

Celia did what she could to help as Roy unstrapped her bags from Baldur and put them on Dagur instead. He mounted again, fitted himself between the goods loaded on the gelding. For a moment, he let his gaze rest on Celia, then looked up the path and appeared to hesitate. With a quick, decisive motion, he unsnapped a holster on his gun belt, pulled out one of his heavy pistols and handed it to her. "I won't be long, but take this, just in case. This is the only crossing for hundreds of miles. There may be other travelers."

With that, he wheeled Dagur around and urged the gelding into the stream.

Her heart pounding with a sudden sense of danger and loneliness, the pistol an alien weight in her hand, Celia watched him cross. The water whirled around the horse's legs but never came higher than his belly. Roy lifted his boots out of the stirrups to keep them dry, his balance perfect in the saddle. It only took him a couple of minutes to wade across. On the other side, he turned to wave at her, then dismounted and began to strip the load off the horse.

Beneath her, Celia could feel Baldur's muscles bunch. Before she could react to the motion, the mare was surging down the riverbank. The heavy revolver clutched in one hand, Celia pulled at the reins but Baldur ignored her command and rushed headlong into the stream. Celia's fingers tightened convulsively over the grip of the gun, limiting her ability to control the bridle reins. As the water began to foam around her, she let go of the reins and clung to the saddle horn, her only thought to remain seated.

"Roy!" she yelled. "Roy! I can't stop the horse. I can't stop Baldur."

Barely had her cry faded in the air when she felt Baldur stumble beneath her. Water came up to Celia's thighs, soaking her velvet riding skirt, molding the heavy fabric to her legs.

"Go to the right," Roy shouted. "You're too far to the left."

Frantic not to drop the gun in her hand, Celia fumbled for the reins, but too late. She could feel the horse's hooves scrabbling against the slippery rocks at the bottom of the river, and with a lunge

Baldur leaped into the stream and began to swim, the powerful body of the horse churning through the water.

"Stay in the saddle!"

Celia could hear Roy's voice over the gushing spray the horse stirred up but she lacked the strength to fight against the weight of her skirts and the pull of the current. She felt herself being swept out of the saddle. With one hand, she clung to the saddle horn, her fingers curled around the slippery protrusion. Her other hand never loosened its grip on the cold steel of the Smith & Wesson revolver she knew was important to Roy. Even as the weight of the waterlogged velvet and the swirling water dragged her under, even as childhood images and memories of her parents flashed before her eyes, she held on—held on to the piece of cold, hard metal that connected her to Roy Hagan.

Frantic, Roy watched Celia slide out of the saddle. He rushed to the river's edge, was about to wade in when he saw her in the foaming swirls of water surrounding the horse. Her bonnet dangled by its straps, floating behind her. Her upsweep had unraveled and her hair hung in wet strands, the ends undulating in the water like a cloud of seaweed. He could make out one small, white hand wrapped around the saddle horn, trying to hold on.

His heart hammered so hard it hurt. He could not breathe, could not breathe. Terror and uncertainty stretched each second into an eternity. The whole world seemed to be in that small hand, holding on to the saddle horn, clinging to stay afloat. Baldur was craning out of the water, legs churning, closing the distance to the shore.

Horses were good swimmers, but their powerful bodies created a turbulent current. A rider who fell from the saddle could be sucked beneath the surface by the undertow. If Celia lost her grip, she would not only be swept away by the river, but she might be hurt by the kicking hooves of the horse, increasing the possibility that she might drown.

And yet, Roy did not dare to go to her. Celia's best chance was to hold on. If he tried to swim out to her, he might startle the horse into a sudden lurch and cause Celia's grip to slip. If that happened, the current might sweep her away before he could rescue her.

Finally, Baldur reached the shore. Panting, water cascading down her flanks, the gray mare stumbled out of the stream and scrambled up the bank. Celia hung draped against the side of the horse until they were clear of the water. Then she released her grip on the saddle horn and slumped down on the muddy slope.

Roy rushed over, crouched beside her. "Are you all right? Are you all right?"

Gently, he slipped one arm around her shoulders and raised her to a half-sitting position. Her face was marble white, her lips tinged with blue. Icy shivers racked her body. She spoke through chattering teeth. "I didn't...didn't drop it."

"Drop what?" he asked, before he noticed the pistol she was gripping, almost hidden in the folds of her dark blue velvet skirt. "You fool," he said with a flare of anger. "Why didn't you just toss it away?"

"Didn't drop it...didn't drop it..."

She kept repeating the words, as if she hadn't heard him. Just as well, Roy thought, furious at himself for the thoughtless outburst. Gingerly, he pried the pistol out of her grip and shoved it into the empty holster at his hip. "Let's get you dry."

He gathered her in his arms and straightened on his feet. As he carried her over to the flat piece of ground at the base of the cliffs, her waterlogged clothing soaked his shirt. He laid her down between a boulder and the single struggling cottonwood, went to the pile of goods he had unloaded earlier and unraveled her two pink blankets as well as his own gray one.

"You need to get out of those wet clothes."

"Here? Out in the open?" Her head swiveled

left and right, damp strands of hair flapping about her shoulders as she craned her neck to survey the trail that led up to the plateau above the valley. "Someone could come."

"I'll make a shelter to give you privacy."

He created a small enclosure by tying the gray blanket to the spindly tree and wedging the opposite end against the tall boulder with a piece of driftwood. By now, the sun had set, giving way to dusk. The temperature was plummeting. Roy cursed himself for not waiting to cross the river in the morning, when they could have benefited from the warmth of the sun.

Rushing around while Celia was getting undressed, he took care of the horses and collected a few pieces of driftwood to start a fire. The urgent tasks completed, he came back and peeked over the edge of the blanket. "How are you getting on in there?"

Celia lay slumped on the ground, still in her wet clothes. Her skin was deathly pale, her eyes closed, her body racked with shivers. She appeared barely conscious. Roy fought a flare of panic. He had little experience of well-bred ladies, but he expected them to be delicate creatures, prone to chills and fevers.

Not wasting any time on worrying about propriety or that he might give offense to feminine sensibilities, he ducked beneath the makeshift curtain. With quick, expert motions, he built a fire and lit it. Once the flames were crackling, he knelt beside Celia.

"You've got to get out of those wet clothes. Let's start with the shoes."

He undressed her like one might undress a sleepy child, talking softly, asking for guidance as he located rows of hidden hooks, untied knots and released buttons. All through the task, Celia made no resistance. Stiff and cold beneath his hands, she responded to his commands, lifting her arms, turning, helping him to shed the layers of soaked clothing.

By the time he had her stripped down to a thin cotton chemise and drawers, Roy found himself shaking with pent-up tension. He tried not to look, did his best to curb his masculine instincts. But the fine, hand-embroidered garments became nearly transparent as the damp fabric clung to her skin, revealing a dark triangle at the apex of her thighs and the rosy circles at the tips of her breasts.

Exercising every bit of restraint he could muster, Roy looked away. He spread his long duster on the ground, settled Celia to sit upon it and wrapped one of the pink blankets around her shoulders. When he spoke, his voice was strained. "I'm going to turn my back now. You get out of those wet things, all the way to your birthday suit.

Bundle up into the blanket and I'll rub you warm. Let me know when you are ready and I can turn around again."

As he stood with his back to her, his ears picked out every rustle of fabric, every swish of damp hair as she undressed. The river rippled only yards away, the wind blew in gusts along the valley, a hawk screeched overhead, but those sounds faded away as his senses attuned to the woman behind him removing the last scraps of clothing that covered her nakedness.

"I'm ready," she informed him.

Roy's heart was beating wildly, his hands trembling. While he'd undressed her, the aftermath of terror and the surge of relief that followed had helped him keep his rising desire at bay. Now, as he turned around and saw her sitting on the ground, the blanket draped over her shoulders, his body reacted with a sudden violence to the knowledge that beneath the blanket she was naked, totally naked, without a stitch.

"Let's get you warm." Moving with an odd reluctance, he sank on one knee beside her and began to rub her body through the blanket. Arms, shoulders, legs. He tried to think of something else, tried to forget that she was unclothed, but his mind refused to obey.

Celia spoke in a soft whisper. "I'm sorry."

"No need to be sorry," he replied, striving to

keep his tone bland. "You couldn't help it. Baldur is used to following Dagur on the trail. When the mare saw me unsaddle the gelding, she knew the day's work was over, and she was impatient to join him."

"I didn't mean that."

Curious, Roy glanced up at Celia's face. Until now, he'd been staring at the solid surface of the boulder beside him. At the barren earth in front of him. At the deepening shadows around them. Anywhere but directly at her. And now he froze. His hands ceased their rubbing and stilled, his fingers circling one slender ankle.

The blanket that covered Celia's nakedness had slipped down a fraction. Her back was straight, her legs lightly folded as she sat on the ground, her shoulders rising from the folds of the fabric like the statue of a goddess. Roy caught a glimpse of the upper slopes of her breasts, a pair of rosy pink nipples. It was clear to him that she knew what he could see. And she was letting him look. A lady and an outlaw. And she was letting him look.

He spoke through a tightened throat. "Celia... don't tempt me. Don't test your feminine charms on me. You're taking too many chances."

"No." She shook her head, her expression fraught. "I'm sorry, truly sorry for what I said earlier...about you testifying that my father is innocent. I didn't mean it like that... I was thinking that if you turned yourself in and served your sentence, you would be free." Her voice grew bolder, her tone more confident. "And don't lie to me. Don't tell me that you haven't thought about it yourself. That you haven't been dreaming of a better life."

The strain of looking at her and not touching added to the bitterness inside Roy. Of course he had dreamed! But he knew how unattainable, how impossible those dreams were. Her naive confidence was like wishing on a star and trusting for the wish to come true, and because of that foolish faith his response came out on a surge of anger.

"You act as if you care about me, but you don't. Not really. You're simply latching onto me as the first person who broke your loneliness. When I found you hiding in your house in Rock Springs, I told you that you were happy to see me. And you were. But not because of anything to do with *me*. Because I was a human contact. Someone to talk to. I know how terrible it can feel to be completely isolated, and how easy it is to cling to anyone who eases that isolation."

"I was happy to see *you*."

Roy ignored the comment and resumed his task of rubbing Celia's icy limbs. Slipping his hands beneath the blanket, he tried to close his mind to the shape of her leg, the soft texture of her skin, the subtle scent of her. As he worked to get her warm, he talked softly, telling her of his past, as much to unburden himself of the painful memories as to make her understand what he meant.

"My mother grew up on a horse ranch, and when she was sixteen she ran off to join a traveling circus. A year later, she came back, heavy with child. My grandparents found a man to marry her. He didn't love her, but he wanted the ranch. She was an only child and would one day inherit the property.

"I was born with different-colored eyes, and my grandparents took it as a sign that I was cursed, because of my mother's wanton ways. My stepfather hated me for what I was—another man's bastard. My mother…" He shrugged, unsure as he had always been. "Perhaps my mother loved me, but she feared the opinion of others, and her fear was greater than her love."

His hands stilled as the memories flooded over him. He told Celia of his lonely childhood, of being an object of fear and suspicion. "I went to school but I had no friends. At home, I had to eat at a separate table in the corner of the kitchen. My family, including my mother, barely spoke to me. And then, when I was ten, both my grandparents died of a fever, and my mother broke her neck practicing her tricks on a horse. I was left alone with the stepfather who hated me."

Roy paused and gritted his teeth, the old pain

still sharp. He told Celia how he had been banished from the house and was no longer allowed to attend school. He'd lived at the stables. Every morning, his stepfather had chalked a list of chores on a slate and put it by the back door of the house. In the evening, if Roy had completed the tasks, a plate of food would be left on the doorstep. If he failed to do the work, he'd go hungry.

From the way Roy could feel Celia's body shaking, he could tell she was weeping, silent sobs that rocked her shoulders. A beautiful woman, weeping for him. The thought eased the impact of the stark memories. He wanted to see her expression, wanted to see the empathy on her face, but he found that he couldn't look at her, for he couldn't trust himself not to reach out for her and take the comfort she was offering.

His voice hoarse now, as if it hurt to speak the words, but he went on, "When I was fourteen, my stepfather ordered me to leave the ranch. He was going to remarry and he didn't want me around his new wife. So he told me I had to be out by nightfall. I could take one horse with me. That's how I came to be riding the black stallion that got me mixed up with the outlaws."

Shaking his head ruefully at the memories, Roy suppressed a bitter smile. "At first, I was overwhelmed by the companionship, the camaraderie. Every outlaw at the camp seemed like a friend. I thought I loved them all. But as the weeks turned into months, and months turned into years, I grew to know some of them as the meanest, cruelest, sorriest excuses for a human being that ever trod the earth." His voice cracked, all artifice stripped away. "But when you've been all alone, isolated from the world, like you were in your house, any man who comes along will seem like a hero. It's not *me* you are hankering after. It is the comfort of companionship after having been ostracized by others, condemned to the prison of solitude, an outcast through no fault of your own."

Finally, he chanced a glance up at Celia's face. Tears were trailing down her cheeks, and her expression was gentle. In her misty eyes he could read pity, but also tenderness.

The truth he had tried to forget slipped out. "My mother...before she died, she was preparing to go away. I knew it, because I'd spied on her when she took a horse to a clearing in the forest. She was practicing her circus tricks, jumping on and off at full gallop, making handstands on the back of a horse. She was planning to leave, and she wasn't going to take me with her. Even if she had lived, I'd have been alone."

With a gentle smile, Celia opened her arms to him, the blanket spread wide, her bare breasts shining milky white in the falling darkness. "You don't have to be alone anymore," she told him softly. "At least not right now."

Roy abandoned the fight to stand aloof. With a harsh groan of emotion, he pulled Celia against him. Eyes closed, he kissed her—her mouth, her cheeks, her neck—hungry kisses that tasted salty from her tears, tears she had shed for the child he had once been. He hugged her tight to his chest and clung to her, as if trying to mold them into one so he would never have to let her go.

"Your shirt is damp," Celia murmured. "Take it off."

Reluctantly, Roy broke the embrace. It awed him to think that Celia welcomed his kisses, his touch. The knowledge filled him, soothing the childhood hurts that had never healed, making him feel complete for the first time in his life. Light-headed with a sense of elation, he released her, got to his feet and fetched more wood for the fire. Then he pulled his shirt over his head, hung their wet clothes over branches in the tree and came back to her.

Celia was lying down now, huddled beneath the blankets. Roy settled beside her, stretching out on his side. Without hesitation, she lifted the edge of the blankets, inviting him to join her. Inviting him to take whatever he wanted from her.

"Celia…" The protest died on Roy's lips. Slowly, as if giving in to a greater force than his reason, he joined her inside the warm cocoon of blankets. With a rough sound of longing, he reached out and let his hand slide over her soft skin. Inch by inch, he traced her shape. The slope of her breasts. The dip of her waist. The slight rise of her belly. He'd never felt anything so delicate beneath his callused palm.

Emotion rose within him, like a storm he could not hold back. It had never been like this when he sought comfort in a whore's bed. The very fact that he had paid for the pleasure, that he was one man in the string of many, to be forgotten as soon as the door closed behind him, had reduced the act to merely a physical release, without the sense of acceptance, the sense of validation he had sought his entire life.

As his hand swept back up over Celia's breast, she arched her spine and emitted a startled sound of pleasure. "Tell me," Roy said in a hoarse whisper. "Tell me what you like. Tell me what feels good for you."

"That…what you just did…do it again…" Despite the darkness, Roy could see her blush, understood that although she was brave enough for the act, she lacked the boldness to put her desire into words.

"All right," he replied. His reticence gone now, he cupped her breasts, stroked his thumb across the peaked nipples. When Celia made those low, husky sounds again, it broke the last of his restraint. Bracing his weight on his elbow, he eased half on top of her, his leg sliding between hers. When Celia's thighs parted in invitation, a wave of desire swept over Roy like a dark cloak that covered him, blotting out his decency and common sense.

He could feel his pulse pounding in his ears, could feel his blood surging in his veins. His entire body trembled with need. Within the confines of his clothing, his erection strained and throbbed, pressing against the soft swell of Celia's belly. Reaching down between their bodies, Roy fumbled with the button at his waist, driven by the prospect of release.

The sudden shifting of his weight on top of Celia's body must have hurt her, for she let out a whimper of pain. Roy could feel her wriggle, trying to get more comfortable. Like a light being snapped on in a darkened room, he suddenly saw himself in his mind, sprawled over her, intent on taking his pleasure, no matter what the cost to her.

With a supreme effort, he stopped. Lifting his weight away from her, he rolled onto his back. By now, stars had appeared in the sky. Bright, shining stars. And each of them seemed like a mark of judgment, telling him what a bastard he was.

Roy waited for a moment to calm down his ragged breathing. When he knew the words would come out casual, without the tremor of yearning or the huskiness of desire, he gathered his determination to prove those judgmental stars wrong.

"Celia, we must stop. Right now, before things get out of hand."

"I don't want to stop."

Roy let out a heavy sigh, tried to hold on to his resolve, prayed for strength. "There are few things in my life that I can take pride in, but I can honestly swear that I've never hurt a woman. If we take things too far, I'll end up hurting you."

"You could never hurt me."

"I will, if I get you with child."

For a moment, only the rush of the river filled the silence. Then Celia spoke very quietly. "When a woman is left a spinster, unwanted by any man, she misses out on life. Not just the role of a wife and mother, but she also misses out on physical passions." She leveled her gaze at Roy, her eyes full of uncertainty. "What I feel now...what I want now...is a taste of that passion. How can it be so very wrong?"

Roy studied her expression in the darkness, saw a mix of longing and doubt. "It's not just a question of hurting you, Celia," he told her softly. "I won't risk bringing a child into this world and having him suffer because of my sins. Even if you might be able to hide the fact that he is an outlaw's bastard, the child would grow up without a father to protect him. I will not have you taking such chances. I will not have *us* taking such chances."

"But couldn't we just…"

"No, Celia." His tone was blunt. "If we start something, I may not have the strength to pull back when I should. But I know that I must not take your innocence, or create the possibility of a child. If we don't stop right now, it will only bring suffering to both of us."

In the flickering firelight, Roy could see Celia's expression grow somber. He sighed, a heavy sound that held as much frustration as regret. Easing over to his side, he hauled Celia into the shelter of his body, her back pressed to his naked chest. He draped one arm across her waist to anchor her close to him and spoke in a soothing tone into her ear.

"Sleep now, Celia. That's one thing I can offer you tonight. I can watch over you while you sleep. Keep you safe. Safe from the world. Safe from me. For you should understand that right now the greatest danger you face is from me."

Chapter Nine

Dressed in her wrinkled velvet riding costume that had lost its elegance, Celia crouched by the river's edge and rinsed her face and teeth. To her surprise, she felt at peace with the world, even though her father was languishing in prison and tomorrow she would have to say goodbye to Roy. It seemed as if the warmth and closeness of spending the night in Roy's arms had created a shield that limited her horizon to this moment only, to this second, isolating her from worries that might lurk around the corner or wait for her back in civilization.

Refreshed by the cool water, Celia straightened and glanced over to where Roy was cooking breakfast. A jolt went through her at the sight of him. Last night, she had offered herself to him, and only his sense of honor and caution had prevented her from becoming a fallen woman.

Perhaps it was just as well that they would be parted. Given the opportunity, she might tempt him again, and the next time he might not show such restraint.

With a wry smile at her thoughts, Celia set off to join Roy, who had dished out the pan bread and was packing up their bedrolls, getting ready to leave. She halted when a hint of something pink beside a stone caught her attention. On a closer inspection it turned out to be a tiny clump of wildflowers. With a touch of guilt about depriving other travelers of their beauty, Celia stepped closer and reached down. She'd pick just a few. They would look lovely tucked into her upsweep.

Beside the stone something flashed, like a rope uncoiling, striking at her. A sudden pain gripped her hand, as sharp as a vise snapping shut over the delicate bones. Celia yanked her arm away. Petrified, she stared at the twin puncture wounds on the back of her hand. On the ground, something slithered away with a rattling sound.

A rattlesnake.

She'd never seen one before, but there could be no mistaking the sound, or the burning pain in her hand and the two bleeding holes by her knuckles. Mesmerized, her gaze riveted on her throbbing flesh, Celia stood frozen in terror. In her mind, she could see the venom spreading like a stain beneath her skin, like an arrow racing toward her heart.

She found her voice. "Snake!"

Unable to move, she couldn't whirl around, couldn't run, as if turned to stone by the fear. Behind her, she could hear the thud of footsteps and then Roy's frantic voice. "Where? Is it gone? Did it bite you?" He skirted around her, his booted feet stomping at the ground, his gaze scanning every nook and crevice by the rocks. When he could be sure the snake was gone, he spun toward her, his face pale, his uncovered blue eye fraught.

"Did it bite you? For God's sake, Celia, *did it bite you*?"

Wordlessly, she held her hand out for him to see. To benefit from complete vision, Roy tore the patch away from his brown eye, blinking in the morning sun. Gently, he slipped his fingers around hers and leaned closer to study the puncture marks.

"Did you see the snake?" He glanced up at her. "Tell me what you saw. How did it feel? How does it feel now?"

"It was like getting my hand caught in an animal trap. Sharp, strong pain. I didn't see the snake until after…it made a rattling sound when it slithered away…it was black-and-white, I think…with a pretty pattern along its body."

"Diamondback rattler." Roy tugged her arm

downward until it hung straight at her side. "Don't move. Keep as still as you can. Some snakebites are dry, without venom."

Celia hovered on her feet. "It hurts…and I feel hot and cold…like a fever." Even as she spoke, she could feel a touch of light-headedness, the onset of nausea. The barren, rusty-red hills surrounding the valley seemed to undulate in her sight, like a mirage.

Roy swore under his breath and sank to his knees in front of her. "Stay still," he instructed, his attention on her hand. "It will slow down the spread of the venom. Take slow, deep breaths, and try to keep calm." He pulled his knife out of his boot. "This will hurt, but try not to move."

Celia tensed herself against the pain. A deep, grudging anger at fate rose inside her, consuming her with such intensity it helped her to block out the sensation of the blade piercing her skin. Was this all she was going to have? A glimpse of happiness, a taste of what life could be, and then every dream and hope snatched away by a slow, painful death.

Roy emptied his mind, the way he'd learned to do as a child when the world around him became too hostile, too cruel to bear. Focusing on nothing but the twin puncture marks on the back of Celia's hand, he made a small, careful cut with the tip of his knife, enlarging the snakebite to let the blood flow out. When the bleeding slowed to a trickle, he pressed his mouth to the wound and sucked out the blood, keeping her arm as immobile as he could.

If only he knew more about doctoring! Some advised to suck out the poison. Some burned the skin around the bite with a hot iron, but the breakfast fire had already reduced to ashes. It would take too long to get the flames going again, to allow him to heat the blade of his knife. So he did what he could, sucking and spitting until the flow of blood dried up.

Celia was swaying on her feet, her face ashen. Roy picked her up in his arms and carried her to the remains of the smoldering fire and lowered her to a sitting position on the ground. "Can you stay upright? It's important to keep the area of the bite below your heart, to slow down the spread of the venom."

"I'll... I'll try."

Kneeling in front of her, Roy smoothed her hair back from her brow. Her skin was cold, clammy with perspiration. "I'll get the horses," he told her. "You stay here. Keep as still as you can."

He fought the anguish, the terrible fear. If he gave in to it, it would cloud his mind, stop him from thinking straight. But he'd been right last night. He was no good for her. Already, he'd nearly caused her to drown, and now this... At the thought of what the next few hours might bring, Roy's eyes stung. Refusing to admit it was the pressure of tears, he slipped the cotton patch back over his brown eye.

"It hurts," Celia whimpered. "My hand hurts."

Roy didn't know how to put these things to a woman, so he chose to be blunt. "Rattlesnake bites don't kill at once. It will be a day or two before we know how bad it is. It would be better not to move you at all, but there's a place an hour's fast ride away. Miss Mabel's Sunset Saloon. You'll be more comfortable there, and she knows about doctoring."

"Miss Mabel's Sunset Saloon...a bordello?"

"Not anymore. Not really. The women there are too old for the job. It's a saloon, the only one for fifty miles. The only proper building for fifty miles, to think of it. Miss Mabel pulls teeth, sews up cuts, digs out bullets. She is a doctor and a priest in one—she listens to those who want to confess their sins, comforts those strong enough to live, writes letters on behalf of those who are about to die. She'll help you."

"Am I going to die?"

"No," Roy said grimly. "I won't let you."

He brushed a quick kiss on Celia's lips and went to saddle the horses. For a better division of weight, he loaded all their packs on Baldur. After he was ready, he dressed the wound on Celia's hand, and then he lifted her onto Dagur and settled in the saddle behind her, cradling her across his knees.

Balancing between the conflicting needs to make haste and to keep the injured girl as still as possible, Roy set off along the trail up to the plateau. A terrible weight pressed upon his chest, like a stone crushing his lungs, choking his breath. He'd never had anyone. If this was how it felt to lose someone you cared about, perhaps loneliness wasn't such a bad thing, after all. He tightened his arms around Celia and increased his pace. At least at Miss Mabel's she would have a comfortable bed and laudanum to take away the pain.

Miss Mabel's run-down pleasure palace was a big, turreted frame house with echoes of grandeur from the nearby gold-mining town that had played out almost a decade ago. The town itself had been looted and vandalized, the buildings burned for firewood. Miss Mabel's bordello stood on a hillock to the north, a relic from the past, surviving on the occasional passing trade and the patronage of outlaws who rode down from their canyon hideouts.

Roy pulled Dagur to a halt outside, dismounted, tied the horses to the hitching rail and gathered Celia in his arms. Over an hour had passed since she'd been bitten. She was conscious, but pale and listless. Not pausing to knock, Roy lifted one booted foot, kicked the front door open and strode into the parlor, a huge, shadowed room furnished with ornately carved gambling tables and sagging velvet sofas.

"Miss Mabel!" he roared.

Deeper inside the house, a door banged. With a rustle of green satin skirts, a small, fine-boned woman with graying hair twisted into an elaborate chignon burst into the room.

"There's no need to holler—"

"Snakebite," Roy cut in. "Diamondback rattler."

Miss Mabel took in the situation at a glance and spun around. "This way."

Roy followed her up the stairs. The crimson carpets were frayed, droplets missing from the crystal chandeliers, the gilt-framed mirrors mottled with age. When something broke or wore out, it didn't get replaced. Every dollar Miss Mabel could save went toward providing a pension for her ladies, now retired from their profession.

Only two of the prostitutes remained, and when they were fixed up with enough funds to live out their days in comfort, Miss Mabel intended to leave. And before leaving she planned to put a match to the house, to stop it from turning into a den of vice and unruliness.

"Which part of her body and how long ago?" Miss Mabel asked as she flung open a door to an airy, sunlit room with a big brass bed made up with freshly laundered linen sheets.

"Back of her hand. Almost two hours ago."

"What have you done so far?"

Gently, Roy propped Celia to sit on the edge of the bed. She was awake, but her skin was deathly pale, her eyes dull and vacant, and her sluggish, docile manner seemed unnatural. Roy supported her while he described how he had tried to suck out the venom and how he had done his best to keep her still during the ride over.

With an impatient gesture, Miss Mabel ushered him out of the way. She crouched in front of Celia, took hold of the injured hand and studied the wounds, now a pair of small crosses from the tip of the knife instead of the round holes from the fangs of the snake. Carefully, Miss Mabel examined the skin on Celia's arm, and then she took each of Celia's hands in hers and compared them, sliding her fingers over the forearms, feeling their shape.

"What is this girl to you?"

The question took Roy by surprise. He swallowed. *If I could have a woman of my own, she'd be the one I want.* The knowledge had been burning inside him every mile as he raced along the trail, but he hesitated to put it into words, to acknowledge the emotion that would make the loss even harder to bear.

"A friend."

"Well, Mr. Hagan," Miss Mabel said with a quick glance up at him, accompanied by a wry smile. "If I promise you that she'll live, will you clean the well and chop the logs out by the barn?"

"She'll…she'll live?" Roy blinked, that burning sensation in his eyes returning. The pressure in his chest seemed too great to tolerate, as if the air had become too heavy, his body no longer obeying his commands. "Are you certain… I mean, how can you know?"

"See here." Miss Mabel traced her fingers along Celia's forearm. "Had it been a bad bite, this arm would be twice the size of the other. The skin would have turned blue by now, with the flesh inside dying. I guess the snake might have just killed something for his breakfast and he was low on venom, or he didn't consider her big enough a threat to use up his supply."

"How can you be sure? She seems real sick."

"She is in shock, her faculties dulled by fear. That needs no medicine apart from a pot of hot, sugared tea." Miss Mabel flapped her hand. "Go. Get out. I need to strip her naked and get her into a nice, hot bath. If she is nothing but *a friend* to you, I can't let you watch."

Roy shuffled on his feet. "I…"

"Go," Miss Mabel said, with a touch of kindness now. "You'll just get in the way. You'll be much more use cleaning out the well, and the physical exertion will do you good, calm your nerves. By tonight, she'll be feeling better, and you can fuss and hover at her bedside, the way a man does with his *friends*."

Roy swung the ax to split a log stump in two. Midmorning sun baked down on him, dispelling the last of the night's coolness. Sweat poured in rivulets down his naked back and chest as he labored at the woodpile, attempting to keep his emotions under guard.

The hour when he'd raced against time to bring Celia in, not knowing if she would live or die, had been the longest of his life. For the first time in his troubled existence, he'd felt plunged into a darkness so deep it seemed impossible there would ever be light again. If that was what caring for a woman did to a man, he wasn't sure he was equipped for it.

"Mr. Hagan!"

Roy dropped the ax and hurried to the kitchen door. Miss Ada, one of Miss Mabel's aging ladies of the night, was hovering on the doorstep.

"Is she all right?" Roy blurted out.

"Calm down, Mr. Hagan. Miss Celia is having a bath. I thought you might like some lemonade."

Roy accepted the tall glass the woman was holding out and gulped down the cool, sugary drink while Miss Ada looked upon him with approval. Tall and thin, with russet hair streaked with gray, Miss Ada tended the bar, probably consuming more whiskey from her rose-patterned teacup than all the customers combined.

"It's very quiet around here," Roy commented as he handed back the empty glass. So far, he'd seen a pair of prospectors and a trader with a mule train. "Is anyone from Red Bluff Gang about?"

"No." Miss Ada turned the glass over in her hands, looking puzzled. "Haven't seen anyone in two weeks. Must be something big going on."

Roy replied with a grunt and returned to the woodpile. He would have preferred to leave Celia in Miss Mabel's care while he fetched the money for her, but to collect what was owing to her father she would have to make her demand in person. Further, if there was some big scheme under way, Lom Curtis, the most paranoid of men, might not allow him to ride out and deliver the funds to Celia. The best plan was to take her to the hideout and send her away again as fast as possible, before she came to any more harm.

Water trickled down from Roy's damp hair as he made his way up the stairs. When he'd finished at the woodpile, ready to tackle the task of cleaning the well, Miss Henrietta—the third woman living in the ramshackle bordello—had appeared by the kitchen door, calling out his name and clutching a pile of towels and clean clothing.

"No point in wasting the water you'll need to haul up," Miss Henrietta said and shoved the stack of garments at him. Big boned, robust, with long, flowing hair that remained jet-black despite her age, Miss Henrietta ruled inside the kitchen. She also kept order on the premises and, when required, was capable of ejecting troublemakers.

Roy accepted the towels and the clothing. After cleaning the top of the well shaft of mud and algae, he hauled up bucket after bucket, until the water ran clear. While doing it, he stripped naked and used a coarse piece of linen cloth to scrub his body clean, standing out of sight behind the well canopy. Not the luxury of a hot bath but refreshing nonetheless, and on his way to look in on Celia he paused by the kitchen door to thank Miss Henrietta for the clean clothing.

"No need to thank me." Miss Henrietta waved a carving knife to emphasize her words. "Thank all the lazy men who discard their dirty garments instead of bothering to have them laundered. Gives us something to hand out to unwashed mud hogs like you." The knife pointed at his chest. "And pull that patch away from your eye, Roy Hagan.

That pretty lass of yours told me she likes to see all of your face."

That pretty lass of yours.

The words echoed inside Roy's head as he knocked on Celia's door, both eyes uncovered. He knew he had no right to encourage her to think there could be anything between them. And yet, the way his hand shook on the doorknob betrayed how much he wanted Celia to belong to him, how fervently he wanted to give her the happiness she deserved.

"Come in!"

He twisted the knob, pushed the door open and walked through. The shutters stood open, but some kind of thin, gauzy drapes had been drawn across the wide window. Late-afternoon sunshine filtered in through the yellow fabric, painting the room with a golden glow, but the light was muted enough not to hurt his brown eye.

"Roy!" Celia tossed the covers aside, jumped out of bed and ran to him. Her cheeks were flushed, her eyes shining. Her hair tumbled in a flurry of curls down her shoulders. She was wearing a white nightgown, very prim and proper, high at the neck and down to her toes, but beneath the garment he could see the outline of her breasts.

"Are you all right?" he asked.

"I'm fine. Look. Look." She lifted her hands and thrust them out in front of him, loosely fisted to display the back of her knuckles. "No swelling at all, no sign of venom. Miss Mabel says your knife did more damage than the rattlesnake."

"I'm sorry I cut your skin."

"Sorry? *Sorry?*" Celia waved her arms about, more animated than Roy had ever seen her before. "For trying to save my life?" She paused, the residue of fear flickering across her features. "Miss Mabel says that if it hadn't been a dry bite, even if I survived, she may have been forced to amputate my hand, because the venom makes the flesh rot. But I'm fine, fine."

Lifting her arms high overhead, Celia shrugged away the lingering traces of terror and danced around the room, looking like an angel in the golden light. She finished her circle and came to a halt in front of him. Her expression grew serious. "While I thought I was going to die, two things weighed on my mind. I didn't want my father to know that I was dead. And I regretted that we hadn't made love last night." Her voice fell and she looked down at her bare toes. "I hated the thought of dying a spinster, unloved and unwanted."

"Celia… I want you…but you know we can't…"

"No." Vehement now, she lifted her gaze up to his face. "I've always dreamed of being happy. Always, I've waited for a better tomorrow. But now I understand that tomorrow might never come. I want to be happy *today*. I want to be happy *now*, even if it is just for a fleeting moment."

Celia took a step toward him. She tripped on her feet, her bare toes catching on the long hems of her nightgown. Roy reached out both hands to steady her. Holding her by the upper arms, he restored her balance, but her body seemed oddly languid, and now that he thought of it, there was a slight slurring to her speech.

"Celia, have you been drinking?"

She flashed him a mischievous grin. "Perhaps I have. Miss Ada gave me a cup of tea that tasted peculiar. She said it would put hair on my chest. Not that I'm enticed by the prospect."

As Roy looked down into her radiant face, he felt his resistance crumble. Celia seemed so happy, her emotions flowing as freely as a waterfall. He had taught her that, had given her the courage to embrace her feelings instead of bottling them up. And yet he was refusing to give in to his own feelings of need and longing. Not just because he wanted to protect her from harm, but because of his own ingrained fear of hurt, caused by his history of rejection and abandonment.

He spoke gruffly. "I can't promise you a future."

"Who cares about a future?" Although Celia's tone was flippant, her expression was serious, almost fierce. "I want to live in the present. I want happiness *now*."

"Then I'll do my best to give it to you," Roy replied. His grip tightened on her upper arms as he slowly pulled her toward him. When he could feel her hips butting against his, he marshaled the last remaining shreds of his caution and eased their bodies apart. "Celia, there are ways a man and a woman can give each other pleasure without risking a child. I can show you those things, but when the time comes you must make me stop. Don't let me take it all the way to the end. Promise me that."

He could see curiosity in her eyes, perhaps even a flash of rebellion at the boundaries he was setting. But she gave him the promise he had demanded. A muttered, reluctant promise, but a promise nonetheless—a promise he hoped she could keep.

The final traces of resistance swept away, Roy pulled her close once more and lowered his mouth to hers. He kissed her with all the hunger that had built up inside him during their days together on the trail. And more than that, he kissed her with a longing born from his years of loneliness within a family that had rejected him. A longing that had grown and flourished in the harsh environment of an outlaw camp.

Fresh from her bath, Celia smelled of her fragrant soap, combined with a hint of whiskey from Miss Ada's spiked tea. Roy inhaled deep breaths of her scent. Her hair was still damp, and he buried his hands in the thick curls, feeling their silken weight.

He could feel her arch up against him, the feminine contours of her body sharpening his desire. With a growl of impatience, he broke the kiss and lifted his head so he could look into her face. Her complexion was flushed, her eyes shining. Her lips were parted and moist from his kisses. Torn between the reluctance to let her go and the need to get even closer to her, Roy took a single backward step. For an instant, he stood still and let his gaze sweep down her body, hidden by the folds of the long nightgown.

It was wrong; he knew it. In his mind, he went over every objection, including the possibility that they might let things go too far and create a child. But his need was too great, his longing too fierce. Just as Celia had insisted, he'd allow himself to live for now and let tomorrow take care of itself.

Brushing aside the last of his scruples, Roy gathered the flowing fabric of Celia's nightgown in his hands and slowly pulled the garment up over her head, until he could toss it aside and let his eyes feast on her nakedness.

The golden light that filtered in through the yellow muslin curtains made her look like a wood nymph, a fairy-tale creature, beyond the touch of a mortal man. Her breasts were full, her hips rounded, a womanly figure. While he stared, transfixed, a cool breeze through the open window stirred the air in the room. He could see Celia shivering.

"You're cold."

He barely recognized the low, husky timbre of his own voice. Saying nothing more, he picked her up and carried her to the big brass bed and settled her under the covers. She wriggled to lean against the pillows and watched him, excitement battling apprehension in her expression.

"It's all right," he said. "We both want it."

His eyes never left hers as he removed the borrowed clothing he had only a short while ago put on. Fully naked, he paused and stood by the bedside, letting Celia look at him, just like he had looked at her only seconds ago.

With a hesitation that held a hint of alarm, her gaze drifted downward, came to rest on his straining erection. From the fascinated curiosity on her face it became evident to him that she had never seen a naked, aroused man before.

"Have you ever...?" Celia's voice quivered.

"Yes... I have."

Part of him wished he could deny it, that she could be his first, just as he would be her first, but he was a man with normal desires, approaching thirty, and despite his isolated life he had found several occasions to satisfy his physical needs. With a fleeting smile, he added, "I know what to do. It is better if one of us does."

"I know what to do, too." She flustered, red flags of embarrassment burning on her cheeks. Her attention shifted back up to his face. "I mean, I've read about it...in books that a lady isn't supposed to read."

Roy pushed the covers aside and climbed up to sit on the mattress, facing her. He could sense the mental struggle within Celia, could almost read her thoughts. That starched-up lady part of her was stirring up trouble, reminding her that decent women didn't let a man into their bed without the bond of marriage.

And despite everything he had told her before, despite the impossibility of a lasting union between them, he wanted to give her some token of belonging, some reassurance that what was about to take place between them meant something more than just a moment of clandestine passion.

"Have you ever read up about Indian marriage customs?" he asked.

Celia nodded. "Apache braves stake their horse outside a girl's wickiup. If she brings out a bucket of water and the horse drinks it empty, they are married."

He reached out, curled his hand at her waist

and slid it upward until it met the rounded swell of her left breast. "Some other tribe… I don't know which…they press their hands over each other's heart…" he flattened his palm against her rib cage "…and once their hearts beat in the same rhythm, they are married."

For a long moment, he waited for her to respond. He could feel her swift heartbeat beneath his palm, could feel the heavy drumming of his own pulse in his veins. He was about to reach out with his free hand, wrap his fingers around Celia's wrist and guide her, but just then she moved of her own volition and pressed her palm to his chest.

"Can you feel it?" Roy whispered. *"Ta-dam… ta-dam…ta-dam."*

"Yes."

"Your heartbeat needs to slow down," he told her. "Take deep breaths."

He could feel Celia's chest rise and fall as she regulated her breathing, could hear the faint sound of each unhurried inhale and exhale. Letting his mind leap ahead, he pictured their bodies intertwined, imagined the pleasures they would share.

Beneath his palm, he could feel her heartbeat slow down, while his own pulse was accelerating. He closed his eyes and let the mental images of their physical union take hold, adding to the almost-painful force of his arousal, increasing the urgent pounding of his heart.

"Now," he said. His eyes blinked open. "Can you feel it?"

"Yes," she replied. *"Ta-dam. Ta-dam. Ta-dam."*

For a few moments longer, they sat still, their palms pressed against each other's warm skin while their hearts beat in complete symmetry. Tenderness welled up within Roy. The apprehension he'd seen in Celia's eyes while she'd studied his naked, masculine form was gone now. That small private ceremony between them, that small piece of make believe had overcome her moral scruples, given her the reassurances she longed for.

His mind flickered back to his first night with a woman. The feel of her feminine shape, her soft skin beneath his hands, the pleasure of burying himself in her welcoming body, had seemed like a miracle. But what had truly overwhelmed him was to be so near to another living person. To feel the warmth, the comfort of closeness, the human response, the sense of life meeting life, sharing a moment of togetherness.

As a child, he'd never been held, never been hugged. When he was a baby, his mother must have taken care of him, but he could not remember. Usually, he'd only been touched by another person when someone hit him or shoved him or kicked him. When he grew to be a man, he experienced a handshake, even a masculine pounding on the back, but those tokens of camaraderie were too fleeting to fill the sense of isolation within him.

A tumble in a whore's bed had eased his solitude for a moment, but as soon as he'd pulled his clothes back on again and walked out of the room, that feeling of being alone had always returned, like a chilly mist that lingered inside him, never lifting.

But now, as he sat facing Celia on the bed and felt the bond of trust between them, something in his troubled mind eased. He turned his wrist, a small movement that brought his hand into full contact with her breast. The intimacy of the gesture swept over him, sending a rush of desire through him. His eyes not leaving hers, he brushed the pad of his thumb across the peaked nipple. Celia gave a small moan of pleasure and tipped her head back, exposing the pale column of her throat.

Leaning forward, Roy pressed his mouth to the hollow between her collarbones. Beneath his lips, he could feel her pulse speeding up again. He let his lips roam over her neck, the shell of her ear, the line of her jaw, until he finally settled his mouth on hers.

She parted her lips to welcome him. Her hands

raked into his hair, anchoring him close. Roy let his arms circle her and hauled her tight against his chest. Despite Celia's feminine curves, there was a frailty about her, a difference in their strength that reminded him of the need to be gentle.

Minutes ticked by before Roy eased their bodies apart again. The impact of daylight on his normally covered brown eye added to his already-overloaded senses. In awestruck silence, he studied Celia's features. Her hair shone like molten gold in the yellow light that filtered in through the curtains; her skin looked smooth and white, like alabaster.

What have I done to deserve this moment, to have this woman offer herself to me, in the afternoon sunshine that allows me to see her nakedness, her beauty?

Was there a balance of misery and happiness in each person's life, and after all his suffering this was his reward? If so, he did not resent the acts of cruelty he had faced, for they had earned him this moment.

All of a sudden, his own pleasure seemed unimportant. More than anything, he wanted to give Celia a taste of the passion she craved. He eased her down on the bed and leaned over her. Slowly, as gently as he could, he began touching her, stroking her, until she trembled in the throes of her own need.

"What is this?" she murmured, her tone thick and husky. "It feels like my skin is too tight and I'm burning all over and I'm throbbing in places a lady should not mention."

"It's all right," he replied. "Just close your eyes and feel it."

Her eyelids fluttered down, creating a barrier of privacy that Roy hoped would allow her to give in to the physical sensations. Carefully, aware of the rough skin and thick calluses on his hands, he reached down between her legs and teased and rubbed the slick ridge there, watching the reaction on her face until he could see an intense frown that told him she was ready, and with a final caress he sent her over the edge.

The violence of her release took him by surprise. With an inarticulate cry, she bowed up on the bed, her body taut and still. Then she sank back down to the mattress and a series of tremors rocked through her while her cries faded to throaty murmurs.

Alarmed, Roy leaned over her and studied her features. Her mouth was open, her eyes tightly shut, her breathing rushed. "Celia, are you all right? Did I hurt you?"

Her eyes blinked open. Her gray eyes, normally so luminous, were as dark as storm clouds. He could read awe in them, perhaps even a trace of shame at her wanton reaction, but then her lips curved into a smile, the kind of secret, tremulous smile that came from finally having discovered the pleasures shared by most of mankind.

"Are you all right, Celia?" he said again. "I didn't hurt you?"

"Yes, you did," she told him softly. "You made my heart shatter. And when it came back together you were trapped inside it. Whatever happens, you will always be with me. You will always be in my heart."

"Celia…" Roy let out a sigh, a sound of frustration as much as of regret. "You know that this can only be what you said it would be. Happiness for now. For tonight."

Gently, she reached up and touched his cheek. "I know. I meant that I will have a memory of you, of this moment, locked in my heart. It will be something beautiful I can carry with me, wherever I go, whatever happens to me."

The mention of the future, of how they would have to go their separate ways, flooded Roy with a sudden sense of gloom. He rolled onto his side and pulled Celia into the circle of his arms and held her tight. She burrowed against him, her face pressed into the crook of his neck, her warm breath fanning over his skin. Soon the rhythm of her breathing grew even and he knew she'd fallen asleep.

For hours, Roy held the sleeping girl in his

arms. Evening cool invaded the room, easing the heat in his body. Suppertime came and went but Celia slept through it all. No one knocked on the door. Twilight fell. Sounds drifted in through the open window—birds singing their evening chorus, a coarse male voice shouting a greeting and mules clipping along the trail as another trader passed by.

Night darkness thickened, and still Celia didn't stir. Roy held her, feeling her heartbeat, breathing in her scent, enjoying the feel of her naked body against his.

He knew it had been wrong to let the intimacy between them deepen but he could not bring himself to regret the night. She deserved those brief moments of happiness. They both did. The best he could do now was to get Celia the money she was owed and send her off to find some place of safety. Somewhere she could forget about him and set about building a secure life for herself. An independent, affluent life, even if a lonely one. A life that did not expose her to the dangers of an outlaw camp or to the grief of watching her man dangle lifeless at the end of a rope.

Chapter Ten

Yawning, Celia sat up on the bed and stretched. The room still held the nighttime cool, but she could see the dawn light filtering in through the yellow muslin curtains. Roy was gone. She closed her eyes and recalled the feel of his naked body against hers, his mouth on her skin, the incredible sensations he had triggered within her…

But reality intruded. Her mind raced ahead, to the outlaw camp, to the life beyond. She had told herself it would be enough to seize happiness for now, even if just for a fleeting moment, but was that really true? Was happiness even happiness at all, if a greater sense of emptiness followed in its wake? It had been easy to say she wanted a life as an independent woman, but such a life might be lonelier and bleaker than she could tolerate.

A knock at the door interrupted her thoughts. "Miss Celia?"

She snagged her nightgown from the floor and pulled it on. "Come in!"

Miss Henrietta shouldered the door open and bustled in carrying a breakfast tray. "Mr. Hagan's gone to get the horses ready. You get this lot inside of you. Might be a long time before you'll taste decent cooking again."

While Miss Henrietta deposited the tray on the bedside table and hurried out again, Miss Mabel strode in through the open doorway. She carried Celia's dark blue riding suit draped over one arm. "Your outfit pressed quite nicely. It's possibly a little shrunken, but I could see no stains or rips."

"I don't know how to thank you for everything…"

"Hush," Miss Mabel replied with a flap of her hand. She came to stand beside the bed, pulled over a small wooden chair and sat down, her eyes intent on Celia's scar. "No, don't avert your face," she scolded when Celia turned aside, using the excuse of reaching for the coffee cup on the breakfast tray.

Celia touched her cheek. "I try to ignore the curious stares…but sometimes I'm so aware of them, it feels like there's a branding iron scorching my skin."

"How would you like it if I could make your scar disappear?"

Startled, Celia sat straighter on the bed. "Disappear? But how?"

"Well…" Miss Mabel bent over her and rubbed the puckered skin with her fingertips, examining the texture. "Not quite disappear, but I can make the color blend in." She produced a small porcelain jar from her skirt pocket. "This cream will darken your skin. If you brush it over the scar, very carefully, making sure you get none on the unmarked skin, the scarred area will darken to match the rest of your face. Use it every day for a week or so, until the scar turns the same color as the surrounding skin, and then occasionally to maintain the shade. I'll show you how. Tip your head aside."

"What's in it?"

"Cinnamon and cocoa beans and a tiny bit of a poisonous herb called bishop's weed. Now, tip your head."

Bishop's weed.

Celia rolled her eyes at the name. It had been a bishop who caused her to suffer because of her scar, so the herb might be a fitting remedy. She tilted her head to one side and felt the deft strokes of a brush on her cheek. While Miss Mabel applied the cream, as carefully as if painting a masterpiece, the elderly madam spoke quietly.

"So you have become an outlaw's woman… No, keep still. Don't shrug… You plan to marry him…? Keep still, I said… You know, sometimes it is better for a woman to be like a man—to take a night's pleasure and ride away."

"I plan to become—"

"For God's sake, didn't I tell you to keep still?" Sounding angry now, Miss Mabel went on with her quiet muttering. "So, perhaps you think you'll set up house somewhere and Roy will come by every couple of months, like a clockwork. You'll pretend that your husband is out at sea, or a drover on the trail, and you'll bring up a litter of children all on your own, perhaps working in a store to make ends meet, happy in your part-time marriage…" Miss Mabel straightened by the bedside and her tone grew brusque. "There, all done now."

Celia looked up. "Why would you mock such a dream?"

"I'm not mocking your dream, if that is what you are dreaming of. I'm trying to warn you that reality might turn out different." Miss Mabel clipped the lid back on the jar. When she turned to deposit the jar on the bedside table, Celia caught the glint of tears in the older woman's eyes. Understanding hit her with a jolt.

"You did it," she said in a low voice. "You chose that kind of life and something went wrong."

Miss Mabel hesitated. She fingered the lace at the end of her sleeves, then seemed to shrink as she let out a long, shaky sigh. "His name was Jim Rowland. He was wanted for a stagecoach robbery. Not for murder. Never murder.

"For seven years, we lived like that. Every time someone spotted him, we moved on, to some other town, just to make sure. We had a little boy… Johnny…and then, one night, when Jim came to see me, there was an incident in town…a fire at the livery stable. Jim stopped to help, and in the light of the flames someone saw his face, recognized him from a wanted poster.

"They came for him before dawn. We had a small cabin on the outskirts of town. Just one room, with a sleeping loft above. The posse rode up outside, holding lighted torches, and they yelled for him to come out, his hands held high. We'd always agreed that if that ever happened— if the law caught up with him—he'd give himself up without a fight.

"So Jim called back to say that he'd come out, he would just get his clothes on first. We had been in bed, and we were naked. But the men in the posse were drunk and trigger-happy. They decided it was a ruse and stormed the cabin. They fired at Jim while he was balanced on one foot, pulling on his trousers."

A shiver ran through Celia. "Dear God. Did he die?"

Miss Mabel shook her head from side to side,

silent tears streaming down her face. "Not from the bullet. They took him to a doctor. Kept him alive, just so that they could hang him with all the pomp and fanfare that goes with those occasions. But my little boy died. Some of the men who burst into the cabin were firing their pistols in the air, just for the fun of it. Johnny was sleeping in the loft. A stray bullet hit him. I found him in the morning…after…after the men in the posse had finished with me and tossed me back on the cabin doorstep."

Celia lifted her hand toward the weeping woman, not quite touching—a comforting gesture that in its very futility summed up the helplessness of any consolation against the memory of such pain, such loss and suffering. "Oh, Miss Mabel," she whispered. "I'm so sorry."

"Sorry doesn't help. Being careful might." With a snap of her spine that made her green satin gown rustle, Miss Mabel appeared to collect herself. "I'm not in the habit of spilling my grief out to strangers, but you need to be warned. Don't choose such a life, unless you have the guts to watch your man die. Unless you have the guts to be branded an outlaw's woman and be treated with the lack of respect it invites." The older woman got to her feet and took a step toward the door. "Get dressed now. You'll need to ride out as soon as you've had your breakfast."

As Celia watched Miss Mabel go, she caught a movement in the corridor outside, heard a muffled greeting. Then Roy walked into the room. The grim expression on his face told Celia that he had been listening, had heard Miss Mabel talking about her past—a past that might be an indication of what they could expect in their future if they were foolish enough to seek a shared life.

Celia didn't try to engage Roy in conversation as they took their leave, got on their horses and rode off into the maze of red rock canyons. The narrow passages that scored the barren plateau branched off, petered out and bisected one another, like a labyrinth. Despite the confusing trails, Roy appeared to know his way to the hideout, although sometimes he had to pause and study the symbols chiseled into the rock.

When the sun was directly overhead, they paused for lunch. Roy lifted Celia down from the saddle. She could feel a new tension in him, could read the bleakness in his expression. For an instant, she clung to his shoulders and asked the question that weighed on her mind.

"Do you regret bringing me with you?"

"No." Roy stepped away to rummage in his saddlebags and spoke with his back to her. "There is no point in regretting the past. It can't be changed. But I worry about the future. That I may have some influence over. And as soon as you've collected the money you're owed I want you out of here."

"But—"

He turned to face her. "No buts, Celia. From now on, you obey orders."

"I..." Her words petered into silence. There was an edge to Roy's manner she found unsettling. Perhaps it was what lay ahead, their arrival into the outlaw camp, but instinct told her it was more. Something troubled him. She had sensed the change in him after he had overheard her conversation with Miss Mabel, when the older woman had talked about the tragic death of her husband and young son.

"All right," she said quietly. "I shall obey."

And she *would* obey. And she would ride out, leaving Roy behind. But before they said their farewells, they would make plans for how she could keep in touch with him, to let him know how she was managing their joint investments. It might be merely a business relationship, but she would relish that small bond, that sense of togetherness.

Frowning, Roy scanned the trail ahead. Hearing Miss Mabel talk about the horrors of her past had stirred the ugly memories. It had been the first hanging he'd ever witnessed. Afterward, he'd been sick on a street corner, shaken by the cruelty of the occasion, racked with pity for the grieving widow. The thought that such a fate might one day befall Celia if he tried to hold on to her filled Roy with a grim determination to send her away. With enough money to use as a starting stake for her financial speculations, she would be safe, could build a comfortable life for herself, isolated from the dangers of the outlaw life.

However, apart from the past horrors and future uncertainties, another worry churned around in Roy's mind—the curious fact that Lom Curtis and his men had not ridden out to Miss Mabel's Sunset Saloon in weeks. It made no sense. And, as if trouble had to come in packs of three, how would Celia react to learning the truth about her father?

His nerves increasingly on edge, Roy led the way deeper and deeper into the ragged canyon breaks. Late in the afternoon, when the sun was already sinking in the sky, they entered a narrow gorge. A rifle shot echoed in the air. Roy pulled Dagur to a halt. From the top of a tall buttress ahead came a coarse shout, "Who goes there?"

"Roy Hagan. Red Bluff Gang."

"Wait there." Two more rifle shots shattered the quiet.

Surprised, Roy wheeled his mount around and faced Celia. "This is not normal practice. Be careful. Something is going on. Stay behind me." He pulled one of his pistols out of the holster and wheeled Dagur around again, pointing the horse in the direction of the hideout.

Hoof beats drummed in the distance, slowing down as a rider entered the gorge from the opposite end. A gleaming bay gelding with four white socks pranced into sight. In the saddle, the rider sat proudly, dressed all in black, a silver band gleaming in his hat.

Roy holstered his gun, twisted around to call out to Celia. "It's Dale Hunter. He's a friend, a good friend. No need to worry."

Dale trotted over. Lithe and dark, he had a wedge-shaped face and green, catlike eyes that never missed a thing. He wore his jet-black straight hair long enough to skim his shoulders. His handsome looks came from his mother's well-connected Creole family, but to protect his identity he liked to pepper his speech with Spanish, passing for a Mexican.

"How are you, *amigo*. Got yourself a wife?"

"No." Roy glanced back at Celia. "She's a lady. Not for the likes of us."

Dale Hunter grinned. "Speak for yourself." His expression grew serious. "Where you been, *amigo*? No one knew what happened to you."

"Got laid up. Lom Curtis put a bullet in me. Didn't he tell you?"

"Didn't have the time. Lom Curtis is dead."

Dead. A thrill went through Roy. If Lom Curtis was dead, it might be possible to break away from the Red Bluff Gang. All those dreams that had seemed unattainable before suddenly appeared much closer, perhaps even within reach.

"Don't think you can dance on his grave," Dale Hunter went on. "The man from Prescott has arrived to impose order. He goes by the handle *Mr. Smith*. Wears a wig and a fake beard, so ill-fitting it must be his intention to make everyone aware he's in disguise." Dale's dark eyes flickered over to Celia. "Aren't you going to introduce me to the *senorita*? If you ain't marrying her, I might take her off your hands."

Roy couldn't help but laugh at Dale's carefree prattle. "Her name is Celia Courtwood. And, as I already told you, she's not for the likes of us. She has some business at the camp, and when that is taken care of she'll ride out again."

Dale feigned disappointment. Then his expression sharpened. "I can't be seen talking to you for too long, so I'll be quick. Lom Curtis got into an argument with Big Kate and hit her so hard she fell against a rock and cracked her skull. Miss Gabriela tried to intervene and Curtis let her taste his fist. The big Swede, Andersen, got mad. He shot Lom Curtis and claimed Miss Gabriela for himself. Two weeks later, Mr. Smith appeared. You recall how we used to puzzle where Lom Curtis went every Friday? I reckon he rode to the nearest telegraph office and wired a report to Prescott. When no message came through, Mr. Smith knew there was trouble in paradise and came out to do a bit of housekeeping."

"Is he paying the men their cut?"

"You won't believe this, but he acts like an accountant, keeping books and asking the men to sign a receipt when they collect their share from the take."

"Do you think he might allow me to cash in and pull out?"

Dale made a sour face. "Forget it. He is worse than Lom Curtis ever was. Why do you think he keeps such careful records? If he can't kill you, at least he can get you convicted so you'll spend the rest of your days at the penitentiary." With a mocking salute, Dale Hunter turned his horse around and trotted off, leaving his warning hanging like a dust cloud in the air.

As they rode out of the gorge, Celia caught a glimpse of the rifleman standing at the top of the tall buttress. Short and stocky, he appeared unkempt, dressed in tattered clothing. The way his eyes followed her, like a raptor stalking its prey, sent shivers up her spine.

They emerged into a narrow, almost-treeless

valley with a creek running through the center. At first glance, it might have appeared to be an ordinary ranch. A single-story main building. A bunkhouse. A cook shack with tables and benches beneath a canopy. Two small cabins. Beyond the buildings, at least two dozen horses pranced in a row of pole corrals.

And men. There were men everywhere. Standing. Sitting. Strolling. Smoking. Talking. And staring. Staring at her, as if they had never seen a woman before.

Celia stiffened in the saddle and gritted her teeth to hide her fear. From the corner of her eye, she surveyed the scene. Upon a closer look, the sense of normalcy vanished. All the men were heavily armed. And it was not ranch chores that occupied them, but gambling and drinking. Only a few were busy with productive tasks: cleaning their guns, mending their tack or seeing to the necessities of existence, such as cooking and chopping firewood.

Dale Hunter stood waiting for them outside the main building. He waved them over and gestured for them to dismount. "Mr. Smith is inside. I'll take care of your horses." He moved closer to Roy, lowered his voice. "I'll see you after you've talked to him."

Her muscles sore after the long ride, Celia stretched her legs. She followed Roy's example and handed Baldur's reins to Dale Hunter. Before leading the horses away, he nodded at her and touched the brim of his hat, a gentlemanly gesture that seemed out of place in this gathering of rough, lawless men.

Celia turned to Roy. "Shall I wait outside?"

His expression grew guarded. "You'll need to come inside with me…and Celia…if you hear something startling, something you find impossible to believe, don't argue. Just play along. Afterward, I'll explain. I promise to answer all your questions. Only don't speak now, in front of Mr. Smith. This is very important."

Roy's grave tone added to Celia's unease. She searched his expression for some hint, some clue of what he expected her to learn, but she found none, only a blank mask that made her instincts riot. She wanted to ask, get the answers before facing the outlaw leader everyone seemed to fear, but the look in Roy's single blue eye warned her to hold her tongue.

"I understand," she said quietly. "I will keep quiet."

"Good," Roy replied. He turned around and strode toward the entrance.

The house, built of adobe brick, had no porch, but their boots made an ominous click on the stone patio by the front door. Her heart pounding, Celia listened to Roy knock on the thick oak door. She caught a flash of metal and realized a rifle barrel had been pointing out through a slit in the panel. An instant later, the door swung open. The thick timber panel was hinged outward, making it harder for an intruder to ram it down.

The man who opened the door held the rifle level in the crook of his arm, and behind him another man had his pistol out of the holster. Both stepped forward. Celia watched Roy exchange a greeting with each of them.

"Glad to see you're alive," said the taller man. Despite the friendly comment, the man's expression held no joy, his tone no warmth.

The stocky one with square features nodded to Celia and introduced himself as Zeke Davies. Appearing unsure of himself, he cast a nervous glance at the open doorway behind him and moved out of the way to invite them to enter. "Mr. Smith is waiting."

The house, although neatly constructed, was bare inside. The parlor contained a low wooden table and a pair of crude, homemade armchairs. The windows had no glass, only shutters, which were closed now, allowing in limited daylight. When the man with the rifle closed the front door, they were pitched into near darkness.

"This way." Davies picked up a lit lantern from the table. He guided them across the room to a closed door and paused to knock on it.

"Who is it?" a voice called from the other side.

"Hagan. Has a woman with him."

"Take his guns."

Celia could feel her heart thudding, could feel a dampness coating her palms as she watched Roy unbuckle his gun belt and hand over his pair of pistols. The light from the lantern threw leaping shadows on the walls, creating a confusing, hellish atmosphere that made her fears escalate.

"I've got his guns," Davies called out.

"And the woman?"

Davies flustered. "Ma'am... I'm sorry." He stepped forward and gingerly patted at her velvet skirts, checking for a firearm hidden beneath. Even in the darkness, Celia could see the mortified flush on the man's face, could feel the respect in his touch. It occurred to her that Roy might not be the only outlaw with a sense of honor and decency.

"I carry no weapons," she informed him. "No gun, no knife."

Davies finished his search and stood straight. "The lady is clean."

"All right," the voice from the other side of the door called. "Let them in."

The lock clicked, and the door inched open. A big man filled the gap, holding a pointed pistol at waist height. Slowly, he eased backward and swung the door wider. With a small jerk of his gun barrel, he invited them to enter.

The room was equally lacking in daylight, the air stale with smoke and sweat and the lingering odors of consumed meals. The only furniture was a huge desk, a chair behind it and a safe in the far corner. Two lanterns hung on the wall, positioned so that they left the face of the man sitting behind the desk in shadows.

Wasting no time on introductions, Mr. Smith— for the man behind the desk could be none other— launched into questioning Roy about his injuries and how he had recovered from them.

While Celia listened, she studied Mr. Smith. Lean, with the proud carriage of a soldier, he bore the stamp of authority. Between the black beard attached to his chin and the hat brim pulled low and the thick spectacles that shielded his eyes, it would have been impossible to make out his features, even in broad daylight.

Whoever Mr. Smith was, he was going to a great deal of trouble to protect his identity, however, from his voice Celia surmised that he was likely to be well past his youth. The cultured tone and the vocabulary he used revealed him to be an educated man.

He gestured at her. "And the woman…?"

"She is Miss Courtwood," Roy replied. "The bank teller's daughter."

Mr. Smith directed his attention to her. As he turned his head slightly, the lamplight glittered on the lenses of his spectacles, giving Celia a glimpse of the coldest, cruelest gray-green eyes she had ever seen. He tipped his hat to her, and his hair peeked into view, allowing her to determine it to be light brown and wavy. Unless, of course, he was wearing a wig beneath his hat, to complete his disguise.

"Miss Courtwood," he said. A gentleman's greeting.

She gave a brief nod to acknowledge the courtesy but offered no reply.

"I guess you've come to collect your father's cut in the takings," the man behind the desk went on. "He is due a half share, one thousand dollars. Less than a full share but he took lesser risks. You might like to know that I offered to send a lawyer to defend him. It was his choice to plead guilty."

For a moment, the words made no sense to Celia. They buzzed around inside her head, like a swarm of bees. And then they stung. Layer by layer, the truth revealed itself to her. She whirled around to look at Roy. He met her gaze without a flinch. The guilty look in his eyes, combined with the hard, closed expression on his face gave her the confirmation she needed.

He had known. Known about her father's involvement in the crime all along. The understanding swelled in her mind, a sense of betrayal and resentment gathering like a flash flood might gather behind a dam about to break.

"Celia." Roy's voice was low, reminding her of his warning.

Don't speak now, in front of Mr. Smith. This is very important.

She clenched her hands into fists at her sides, reaching back for the straitjacket of a dutiful daughter she had worn for so long, using it as a means to suppress any unruly shows of emotion. Little by little, she conquered her flare of anger, shutting it away.

"Yes," she said in a strained tone. "I've come to collect my father's…*cut in the takings*. But I'm sure you understand that I don't wish to have my name entered in your account book. Mr. Hagan will sign for my share."

With a polite farewell, she marched out of the room, the heavy velvet skirts swishing around her feet. The way Mr. Smith arose behind the desk confirmed to her that he was a man of position, a man of respect in his real life. Good manners in the presence of a lady seemed instinctive to him, so deeply ingrained that he adhered to them, even while they might jeopardize the effectiveness of his outlaw disguise.

After her abrupt exit, Celia stood irresolute outside the ranch house. She let her gaze drift over the men playing cards at the long table beneath the canopy by the cook shack. Earlier, she had felt threatened by the aura of violence about these men, but now, as she studied them, she imagined her father as one of the crowd.

How had these men ended up outside the law? Perhaps it was not some streak of evil driving them, or greed, or even laziness. Perhaps, as it had been with her father, their only means to provide for their loved ones had been a criminal act.

She could feel the men's eyes on her, but their attention no longer seemed quite so sinister. Instead, in their hungry glances she recognized the longing of men denied the company of women, denied the chance of a family and home.

Behind her, footsteps thudded on the stone patio. She turned to face the house. Roy was striding toward her, the pockets of his canvas duster dragged down with the weight of something inside. Her gold. Her father's gold. One thousand dollars' worth of it.

The thoughts she had worked hard to suppress a few moments ago surged back to the surface, filling her with unspent emotions. Her hands fisted at her sides. She waited until Roy came to a halt in front of her, and then she spoke in a low, harsh voice.

"You knew. You knew all along."

"I suspected. Couldn't be certain."

It built and built inside her, the pressure of those feelings unacknowledged, denied. Her lungs were heaving, her chest rising and falling. There seemed to be a storm going on inside her head, her thoughts in jumbled disarray, as if she feared her own feelings.

"Let it out, Celia," Roy said quietly. "Let your anger flow. How can you let your love flow if you bottle up the rest of your emotions?"

She closed her eyes. In her mind, she could see her father at the bank, the haughty arrogance of the manager, Mr. Northfield. She could see the bishop, the preacher, and she recalled their misguided fanaticism that had condemned her because of a small childhood injury. She could see the townspeople, so cowardly in their rejection of her.

The strange feeling inside her flared into full existence, like a firecracker exploding, and she faced the emotions that were whirling with such violence inside her. She accepted those emotions, understood them. And refused to feel guilt or shame over them.

Tipping her head back, she burst into a deep, roaring laughter. The sound rippled over the narrow valley. From the corner of her eye, she could see the men pause in their card game and stare at her. A madwoman. That's what they must be thinking. But she didn't care. Never again would she lend too much weight to what others thought of her. Never again would she give others the power to rob her of her dignity, to rob her of her self-worth.

Roy reached over to her, curled his hands around her upper arms and gave her a gentle shake. "Celia, what's wrong? Talk to me."

Her body still shuddering with laughter, she fought to bring her outburst of wicked, petty pleasure over a revenge achieved under control. When she had calmed enough to talk, she met his worried gaze and tried to explain.

"What I feel is not anger. It is something else." Animated now, the confused thoughts tumbling into place, she went on, "It felt so futile, so wrong, when I thought my father had accepted the blame for someone else's crime…but now I know there is no injustice in his imprisonment…he did what he thought necessary to provide for me, to secure my future, and he paid the price."

She paused, her lips curving into a grim smile. "And, in some way, my father's actions seem like payback to the town for ostracizing me. I know what he did was wrong, I know it was dishonest, but somehow it seems as if he has made fools of them all. Perhaps he has made a fool of me, too, but I can't help but love him all the more for it."

As her thoughts formed into words, another idea flickered at the back of her mind. Perhaps she had wished to make a fortune so that she could sashay back to Rock Springs and queen it over the people who had shunned her, as Roy had put it. But there was no longer a need for revenge. Papa had already taken care of it.

Chapter Eleven

It would hurt to let her go. The realization hit Roy hard as he looked down into Celia's flushed face. Aware of the curious stares of the men, he spun her around on her feet and ushered her into motion. He could feel the tension in her body, could sense the brittle edge of her high spirits. She appeared mentally exhausted. Danger, outlaws with guns, being bodily searched, combined with the startling news about her father must have taken their toll.

"Let's get you settled."

Taking her by the elbow, he led her along the path to the nearer of the two cabins. A small adobe structure, it had belonged to Big Kate, the aging whore who had serviced the men at the hideout. Mr. Smith had offered them the use of the cabin, but Roy had no idea if anyone had cleaned up inside after Big Kate had died from the beating she'd received from Lom Curtis.

He left Celia standing a short distance from the entrance. "Wait here."

Roy tried the door, found it unlocked and went inside. The single room was spotless, bearing no sign of Big Kate's occupation. Stark, almost like a prison cell, the cramped space contained nothing but a sturdy pine bed with a sagging mattress, a table with a single rickety chair by the glassless window and a big oak chest in the corner.

He lifted the lid on the chest and recognized Big Kate's clothing, carefully washed and folded. Big Kate, tired of the hard life, had been slovenly and unkempt, drunk much of the time, but the air inside the cabin smelled fresh and the earth floor shone clean.

Miss Gabriela must have scrubbed the interior, one last favor between the only two women at the camp. Roy would have liked to thank her for taking care of the task, but none of the outlaws ever spoke to Miss Gabriela unless she approached them first.

He went to the doorway and waved Celia inside. "Try to make yourself comfortable. I have to go and talk to Dale Hunter. I won't be long."

She studied the cramped space. "What about my things?"

"I'll send them over."

He left her in the cabin and took the path down the slope toward the corrals. After only a few paces, he heard someone calling his name. He turned and saw Joe Saldana hurrying toward him. Roy halted to let the tall Mexican catch up.

Saldana slapped him on the back and grinned, white teeth flashing beneath his drooping moustache. "You take a bullet for the father and win the daughter?"

"She came with me because she had no other choice." Roy lowered his voice. "And I want to get her out of here again as soon as possible."

"Good luck, my friend." Saldana jerked his head in the direction of the ranch house. "I've been ordered to keep an eye on you. No one leaves. Not until Mr. Smith has gone back to his honest life and established a credible story to cover his absence."

"No one?"

"No one except Dale Hunter."

Roy hid his unease. He contemplated Saldana. "What happened with Miss Gabriela? I thought with Lom Curtis out of the way you might have... I believed you had some affection for her."

Saldana grew serious. "I do...more than affection...but I can't give her what she needs. Sure, I could make her laugh, lift her spirits for a while, but her melancholy is too deep for me to heal. She needs a strong man to lean on, someone to mollycoddle her. The Swede is the steady, quiet sort, and he worships her. He can be the protector Miss Gabriela needs. He can give her more than I ever could."

"Where is she now?"

"The day Lom Curtis died she moved back into her old cabin. She barely comes out. Her bruises have healed, but she has a broken arm. The Swede takes care of her." Saldana hesitated, looked away into the distance. "When a man loves a woman… truly loves her…sometimes he has to accept that she'll be better off without him."

"I know," Roy said with a sigh. "I know."

They talked for a moment longer. Saldana filled him in on the details since Mr. Smith had arrived. Never without armed guards to protect him against an attack, Mr. Smith held court inside the ranch house, like a king overseeing his subjects. "He'll leave as soon as a new leader is in place," Saldana finished. "My money is on Dale Hunter."

Roy continued toward the corrals, mulling over what he had heard. So Dale might become the new leader. Baffled, he shook his head. They had known each other for a decade. Until their former outfit had been wiped out in the train robbery, they had never taken an active part in the robberies. He had saddled broken horses for the outlaws, wild mustangs bought from the Navaho traders, and Dale had been in charge of hauling supplies to the hideout. But after they joined the

Red Bluff Gang, they'd been given no choice but to participate in the raids.

Roy found Dale by the corrals, watching Dagur and Baldur settle in with the herd. Leaning against the fence, one boot propped on the bottom rail, Dale twisted to look over his shoulder, the raven hair beneath his silver-decorated hat gleaming in the evening sun.

"What is this I hear about you taking over from Lom Curtis?" Roy asked.

Dale returned his attention to the horses. "See how your buckskin stands beside the mare, protecting her from the rest of the herd. You'd do well to observe, *amigo*, and learn to do the same."

"You didn't answer my question."

Dale shrugged. "I got my reasons."

"Anything I should know?"

"To the contrary. The less you know the better."

Roy hesitated. The way Dale glanced at him, a quick, darting look full of doubt and uncertainty, made Roy suspect something was afoot, something dangerous. "Are you sure you can't tell me?"

Dale shook his head. "It has to be this way."

"All right." Roy's unease grew. "But remember, I'm your friend."

"I know." Dale spoke so quietly that the sudden restless burst of motion from the horses in the corral almost drowned out his voice. "I won't forget. I know that if it wasn't for me, you might have broken away from this life before it became too late."

Roy looked past Dale, into the falling darkness. What could he say to that? It was true. Until last year, when they joined the Red Bluff Gang, Roy could have ridden off, sought a new start. Only Dale could not do the same. He had a federal warrant out on him. At the end of the war, when Sherman's troops had marched through the South leaving a swath of destruction in their wake, renegade Union soldiers had raped and killed Dale's sister before burning down the mansion his mother's family had owned for generations.

Twelve years old at the time, Dale had discovered enough facts to identify the four men responsible for the atrocity. By the time he was eighteen, those men were dead and Dale had become a fugitive. Faced with the choice of seeking an honest life or leaving behind the only friend he had ever known, Roy had elected to stay.

"Regrets?" Dale asked softly.

Roy shrugged. "Regrets never change anything. But I need your help now."

He told Dale about Celia and her father, how he'd had no choice but to bring her along to the hideout, to collect what was owed to her. "Dale, I'm counting on your friendship. I need you to escort her away from here, whenever you go out next."

"I'm going for supplies the day after tomorrow, *amigo*. But I can't take her with me. Not this time. Don't ask me why, and don't tell anyone that you asked. Not unless you want me dead." Leaning over the corral fence, Dale gestured at the restless animals with one hand. "Watch your horse and learn, *amigo*. See how he protects the mare. It's a skill you'll need."

"Is there going to be trouble?"

Dale lifted his boot from the bottom rail. He turned around to survey the camp and grinned, cocky and carefree all of a sudden, but Roy could hear the warning in his tone. "Bored, frustrated men. A beautiful woman. Gold and gambling, guns and whiskey. Such an *estofado* is bound to boil over some time. Watch your woman well, *amigo*, while the stew simmers. Watch her well."

Instead of sending someone along with their bedrolls and saddlebags, Roy took them up himself. Celia was busy beating dust from the worn rag mattress with a stick of wood. He dumped their belongings on the floor inside the front door she'd wedged open with a rock. She glanced over at him, sneezed, nodded her thanks and went on, *thump, thump, thump.*

It gave him an odd feeling, witnessing such a scene of domesticity. Restless, Roy wandered off to the cook shack. Jarvis, the ancient, bandy-legged cook was stirring his stew, a staple fare in the poorly provisioned outlaw camp. Long ago, the men had given up trying to identify the meat in the spicy concoction—squirrel, horse, coyote, all served equally well to satisfy hunger.

"I'll put some stew in a clay pot for the lady," Jarvis said, his faded hazel eyes squinting up at Roy. "I could run it over to her before I feed the men."

"I'll take it."

Patiently, Roy waited while the cook finished his preparations and ladled some of the stew into a pot. The men at the long table had put away their playing cards and Roy could feel them watching him with envy. It heightened that odd sensation inside him, making him edgy and nervous. No one had ever envied him before. He'd never possessed anything of value, anything worth coveting, except perhaps a good horse.

He went back up the slope to the cabin. The sun had dipped below the canyon rim. Twilight muted the landscape, making it appear less stark and barren. The temperature was sinking, the chill of a desert night falling. He could tell that Celia had lit a lantern, for a yellow glow shone from the cabin window.

At the door, he paused, stunned. A flood of childhood memories, an avalanche of hopes and longings hit him, rendering him speechless. In no time at all, Celia had turned the primitive dwelling into a home. Blankets covered the bed. A brightly colored shawl framed the window, like a curtain. Clothes hung from pegs on the wall. The dull light softened the rough surroundings, creating a cozy atmosphere.

"I took the shawl from the chest, don't know if I was supposed to… There wasn't anyone to ask, so I went ahead anyway… What do you think, will it do?"

He looked at her, this beautiful woman sharing a cabin with him, creating home comforts he'd never enjoyed before. His chest tightened and his hands trembled so hard he feared he might spill the stew.

"It looks fine," he said gruffly, too afraid to let his emotions show. He stepped across the threshold and lowered the clay pot on the table. "I brought supper."

"Oh?" She pointed at the potbellied stove. "I thought I'd cook for us."

"Firewood is scarce. It needs to be hauled in. You'll have to get your meals from the cook shack, but you can light the stove if there is a frost at night." He shifted on his feet, feeling lost among the forces that pulled him in so many different directions. Not pausing to weigh up his words, he burst into rapid speech. "Mr. Smith has put an embargo on men leaving the valley. You'll be stuck here for a few days. I'm sorry."

Celia silenced him with a gesture. "Do you remember my reaction when you first offered me the money from the bank raid? I acted all high-and-mighty, telling you that I'll not accept your ill-gotten gains. But now we both know the truth. I'm a convict's daughter, suited to the company of outlaws. Staying a few days will do me no harm."

"This is a dangerous place for a woman."

"I know. I'm not a fool." Celia moved toward him. "But if I'm stuck here, there is something I wish to do. My father told me that the greatest comfort I can offer him is to write to him in Yuma prison and tell him that I'm safely settled in some place where people have no prejudice against me. I shall write and tell him that I've received the money from the robbery. It will reassure him that he succeeded in his efforts to secure my future."

Roy wanted to point out that her future would be far from secure until she had ridden out of the canyon hideout with her bag of gold coins, but he did not wish to alarm her. And right now they needed to eat. The greasy stew would taste even more unpalatable if they left it to get cold. So he merely tightened his fingers around hers and spoke quietly.

"Perhaps it makes sense for you to stay a few days. We need to figure out more about this Mr.

Smith, make sure that when you leave, you'll have a safe passage."

For a moment, they contemplated each other, each uncertain exactly what they might expect from those few days. Then Roy released her hands and went to sit in the single chair.

"Get the spoons. Don't bother with the plates. We can eat straight from the pot."

Celia did as told, rummaging in their saddle-bags and holding up the pair of battered spoons as if they were priceless silverware. Roy gestured for her to come closer and pulled her over to perch on his knee.

Laughing now, the moment of tension forgotten, she settled there, and they shared the simple supper, his arm around her waist, their heads bent together over the steaming stew pot. A feeling of contentment stole over Roy. As a child, when he had been banished to sit alone in the kitchen corner, or later, after his mother died, to live in the stables like an animal, he would have given anything for such domesticity, such sense of acceptance and belonging.

While Roy went to take the supper dish back to the cook shack, Celia stood in the middle of the cabin and felt a flicker of nerves. Her gaze drew to the pine bed covered with blankets. Sleeping beside Roy had seemed natural the day before, the euphoria of surviving the snakebite and Miss Ada's whiskey-fortified tea shattering her modesty.

She glanced around the cramped space. It would be impossible for them to undress at the same time without bumping into each other. Quickly, she got out of her riding costume and hung it up on a hook on the wall. Cold air enveloped her. Shivering, she scooped water from the pail by the door into a basin and washed her face and cleaned her teeth.

For an instant, she hovered on her feet, undecided. Then she quickly stripped out of her undergarments and bundled them into the oak chest. The best way to overcome the moral constraints of her upbringing was to meet them head-on. She sat on the edge of the bed, removed her shoes and socks and darted beneath the covers. Just in time, for footsteps sounded outside and there was a knock on the door.

"Celia? It's me, Roy. Let me in."

"It's open."

Roy stepped into the cabin with a gust of cold air. It was fully dark outside now. Celia could hear a burst of rowdy laughter, then a single gunshot. A shiver of fear rippled over her.

"You should have bolted the door," Roy told her.

"But you were close by."

"Always bolt the door if you're alone after dark."

She nodded. The thought of the dangers that surrounded them made her edgy. To her surprise, they also caused a restless anticipation to surge within her. As if the lawless environment was rubbing off on her, making her greedy for physical pleasures.

Her gaze swept over Roy, skimming his wide shoulders, tracing his handsome features. He'd pulled his eye patch aside. His hair curled damp about his face, and she guessed he'd been at the creek to have his evening wash.

He swung a small metal bucket onto the table. "I brought you hot water to wash."

"No need. I had a bath yesterday, and there was little trail dust today."

"Are you sure?"

"I…" A blush flared on her skin. "Perhaps, if you'll help…"

"All right." He removed his gun belt, placed one of the pistols on the bed by the pillow. After shrugging out of his shirt, he took a small flannel cloth from his saddlebags, set the bucket of water on the floor and knelt by the bedside.

With unhurried motions, he dipped the cloth in the bucket, wrung it dry and lifted the edge of the blankets. "Celia…you're naked… I thought…"

"Isn't this how couples sleep together?"

"Celia…" He sank to sit on the floor, the cloth gripped in his fingers. "Celia, I can't…we can't…"

His expression grew fraught. "Don't do this, Celia. Don't lead us deeper and deeper into intimacy. It's all too easy to believe that if love is powerful enough it will conquer every obstacle, but it doesn't work like that."

"I'm not asking for a future."

"No. But you're asking for trouble. Just because you are good and pure, it doesn't protect you from evil. It doesn't insulate you from bad things happening. Bad things happening to you because of me. Because of what I am." Roy's features contorted with some inner pain. When he spoke again, his voice came out strained. "Celia, what Miss Mabel told you…about her husband… I was there… I saw him hang."

His hand fisted around the cloth, sending a rivulet dripping to the floor, but he appeared not to notice. The single lamp burning was on the table behind him, leaving his face in shadows that emphasized his stricken expression.

"It was in my first year at the outlaw camp. I was only fifteen. Jim Rowland—Miss Mabel's husband—had been kind to me. He was an educated man, and he gave me books to read, helped me to make up for the lack of schooling. When he was captured, the rest of us rode out with a plan to spring him from the jail. But it could not be done. There were too many guards. So instead, we watched them hang him."

Celia saw the quick rise and fall of Roy's naked chest as he sucked in a sharp breath. "They made a circus of it. Like the Fourth of July celebrations. People brought picnics. A band played merry tunes. The only thing that lacked was fireworks."

He looked up at her, horror in his eyes. "Miss Mabel stood right in front of the gallows. When they sprang the trap, she collapsed to her knees. There was no one helping her, no one to comfort her. They all shunned her, an outlaw's widow who had deceived them for years. She didn't cry, but she made this terrible croaking sound, as if every breath she took tore at her insides. She had already buried her little boy, and she had no tears left. But I've never seen such grief. Never."

Roy fell silent and lifted the cloth he'd been gripping. Almost touching her bare shoulder with it, he let his hand hover in the air, not quite completing the motion. It seemed to Celia as if that small distance symbolized what he was about to say.

"Afterward, Miss Mabel had no place to go. She ended up in a bordello. Although she did well and now owns the place, I can't risk putting you in a similar position. And I can't risk letting you so deep into my heart that when you go there'll be nothing left but emptiness too great to bear. We'll both have to keep ourselves whole, so we can survive when we are alone again."

Celia swallowed. Roy looked more handsome than ever, the humility of his words contrasting with the blatant masculinity of his powerful body. She reached out, trailed her fingertips over the ridged contours of his muscles and felt the heat on his skin.

"I understand," she said. "But it is already too late. You have already become a part of me. I know that after we say goodbye I'll never stop missing you. The best you can do for me is to build up memories. Give me something to take with me when I go."

Instead of replying, Roy lifted his other hand and cupped her cheek in his callused palm. Celia could feel his hand shaking, could feel the tension in him. She waited. Finally, Roy gave a long, slow sigh. She couldn't see his brown eye well enough in the shadowed light of the lamp on the table behind him, but she could tell his blue eye was bright with emotion. When he spoke, his voice was very low.

"Thank you, Celia. Thank you for this...for making a home for us. The next few days and nights will be the only chance we'll ever have to be together. Let us make the most of them, although we must take care not to create a child."

The cloth in his hand had cooled, and he dipped it in warm water again and wrung it dry in order to not dampen the bedclothes. Then he proceeded to wash her, gently sliding the cloth over her skin. He did not miss an inch of her. His touch wasn't overtly sexual, but the smooth, even motion of his hand stroking her body stirred an edgy need inside Celia that begged to be eased. She began to shift restlessly on the bed. Her fingers fisted into the crisp sheet she had found in the oak chest and used to cover the worn rag mattress.

"Enough?" Roy said.

When she nodded. Roy straightened on his feet and turned to blow out the lamp on the table. The cabin plunged into darkness.

"I can't see," she told him in agitated whisper.

"Oh, but I can." She could hear the laughter in his voice. Fabric rustled. Clothing tumbled to the earth floor. A boot thudded down, then another. In her mind, Celia pictured Roy completely naked, only a step away from her. Somehow, not seeing him added an element of suspense that felt like a powerful narcotic.

A hand closed on her shoulder. "Move aside. On second thoughts, don't."

She felt him climb up onto the bed, felt his powerful frame settle over hers. His skin was hot, his muscles taut. Instinctively, she eased her legs apart to accommodate him, but instead of taking up the invitation, Roy edged downward along her body.

"What are you doing?" she whispered.

"Don't ask and you won't be told lies." She could hear laughter in his voice.

And then the mattress shifted beneath her as Roy adjusted his position. A moment later, she felt it there, right in her secret place, a hot wetness that catapulted her into a dark abyss of pleasure so intense, so decadent, that she would not have believed it possible. On and on it went, waves of sensation that left her writhing on the bed, deaf and blind to all the world except that small part of her body and Roy's mouth upon it.

When the tremors of completion had finally subsided and Celia regained her senses, the mattress dipped again as Roy moved back up along the bed to lie beside her. He pulled her into the circle of his arms. Celia broke free, sat up and gathered her courage. So far, their lovemaking had seemed terribly one-sided, and she wished to remedy the imbalance.

"I want to make you feel like you made me feel."

"Celia…it's not something a man can ask a lady to do."

"You are not asking," she pointed out. "I'm insisting."

It didn't take long for her to convince Roy, and in low, husky tones he instructed her how to go about returning the favor. The complete darkness in the room offered a cloak of modesty while she learned her way around a man's body, discovered how to touch him and give him pleasure. The raw violence of his reaction told her that this release had been as powerful as hers, and she found a new sense of satisfaction from having brought it about.

Afterward, as Celia lay curled up in Roy's embrace, his voice rang inside her head. *The next few days and nights will be the only chance we'll ever have to be together. Let us make the most of them.* She lay awake for long hours, listening to his heartbeat, regret filling her that one of those precious days and nights was already almost gone.

Chapter Twelve

When Celia awakened, the scents of coffee and bacon filled the cabin and streaks of morning light filtered in between the closed shutters. Roy was seated at the small pine table by the window, fully dressed, watching her.

Recollections of the way they had brought pleasure to each other in the darkness of the night flickered through Celia's mind, suddenly making her feel shy. Trying to act confident, she wriggled to a sitting position on the bed. Instinctively, she fumbled at the bedclothes, pulled them up to her chin to cover her bare breasts.

Roy's lips curved into a grin. At his amused expression, the foolishness of her prim action struck Celia. She burst into giggles, and yet the modesty of her upbringing would not allow her to let the covers fall away and reveal her nakedness.

"Turn around," she demanded.

"There's not enough room to turn around. I'll close my eyes, how's that?"

Roy's eyelids came down, the long lashes forming a dark crescent against the tanned skin. He didn't have his eye patch on, but Celia knew that as soon as they opened the shutters he would cover his brown eye. For an instant, she drank in his features, and then she pushed the blankets out of the way and swung her feet to the earth floor. Her toes curled against the cold surface and she let out an involuntary groan, accompanied by a shiver.

"*Brrrrr...* It's freezing."

"I'll get some firewood for tomorrow morning."

She took a deep breath, jumped to her feet and pulled on her clothing with jerky, hurried motions, fighting the chill in the room. She knew that Roy was peeking from beneath his half-closed lids, just as she had expected he would. She didn't mind.

When she was ready, her hair gathered into a knot at the nape of her neck, her face and teeth rinsed, she went to join him at the table and perched on his knee. The bout of shyness conquered, she felt at ease. As long as she remained at the camp, she would try not to think about the future, would not spoil their days together by worrying about the parting.

"We need another chair," she pointed out.

Roy nuzzled her neck. "I like it this way."

"I want my own chair, so I can work at the table. There's a needle and thread in the chest. I can repair your worn-out clothing. And I want to write a letter to my father."

They shared a lazy breakfast, enjoying the sense of togetherness. Roy described the daily routines at the hideout, how the cook banged his pots and pans to announce the mealtimes. Those who didn't hurry to the cook shack risked being left without.

"If you want a lie-in, it's fine, but I'll have to get up before the food runs out. And today I'll have to do some work. A string of unbroken mustangs was delivered while I was away and I need to get started on them."

"Can I come and watch?"

"You can move freely around the camp while I'm close by, and I can accompany you for walks along the valley. But anytime I need to leave you alone, you'll have to be careful. Stay inside the cabin and bolt the door unless I'm within sight."

After they'd finished eating, Roy gathered up the empty dishes. "I'll take these back to the cook shack. I need to catch up with some of the men. I'll talk to Dale Hunter about posting your letter when he rides out tomorrow, and I'll see you again at lunchtime."

With a bittersweet mix of anxiety and contentment, Celia watched him go. She opened the shutters, letting in the crisp morning air. Outside, she could hear masculine voices and laughter, horses whinnying, a crow screeching. Everyday sounds. And then the steady popping of gunfire from target practice pierced all the other sounds, reminding her of the lawless nature of the camp.

Celia closed her mind to the sudden flash of fear. She went to her saddlebags and took out the pen and writing tablet and the small bottle of ink she had packed before leaving home. She arranged the equipment on the table, sat down and composed a letter to her father, deliberating over each word.

Dear Papa,
You longed to see me settled, my future secured, and it gives me great pleasure to tell you that I am married.

My husband is a fine man, a horse wrangler by trade. Currently he is occupied breaking wild mustangs for a fee, but he has some savings that will allow me to make a home where I can bring up our children while he travels around for his work.

Before you went to prison you mentioned a small family legacy coming to me. I am glad to inform you that I have received the

*money. I am fully aware of the measures you
have taken to provide for me, and you have
my love and gratitude.*

*In my eyes, you have never done anything
wrong, and you are the best of fathers, have
always been. I hope your waning health is
not causing you too much distress. I trust
the prison doctor is taking good care of you,
and the warden is an honorable man who
treats you with compassion.*

*I don't expect that I shall have an oppor-
tunity to visit, but you are in my thoughts.
Your loving daughter,
Celia.*

She blew on the sheet to dry the ink, read the
finished letter once more. The reference to a husband and children caused a bittersweet pang of
regret, not just because she was stretching the
truth, but because the lie could never become reality. However, nothing less than marriage would
have the power to reassure her father, and reassuring him was the main purpose of the letter. A
long, rambling account of her travels might have
served to entertain him, but she didn't want her
key messages to be lost among trivia. Further,
she was short on writing paper and wished to preserve her supply, in case no opportunity arose to
acquire more.

Craning out through the window, Celia surveyed the camp for Roy's whereabouts. He was standing near the corrals, half turned away, but she could tell he kept glancing toward the cabin. Surely, that counted as him being *within sight*, and she could go outside.

She checked her appearance in the small mirror she carried in her saddlebags and took the time to apply some of Miss Mabel's cream over her scar. Her hair was neatly gathered at the nape of her neck. She patted her hands over her velvet riding costume, smoothing the fabric. Mr. Smith was a gentleman, with a gentleman's manners, and it might help if she looked like a lady.

Outside, a brisk wind added to the autumn cool, whipping her heavy skirts around her legs. She made her way to the entrance of the ranch house. Davies, the compact, square-faced man with sandy hair who had searched her for weapons the day before, lounged in the open doorway.

Celia gathered her courage. "I wish to speak to Mr. Smith."

Davies pushed his shoulder from the jamb. He stared at her, but there was a reverent, awestruck quality to his perusal. It took him a moment to find his voice.

"I'll tell him."

"I'll wait."

She listened to the cadence of his boots as he

vanished into the building. "The lady wants to see you," Davies called into the inner sanctum. Celia could not make out the muffled reply, but a moment later Davies reappeared and gestured for her to follow him inside.

Again, Mr. Smith's office was shrouded in shadows, the shutters firmly closed, but enough daylight spilled in to remove the necessity of a lamp. An armed guard stood in the corner, blending against the wall. Celia did not bother with a greeting. She merely gave a curt nod and held up the sheet of paper in her hand.

"I wish to send a letter to my father, but I have no envelope. I was hoping you might be able to furnish me with one." She placed the letter on the desk in front of Mr. Smith. "It is only a single page. A small envelope would suffice."

The disguise of a heavy beard and spectacles, combined with the hat pulled low, made it difficult to interpret the man's expression, however Celia thought she saw a flash of respect in his eyes. Without a word, he pulled a desk drawer open, took out an envelope and laid it on the desk.

"Thank you." Celia reached over and picked up the envelope. "I shall go and write the address. I'll only be a few minutes. I understand Dale Hunter is riding out for supplies today. Perhaps you could ask him to post the letter for me?"

"I'll do that," Mr. Smith replied, and Celia caught a hint of a smile.

So they understood each other. Common sense told her that Mr. Smith—a man engaged in criminal deceit—would be worried about a letter addressed to Yuma prison. This way, she was letting him see the contents and be reassured that the message going to her father revealed no secrets, an action which removed the need for him to intercept the letter.

She went back to the cabin, carefully addressed the envelope.

Prisoner Joseph Courtwood
Yuma Territorial Prison
Yuma
Arizona Territory

After delivering the finished product to Mr. Smith in his shadowed lair, she drifted down to the corrals, skirting around the camp to avoid the cook shack, where a rowdy group of men was already engaged in a game of cards.

Four outlaws stood leaning against the corral fence. Edging closer, Celia positioned herself slightly apart from them. Like animals moving in a herd, they all turned to look at her and touched their hat brims. She curbed her fear and gave a stiff nod.

"Good morning, gentlemen."

In a chorus, they returned her greeting. In their thirties or forties, they looked hardened by the lifestyle. Each wore a double rig of pistols. Celia kept her distance and directed her attention to Roy. He was in the corral with three horses, a pair of sorrels and a gleaming black. The sorrels were tethered to a post by their bridle reins. The black had no bridle, not even a halter, but his front legs were hobbled.

Roy glanced over at her, sent her a smile. She smiled back and waved. He lifted a saddle from the corral fence and put it on one of the sorrels, then moved aside. The horse sidestepped, bucked a little, calmed down again.

"Will you ride him?" she called out.

"Came expecting a rodeo, did you?"

When she didn't reply, Roy picked up a saddle blanket and settled it on the other sorrel. The horse swung its neck, managed to grip a corner of the blanket in its teeth and pull down the offending object. Roy plucked the blanket from the dust and replaced it on the sorrel's back, all the while talking in a calm tone.

"There's little to see here today. No bronc riding. I'm just getting them used to a saddle. Letting them know it is nothing to fear. That I am nothing to fear. The black is just watching today. He's more suspicious than the other two, but he trusts them. If they accept the saddle today, he'll do the same tomorrow."

Celia watched Roy and felt her chest tighten. Even if she hadn't known how gentle he could be when he touched her in the night, his patience with the horses would have revealed his caring nature. It seemed wrong to have a man like him trapped in the outlaw life, but there was nothing she could do about it.

Nothing anybody could do about it.

Except perhaps Roy himself.

Their existence acquired a pattern. After breakfast, Celia watched Roy work on the mustangs. In the afternoon, she stayed in the cabin, cleaning and mending. Wishing to preserve her good clothing, she borrowed a wide skirt and an embroidered Mexican blouse from the chest in the cabin. Far too large for her, she wore them with a rope belt tied around her waist, gathering the excess material into folds. Roy told her she looked like a gypsy, with her wild curls tumbling down her back. Pleased by the remark, she unraveled her upsweep in the evenings, knowing he preferred her hair unbound.

Contrary to her fears, the outlaws, perhaps twenty in number, had not bothered her. Most of them seemed reticent, ill at ease in her presence.

They darted curious glances in her direction when she passed, but made no attempt to talk to her.

The only two who alarmed her were Grittenden, the man who had stood guard with a rifle at the head of the gorge on the day she arrived, and another outlaw called Franklin. A small man with sharp, surly features, he appeared to have nothing to occupy his time but to sit on a stone by the path, whittling on a piece of wood, waiting for her to come out of the cabin so he could stare at her. She had asked Roy about him and discovered he was a safecracker, expert at using explosives to break into bank vaults.

Although Celia was aware there was another woman in the camp, Miss Gabriela might as well have been a ghost. She kept to her cabin. Andersen, a big, quiet, fair-haired man around thirty, whom the others called Swede, watched over her like a guard dog, fetching food and water for her, emptying chamber pots, even hanging her clothes to dry.

Once or twice, Celia had caught sight of a timid-looking woman in the open doorway of the neighboring adobe cabin. Medium height, slender to the point of appearing frail, she stood with her face tilted up toward the sun, a lace mantilla covering her glossy black hair. One arm in a sling, her complexion pale, she looked breathtakingly lovely, but an aura of sadness surrounded her, hinting at some past tragedy.

"Could I visit her?" Celia asked Roy.

"Leave it. She'll come to see you when she is ready."

"Why is she so withdrawn?"

Roy hesitated. "I told you. This is a dangerous place for a woman."

He offered her no further comment, and it occurred to Celia that whatever violence had caused Miss Gabriela to withdraw into herself could befall any woman living in an outlaw camp. She wanted to ask about the woman the men referred to as Big Kate, if she had been equally solitary, but her courage failed. For a while longer, she wanted to cling to the sense of peace and security she knew to be false, to gather up memories no future calamity could take away from her.

Dale Hunter set off on another supply run, but neither Celia nor Roy raised the prospect that she ought to leave. Every night, they lay in bed together, wrapped in each other's arms, whispering in the darkness, every minute too precious to be wasted on sleep. And yet, they never allowed themselves to break the boundaries they had agreed to and avoided the final step of intimacy, which might have resulted in pregnancy, altering the course of their lives.

To Celia's surprise, she made friends with Davies, the shy, bumbling man in his thirties who guarded the ranch house. He waylaid her on the path one morning, his hat in his hands. "Miss Celia, you wrote to your pa…would you help me write a letter to my ma…? I never learned how, and I've learned she's taken poorly…"

"If you can't read, how do you know she has taken poorly?"

A flush darkened the man's face. "She wrote me, and Halloran read it for me."

"Why can't Halloran help you write a letter?"

Davies squirmed, his blush deepening. "The sort of thing a man wants to say to his dying ma… I don't want the men to think that I'm a sissy."

"I see." Celia swallowed. She had no desire to fraternize with the outlaws, but something about Davies appealed to her compassion. Perhaps it was the man's lack of intelligence that had made him a target of cruel pranks by the others. Perhaps it was the common bond of having an ailing parent to worry about.

Irresolute, Celia glanced down the slope toward the corrals, where Roy was busy working with the mustangs. Allowing Davies inside the cabin was out of the question, but she did not have the heart to refuse his request.

"If you wait a moment, I'll unpack my ink and

notepaper. Then you can walk over and stand outside my window while you dictate the letter."

She hurried into the cabin and set out her writing tools. Feeling a twinge of guilt at being uncharitable, she examined the thinness of her writing tablet. Hopefully one page would suffice. She sat down, uncapped the bottle of ink and waited, pen poised above the sheet of paper.

Footsteps thudded outside, and then faded away as Davies came to a halt by the window, his burly shoulders blocking out part of the daylight.

"I'm ready," Celia said. "Tell me what you want me to write."

"Well…" The outlaw cleared his throat, shifted on his feet, so that the light through the window altered again. Celia heard a rasping sound. She craned her neck to glance out and saw that Davies was scratching his head beneath his hat, looking miserable.

"I dunno…what to put in the letter…"

Celia spoke softly. "When I wrote to my father, I told him that I loved him, and that he had always been a good father to me. I told him that even if I couldn't visit him, my thoughts were with him. Would you like me to say the same?"

"That's good. Write it just like that…you know…what you said."

With a sigh, Celia dipped her pen in the bottle of ink and began to capture the words on paper.

Why did men find it so difficult to express their emotions? Even as the thought flashed through her mind, empathy stirred within her. There was something decent and sincere about Davies. Once again, it occurred to Celia that Roy might not be the only man in the camp who had fallen into the outlaw life by accident, and was a good person at heart.

Chapter Thirteen

The scent of rosewater alerted Celia before she noticed the woman standing in the open doorway. *Just like a ghost*, Celia thought with a shiver of alarm. Miss Gabriela seemed to have materialized without a sound, as if conjured out of the crisp autumn air.

Still and silent, dressed in a threadbare black gown, a lace mantilla partly obscuring her features, the woman had the quality of a marble statue. And then she moved. The way she glided into the room, like a shadow shifting, made Celia suspect Miss Gabriela had learned to blend into the background, remain invisible.

The lace mantilla fell aside, revealing a face of astonishing beauty. Skin of alabaster, lips of crimson, symmetrical features with a rounded chin and a small, straight nose. Large, dark eyes, which were now filled with fear. The tension about her felt like a palpable force, the way a telegraph wire hums when one stands close enough to feel the vibration.

For a moment, they studied each other. Then Miss Gabriela spoke. Her voice was low and breathless, no more than a whisper. The voice of someone living in constant fear.

"You must leave, Miss Celia. Leave immediately. I sense danger."

A chill seemed to settle over the room. Celia wanted to protest, but the words refused to form on her tongue. In truth, she had sensed it, too. The atmosphere at the hideout had thickened, growing oppressive. The men were drinking hard, and the gambling had gained a wild, reckless edge. Yesterday, an argument had erupted into a brawl. Anytime she went outside, she could see the men skulking about, restless and brooding. The whole place felt like a keg of gunpowder waiting for someone to toss in a match.

"I can't leave… I have nowhere to go."

"You have to go… I have seen how he looks at you… Franklin… I watch out of the window of my cabin and I see him sitting on the stone by the path, whittling with his knife, waiting for you to walk by. Before, I have seen that look in a man's eyes…three times I have seen it, and it brings disaster…bad things will happen…you must go."

"I wish to remain here with Roy."

Miss Gabriela hunched her shoulders, as if preparing to receive a blow. Her eyes darted over Celia's face. "You love him? You love Roy Hagan?"

She hesitated putting such a simple label on her feelings. "Yes."

"Then go. I loved once, too. Felipe…he worked at my father's hacienda. He was poor, my parents did not approve, so we eloped. My father's guards chased us, and Felipe shot one of them. My father called it murder, and we came here to hide. Felipe was not a robber. I brought money with me and we could pay for our food and shelter. But a man looked at me the way Franklin looks at you now. He walked out of the camp with Felipe and he came back alone. I was claimed, like a stray animal can be claimed. I became a prize. And every time there was a killing, the man who claimed me was capable of greater cruelty than the one before. With Lom Curtis, many times I would have ended my life but my religion forbids it. Only now…"

Miss Gabriela glanced back to where the big, fair-haired Swede stood a dozen paces away, watching over her. "Only now I have hope again. Go, while you still have hope."

"I…" Celia made a small, helpless gesture with her hand. She didn't know what to say, how to reply. The horror painted by Miss Gabriela's words felt all too real. The barrier she had built around her thoughts to keep her anxieties at bay cracked, allowing her fears to spill out. She opened her mouth to speak, but by the time she found her voice Miss Gabriela had turned around and melted away on soundless steps.

Roy returned to the cabin at suppertime to find Celia in a state of agitation. She rushed up to him, her frantic words gushing out in a torrent. "Miss Gabriela came to see me…she urged me leave the valley…almost as if she has a premonition… of course, no one can see into the future…and yet I know what she means…the air feels thick with danger…that man, Franklin…he has such mean, reptile eyes…he reminds me of the rattlesnake that bit me…"

"Calm down." Roy deposited the crock of stew on the table and swept Celia into his arms. His heart beat in slow thuds, already heavy from the pain of parting. He'd known all along it was wrong to let Celia stay at the hideout, but he had wanted a taste of happiness, even if just for a short while.

He didn't kiss her, for this was not the time to let passion cloud their thinking. He merely cradled her to his chest, gently rocking her to and fro, until her frightened trembling eased. Leaning back, he raked his fingers into her tumbling curls and met her worried eyes.

"Miss Gabriela is right. You need to leave. I'll speak to Dale Hunter. He is going on another supply run tomorrow. I've been at fault, not to make the arrangements sooner. I'll see him after supper tonight and make sure he takes you with him in the morning."

Celia swallowed. When she spoke, her voice was low. "Chicago. I need to make my way to Chicago. Get settled in a boardinghouse and start studying the market. Including your money, I'll have three thousand dollars. That's a good starting stake."

Roy eased their bodies apart, as if touching her made him too vulnerable, eroded his resolve to let her go. "I'm sorry it's not more. I made some money on another raid, but one of the men in my previous outfit left a widow, and Dale and I sent our share to her."

Celia hesitated. "How can I get a message to you...keep you informed of your investments and send your share of gains to you?"

Roy hardened himself. "It will be safer if you don't contact me." He gritted his teeth. An ache settled in his gut, as painful as a gunshot wound. He let his eyes skim over Celia's features. She was a beautiful woman. Her scar had faded, and without the crazy prejudice she would attract suitors. Perhaps he was better off not knowing, better off not hearing how she was making a life for herself, perhaps a life that included some other man. He felt the cabin walls close around him, felt as if the air had been sucked out of his lungs. "I need to go and see Dale Hunter, make the arrangements."

As he stalked out of the cabin, his body was shaking. How could he have been so irresponsible, to let things get this far? How could he have believed he could enjoy a few days of her warmth, and then go on living as before, as if nothing had happened? He should have known better, should have known that to let her go would hurt more than tearing out a piece of his own flesh, plunging him into a fog of misery that might never lift.

And yet he must.

Must let her go.

Roy found Dale Hunter standing by the cook shack, drinking coffee, one shoulder propped against a canopy post. A few paces away, the men were clearing the table after supper, ready to resume their gambling. Twilight was thickening. Someone was lighting the lanterns while another man was teasing a mournful tune out of a harmonica.

Roy handed the empty stew pot to Jarvis, the aging cook, and sidled up to Dale. "I need to talk to you."

"Hagan. I been waitin' for you." Dale spoke loudly, as if he hadn't heard Roy's comment. "My horse is favorin' his right front leg. I was hopin' you'd take look." He took another sip of coffee, his eyes sending Roy a message over the rim of the cup.

"Sure." Roy shrugged, hiding his unease. "There's just enough daylight left."

They made their way to the corrals in silence. Dale caught his horse, a showy, high-stepping bay gelding with four white socks. Roy crouched beside the animal, ran his hands over each front leg in turn. As he'd expected, there was nothing wrong with the horse. He spoke in a low murmur.

"I need you to take Celia with you when you ride out of here tomorrow."

"Why now, *amigo*?"

"There's trouble brewing. Don't pretend you don't feel it. The men are like a pack of lobo wolves, snapping and circling. For weeks, they've been stuck in the valley, going crazier by the hour. With Big Kate gone, they can't even use a quick tumble in a whore's bed to ease their frustration. It's getting too dangerous for Celia to stay around."

Boot leather creaked as Dale sank down to his haunches beside Roy. He glanced behind them to make sure they were alone. "Listen, *amigo*, and listen good. When I ride out for supplies, I've been meeting with a man from Washington. My mother is friendly with the family of Chester Arthur, the man who became president after Garfield was assassinated. I've been offered a full pardon if I can deliver Mr. Smith. In a couple of weeks, an army unit will storm the valley. It will be a bloodbath. I'll take Celia with me tomorrow, but you must make sure you get out soon after. If you can't escape, hide in the canyon at the first sign of trouble. No one will be spared. It will be a bullet or a rope."

For a moment, Roy didn't move, didn't even breathe. He barely heard the shifting of the horses in the corral, the raucous yells of the men at the gambling table. The single word echoed around his mind, like water rippling in a pond, the circles growing wider and wider.

Pardon.

A full pardon.

A presidential pardon.

"Could I...is there any way I could...?"

Is there any way I could do the same? Move away from this life that is no life at all into another kind of life—a life that I have now had a glimpse of—a life that I didn't even dare to dream about before.

The sudden flare of hope tore at Roy. It would be no use. A woman like Celia might turn to an outlaw for protection when she had no choice, but she was not for the likes of him. He'd been an outcast from birth, never accepted, and a pardon would not turn him into a different man. Celia would be better off pursuing her dream of independence. Better off without him—a man who knew nothing about love, a man scarred by the cruelty of his childhood and tainted by his years as an outlaw.

And yet, he could not stop the question from coming out again, in a whisper so rough he could feel the words rasping in his throat. "A pardon... could I...?"

Dale placed his hand on Roy's forearm, let it rest there for a moment. "I'll do what I can. I've mentioned your name, assured them that both of us deserve a second chance. But there are no guarantees. Even if you survive when they invade the valley, there's no knowing what will happen after. Sometimes the wheels of law can gain their own momentum, spin out of control. Promises may get broken. I'm taking a risk, even for myself."

Roy nodded. Behind them, he could hear a pebble roll, could hear the stealthy sounds of someone moving in the deepening darkness. He raised his voice. "It's just a thorn caught beneath the shoe. I've pulled it out. The horse should be fine to ride tomorrow."

He pushed up to his feet, left Dale with his bay gelding and went to say good-night to Dagur. On his way between the corrals, Roy slipped aside the patch over his brown eye and searched the gloom, trying to see who had been spying on them. Whoever had created that small disturbance was gone, leaving behind only silence and the night shadows.

Celia waited alone in the cabin, turbulent thoughts running through her mind. Chicago. Success on the financial markets. Independence. Never again to face the shame of being rejected by a suitor. Never again to have to rely on the charity of others. Perhaps even to make enough money to buy every piece of property in Rock Springs and rule over the town if she so wished.

Wasn't that her dream?

Without thinking, she lifted her hand to the gold coin in the small silk pouch she still carried around her neck. A talisman. A keepsake. A memory of another dream, one she had tried to forget. As she stood still, her mind strangely frozen, footsteps thudded by the entrance. Then the door swung open. On the threshold, Roy stood framed by the falling darkness.

"You should have barred the door while I was outside."

She ignored his comment. Words that had barely formed in her brain tumbled out. "Making a fortune on the stock exchange and being an independent woman is not my dream. It is not what I truly want. What I have always wanted is a husband and home. That dream turned sour, so I came up with an alternative dream, but it was always second best. I don't want second best. I want my original dream. My real dream."

She could see Roy's eyes widen. He had pulled the black patch aside, and although seeing all his face usually allowed Celia to read his expression, now his features seemed like a blank mask, giving her no hint of his reaction.

"I guess deep down I've never really given up on my real dream," Celia went on. "Why otherwise would I have been so ready to ride out of Rock Springs with you? To open my heart to you? To let you into my bed?"

Not saying anything, Roy went to the table. He lifted the chimney on the oil lamp, struck a match and held it to the wick. From the way the flame flickered, Celia could tell his hands were trembling.

The silence seemed to grow heavier and heavier. Celia drew a deep breath. She'd sworn never to make herself vulnerable to a man again, never to set herself up for a rejection again, but she had to pursue her dream.

"Will you be a husband to me?" she said. "Will you be a father to our children?"

Finally, Roy turned to face her. "Is that what you want, Celia? What you truly want?"

"Yes." There was steel in her voice now. Not

a plea, but a woman fighting for her right to be loved. "If I settle down in some quiet place, will you come and see me whenever you can? I know Halloran has a wife hidden away in some town, and he visits her. Davies told me about it."

Roy seemed to stiffen. He shook out the match with an abrupt gesture. When he spoke, it was in the same kind of fevered outpouring that her words had been. "Do you have the courage for that, Celia? It is one thing to be an outlaw's woman here, among outlaws. What about being branded one among decent folk? You didn't fare too well when they shunned you because of your scar, or your father's role in the robbery. How would you feel if they shunned you because of me? Do you have the courage to love an outcast? My mother didn't. She didn't have the courage to love me, her own son."

At first, Roy's grim outburst felt like a blow, but then the vulnerable note in his voice and the bitterness of his final comment made Celia understand. Pity welled up within her. She was searching for the right response when Roy went on, letting out the hurt that must have festered inside him for years.

"Sometimes, when no one was around to notice, my mother would ruffle my hair, smile at me, give me a kind word. And then, when her husband or her parents entered the room, she would ignore me, as if I didn't exist."

Celia spoke softly. "I'm sorry for the way you suffered. But isn't it strange how everyone doubts my courage to love an outlaw. And here I've been, inviting you into my bed, even without the benefit of marriage. Miss Mabel said it first. *'Don't do it, unless you have the guts to watch your man hang.'* And now you've said it. *'Don't do it, unless you have the courage to stand by me when the world is against us.'*"

She looked up, hoping Roy would see and recognize the steadfastness in her. "I may have been afraid to give in to noisy displays of emotion, but you have cured me of that. And when I first saw you, I desperately wanted to learn your secret, to discover how you had the strength to ignore the curiosity of people over your eye patch. And I've learned that secret, too, have learned not to care about the opinion of people who don't matter.

"But you have no right to doubt my courage to love. I've nursed two ailing parents, seen them grow weaker each day while I witnessed their suffering. I've loved them, knowing that they were about to die. And I loved them all the more because my time with them would be cut short." Celia lifted her chin, forced herself to put into words what she feared most, what they both feared. "Compared to the pain of watching them waste away, seeing you die by hanging would be over quickly. I have the courage to love. To love an outlaw. To love *you*. But do you have the courage to love *me*?"

Do you have the courage to love me?

It felt to Roy as if his very soul had been stripped bare, exposing doubts and fears he hadn't even been aware of himself. "Celia, I…" He made a futile gesture with his hand. All those days on the trail, he'd tried to keep a distance between them. Because he was no good for her. Because a woman like Celia could never truly care for him.

But she had proved that she could.

Celia repeated her question, gently now. "Do you have the courage to love me, Roy?"

He let out a long, slow sigh, his shoulders sagging, as if a heavy weight had suddenly been lifted off him. "What you said about second best…the outlaw life is not what I want, has never been what I want. But I've never felt able to strive for more. Perhaps I felt I had no right to more. Perhaps I was too scared to reach out for more. But you've made me realize that I don't want second best. Just like you, I want my real dream. A dream of a family and home."

He didn't quite have the courage to meet Celia's eyes, but he could find the words.

"If you leave with Dale Hunter tomorrow, you

can wait for me in some safe place, and I'll join you later. We'll go somewhere far away. Montana. Oregon. Someplace where no one can find us. But you'll have to wait for me. It's too dangerous for me to make my bid for freedom right now, with Mr. Smith ruling the camp with his armed guards. But when he goes away, things ought to settle down again. If you leave now, I'll find a way to join you. I promise you that."

Celia moved closer to him, reached out and fisted her fingers in the front of his shirt. Rising up on tiptoe, she studied his face, her expression a mix of hope and relief.

"You promise? You truly promise?"

"I promise," Roy replied.

As long as I'm alive, he added in his mind.

For the rest of the evening, they talked, making plans. Roy had a map of the Arizona Territory, faded and torn at the fold. They spread it out on the table and sat down in front of it, poring over the locations in the soft glow of lamplight.

They chose Winslow for Celia's destination. Some distance to the east, the town was far away from Prescott, where Mr. Smith might come across her when he resumed his real identity. Moreover, Winslow was an important railroad hub, an added benefit in case they had to rely on public transportation.

Once they were finished, Roy lit a fire in the potbellied stove. The small stack of firewood in the corner of the cabin would last through the night. No point in saving it now that Celia would be leaving in the morning.

He stoked the stove until the flames roared, and then he straightened and turned to Celia, who was packing her meager possessions in her carpetbag. Roy pulled his eye patch away and tossed it on the table. Tonight, he wanted everything perfect between them, one final memory to sustain them through the separation.

Celia put her bag aside and came up to him. Her hair was unbound, tumbling in a flurry of curls about her shoulders. While he'd been busy with the stove, she had put on her amethyst earrings, and the firelight made the stones glitter. She bent her head and fumbled with the rope belt that gathered her borrowed skirt around her waist.

"No," Roy said. "Let me."

Because of the cold nights, Celia usually removed her clothing quickly and darted beneath the covers. He'd never undressed her, apart from that one time when she fell in the stream while they were crossing the river. Then, in a hurry to peel away her wet garments, he'd done his best to ignore the rush of desire.

Now he embraced it, let it fill his mind. He bared Celia slowly, while the heat from the fire was building up in the room. As each piece of clothing fell away, he traced her shape with his hands, reveling in the fullness of her figure, the softness of her skin, the subtle scent of vanilla and wildflowers that surrounded her.

She undressed him in turn, her touch sure and deft as she dealt with the masculine garments. "You seem to know your way around a man's clothing," he commented with a faint smile.

"I've done enough mending to figure out how each piece goes on and off."

When they were both naked, they stood facing each other, touching, feeling, caressing. He'd left the stove hatch open, and the firewood crackled and hissed, the flames sending shadows dancing on the rough adobe walls. The heat drew a coat of moisture on their skin. He lowered his head and scattered kisses on Celia's shoulders, on her neck, in the tiny hollow between her collarbones, tasting the slight flavor of salt from the sheen of perspiration.

Slowly, he eased her down on the bed, settled beside her and gathered her close against him. Had he thought about it before, he would have assumed that on their last night together they would throw themselves into a frantic coupling, let their passion burn as bright as the flames in the stove. But it seemed much more important to simply hold her, to feel her heart beating at the same pace as his, the way it had done on that sunny afternoon when they pledged themselves to each other in an Indian ceremony.

"Celia, whatever happens, I want you to know that I—"

"Hush." She silenced him with a kiss. "Don't say it. Not now. Save it for when we meet again, for when you come to find me in Winslow."

Roy nodded, his lips grazing her cheek. He had wanted to tell her that he loved her, but now he understood she preferred to leave the words unsaid. Something to look forward to. Like a superstition, it seemed that if they didn't speak of their feelings now, fate would be obliged to let them reunite, for an emotion so powerful must not be left undeclared.

For long hours, they lay together, occasionally talking in murmured whispers. He let his hands roam over Celia's feminine shape, already worried there was something he might forget: the feel of her breast cupped in his palm, the texture of her hair, the scent of her, the small sounds she made when he touched her just right... Again and again, he memorized them, making sure they would remain branded in his memory forever, for as long as he lived.

"Lie on top of me."

Startled by Celia's request, Roy stilled.

"I want to feel your weight on top of me."

He knew he was courting temptation, but he leaned over Celia, gave her another deep, hungry kiss and stretched out on top of her, his legs sliding between hers. Quivering with the effort of restraint, Roy arched his back and studied Celia's face.

"You promised to stop me from going too far," he reminded her.

"That was then. This is now."

Celia wrapped her legs around his hips, anchoring him in place. Her hips tilted to receive him and her nails dug into his back, urging him on. She lacked the boldness to put her desire into words, but Roy understood. Unable to resist the unspoken invitation, he shifted into position. The promise to hold back had been made in another place, another time, and if Celia felt no longer bound by it, neither should he.

With a murmured request to let him know if it hurt too much, Roy eased himself inside Celia, a couple joining in the most intimate act there could be between a man and a woman. The pleasure of it! It swept through him, and he clamored for more, but he suppressed the instinct to hurry. Carefully, he pressed deeper. When he met a barrier, he paused. Taking his weight on his elbows, he framed Celia's face in his hands and met her anxious eyes.

"Are you sure?" he asked.

She nodded, another wordless response. He lowered his head for a quick, hard kiss, and then he flexed his hips and pushed all the way inside her. He could feel her stiffen beneath him, could feel the gasp of pain she trapped between gritted teeth.

He had no experience of virgins, so he soothed her the way he would soothe a wild horse afraid of humans, afraid of the unknown. With whispered comments, he praised her beauty. He promised her the pain would ease and soon grow into pleasure.

Only when she gave him another one of those silent nods did Roy allow himself to resume his motion. He meant to keep it easy, but the first thrust shattered his control. He had wanted her so badly. It would be over too soon, too soon for her to find her way, too soon for her to learn to match his movements.

But then he felt Celia's hips rise to meet his, and he gave in to the need that drove him. As he moved inside her with deep, steady strokes, he felt Celia tighten around him, heard the small, rhythmic cries of pleasure she tried to suppress and knew he had brought her to completion. With a few final powerful thrusts he took his own release.

The explosion of pleasure robbed him of every trace of sanity. He'd never felt anything like it. For a moment, he believed his heart had ceased beating, and then he felt it pounding against his ribs with such ferocity it frightened him.

Bracing his weight on his elbows, he lowered his head to hide his face against Celia's neck. He was too afraid to let her see the depth of his emotion, the power she held over him. He remained absolutely still until his senses began to function again. Then he lifted his head and searched Celia's face. Her eyes were closed, her skin flushed, her breathing swift.

"Celia?"

"Yes," she replied. The gravity of her voice, the somberness of her expression revealed to Roy that her thoughts mirrored his. By creating the possibility of a child, he had sealed their union with a tie stronger than any vows spoken before a priest. For he would move heaven and earth to ensure that any child of his would grow up safe, with a happy home and a father to protect him.

However, Roy decided not to spoil the moment by discussing the future. There would be time enough in the morning. For the rest of the night, he held Celia in his arms, wishing for each hour, for each minute to last a little longer. But then the rooster crowed in the chicken coop behind the cook shack, and the horses neighed in the corrals. The light outside grew pink and golden, and a new day rushed in—the day that would see Celia ride away from him, with no guarantee of when they would see each other again…

Celia swept one last look around the interior of the cabin to make sure she had packed everything. Feeling sentimental, she let her gaze linger on every inch of the primitive dwelling, every rustic piece of furniture. Despite all the danger and upheaval, it had been a happy home for them.

With a sigh, she picked up her carpetbag and went outside to wait for Roy, who had gone to get Baldur ready for her. In the window of the other adobe cabin a shadow shifted. Miss Gabriela must be watching. By the cook shack, the last stragglers were still finishing their breakfast, but men were already milling about, stealing glances at her. From their increased boldness, she understood they were aware of her departure.

She pressed her hand to the waist of her skirt, imagining the prospect of a new life within her. She and Roy had yet to discuss the potential consequences of last night, but time was slipping away. Perhaps it made no sense to speculate. Until they knew for certain, they lacked a solid basis for making decisions about their future, adjusting their plans to accommodate pregnancy, childbirth and taking care of a baby.

A hard slam of the ranch house door startled Celia out of her thoughts. She turned to look. Dale

Hunter strode down the slope, a grim expression on his patrician face. He spotted her but offered no greeting. His gaze veered away, as if he were unwilling to acknowledge her existence.

Two other men followed him, Franklin and a tall, thin man whose name Celia could not recall. Both looked at her, and something in their eyes filled her with terror. Behind them, Mr. Smith stepped out into the morning light, flanked by a pair of bodyguards. It was the first time Celia had seen him leave the sanctuary of his fortress.

"I hope you don't mind a small delay, Miss Courtwood. Franklin and Longhurst will ride with you and Hunter. Safety in numbers, don't you agree?"

She swallowed, found her voice. "Yes…perhaps."

Davies came out, pushed past Mr. Smith's entourage and hurried toward her, papers clutched in his hand. He came to a halt in front of her. On his face she could see a baffled, troubled look, as if the world around him made even less sense than it normally did.

"Miss Celia, I got an envelope from Mr. Smith, and I have the letter for my ma here, with her address." He thrust the papers at her. "Will you write the address on the envelope and post the letter for me when you have a chance?"

Celia frowned. "I'm sorry, Mr. Davies. There

is no time. We are about to leave. Someone else will have to do it for you."

A desperate, pleading quality entered his tone. "But you promised…"

Celia stole a glance at Mr. Smith, who had not moved from the open doorway. He met her scrutiny, gave her a small, wry smile. "By all means," he said. "There is no hurry. The men have yet to saddle their mounts and round up the packhorses."

With a sigh of resignation, Celia pivoted on her feet, marched back into the cabin and placed her carpetbag on the table. Like a dog on a leash, Davies followed her. He pulled the door until it was barely ajar. It wasn't proper to have him inside the cabin with her, Celia thought, at the same time wondering what foolish notion made her cling to conventional social norms, even while living in an outlaw camp. With two dozen armed men outside, nothing untoward could happen between her and Davies.

Or could it?

Davies edged closer to her as she rummaged inside her bag, searching for the bottle of ink. He craned his head toward her. For a moment Celia feared he might attempt to kiss her. She tensed her arm, her palm tingling with the hard slap she was about to deliver. But then Davies froze in midmotion, his mouth next to her ear, and she could hear him talking in a cautious whisper.

"Miss Celia, they'll kill you. I heard Mr. Smith give the order. Don't go. Find some excuse to stay behind."

Her fingers clenched around the bottle of ink. The claim was crazy; it made no sense. But like a kick in her gut, she recognized it as the truth. She recognized it in the way Dale Hunter had refused to meet her eyes. In the way Franklin and Longhurst had stared at her. In the way Mr. Smith had come out of his lair, to make sure his orders were obeyed.

With mechanical, clumsy movements, she uncapped the ink bottle, set the two letters side by side on the table and began to copy the sender's address from the worn envelope onto the new one. Her brain was racing in fevered circles, looking for a solution, while she drew each letter slowly, playing for time, praying that Roy would return from the horse corrals.

Thank you, God, she whispered in her mind when she heard the thud of boot heels on the path outside. Roy burst into the room, took in the sight of Davies standing too close to her and bristled with masculine indignation.

"What is going on in here?"

"I'm helping Mr. Davies with a letter to his mother." Celia kept her voice calm, then jerked her chin from Davies to Roy and mouthed, *Tell him.* A blank look entered Davies's eyes. She'd noticed before how his mind shut down in panic when he was called upon to make a decision. Poor man, he must have been told all his life that he was stupid, and he had come to believe it, to the extent that he was afraid to think for himself.

"I'll always remember you as a friend, Mr. Davies," she said softly. "Thank you."

Appearing to grow in stature, the short, squat man inched closer to Roy and delivered his message in muffled whispers. A more detailed account by the sound of it, interspaced by questions from Roy. When the two stopped talking, Celia forced a bland tone and spoke in a loud voice.

"Here we are. One completed letter. Now run along, Mr. Davies, so that I can pack my bag once more. Everything is in disarray because the ink was at the bottom."

"Thank you, Miss Celia."

She smiled, a stiff, frozen smile, and reached out to clasp Davies's arm. She gave him a small squeeze to express her gratitude, and then she lifted her hand away from his arm and gestured for him to go back outside.

Left alone with Roy, Celia got up on shaky legs, went to him and slid her arms around his waist. Resting her head on his shoulder, she spoke into his ear. "What can we do?"

"Don't go," he whispered back. "Say you've changed your mind. Mr. Smith doesn't trust you.

He thinks you might go to the law and offer to be a witness, hoping it might help me, or help your father. If you stay at the hideout, he'll have nothing to worry about."

"He is suspicious. If I change my mind, he'll wonder why." She frowned, an idea forming in her mind. Outside, someone yelled, another voice replied. Then her name was called, and she recognized the hoarse, disguised voice of Mr. Smith.

"Miss Courtwood! It's time to go!"

She took Roy by the hand and tugged him toward the cabin door, murmuring her instructions. "Follow me. Don't say anything. Just listen to me and play along."

Keep calm, she told herself as they stepped out into the morning sunshine. *It may save your life.*

With the silent, watchful crowd looking on, she pasted a bright smile on her face, released Roy's hand and hurried over to Mr. Smith. Before she could reach him, she heard the sound of pistols being cocked, saw the weapons of the two bodyguards pointing at her.

Ignoring the show of force, she halted a few steps from Mr. Smith and spoke with a gushing eagerness. "A change of plan, I am afraid. We have decided to get married before I leave. Isn't that wonderful?" She clapped her hands, like a silly schoolgirl. "I've been waiting for Roy to agree to it, but isn't it typical for a man to refuse until it is almost too late?"

Mr. Smith contemplated her through the thick lenses of his spectacles. Damn the disguise that made it so difficult to gauge his reaction. Celia cocked her head to one side. "Aren't you going to congratulate me? It is not every day one of your men takes a bride."

No reaction. She kept smiling, her cheeks aching with the effort. "I'll stay here for another week, and Mr. Hunter can bring a preacher back with him when he returns."

Halloran stepped forward and spoke with the satisfaction of a man who is offering a solution. "There's a circuit preacher that passes by Miss Mabel's every month, on the first of the month. It's only a couple of days away."

"Splendid!" Celia exclaimed. "Dale Hunter can fetch him."

Once again, she felt Mr. Smith's penetrating gaze upon her. Her smile froze. Those cruel, cruel eyes were measuring her, probing, seeing through the charade she was putting on. Her hands clenched into fists and she hid them in the folds of her velvet riding skirt. She'd been full of excitement when she put on her elegant costume and rode out of Rock Springs with Roy Hagan at her side. And this was what the journey had led her to—pitting her wits against a criminal mastermind, fighting for a chance to stay alive.

"No need to fetch the preacher," Mr. Smith finally said. "You and Hagan can ride out to Miss Mabel's, get the reverend to marry you there."

Craning his neck, he surveyed the crowd, sought out Franklin and Longhurst and Dale Hunter. "You three should ride out now. You'll be slower, with the packhorses in tow. Hagan and his woman will set off an hour later and catch up with you. Remember your orders. Now it is twice as important to complete the task."

Chapter Fourteen

Roy listened to the clatter of hoofbeats echoing from the canyon walls. He'd been too young to fight in the war, but this was how he imagined the battle drums would sound—a steady *rat-tat-tat* that seeped into your very heartbeat.

During their final hour at the outlaw camp, while he and Celia had been waiting to ride out, they had barely spoken, too aware of the attention from the men who seemed to sense something in the air—a foretaste of violence about to break out.

The path widened where the canyon walls drew apart. A thick layer of sand on the ground muffled the sound of their passage, allowing them to stop without others realizing that they were no longer in motion. Roy brought Dagur to a halt, waited for Celia to pull up alongside him. He wasn't sure whether to speak up, but she deserved to know what lay ahead. It was better to be prepared.

"You understood what Mr. Smith said?" he asked. "That it is twice as important to complete the task?"

"Yes." She met his gaze without a flinch. "They must kill both of us."

Roy studied her pale face, saw how the scar blended in perfectly now, difficult to notice unless you knew it was there and could home in on the slight unevenness of the skin. The weeks they had shared flashed through his mind. And now he had brought her to this—to die the death of an outlaw. It was his fault.

"I'm sorry…"

"Don't," Celia replied fiercely. "Don't ever say that. I wouldn't exchange what we had together for a lifetime of safe existence. I'd choose this. I'd choose *you*."

Not dismounting, Roy reached over and pulled her out of the saddle to rest across his lap. He kissed her—hungry, desperate kisses. The words could no longer remain unsaid, and he told her that he loved her, had not understood that such a depth of feeling could exist. "It's like I didn't even live before. I was just drifting. Nothing mattered."

"I love you, too. And in a way I'm grateful…" Celia leaned back in his arms, reached up to touch his face. "In a way I'm glad it will end like this… it is better for us to die together than for one of us to be left alone to mourn."

Roy smiled down at her, grim and wistful at the same time. "Don't go burying us just yet. Dale Hunter is on our side. That makes two against two. The odds are better than even."

A spark of rebellion flashed in Celia's eyes. "Three against two. Don't overlook my contribution to the battle. But can you be absolutely sure about Dale Hunter? How strong is your friendship?"

"I'm sure about Dale. As sure as I am of you." Talking quietly, Roy relayed what Dale Hunter had told him, about working together with the law, in the hope of a pardon. "He has just as much to lose as we have."

After one final, lingering kiss, Roy lifted Celia out of his lap and onto her own horse. "I want you to stay back, whatever happens. I'll fight better if I know you're not in the firing line."

Before they set off again, he checked his guns. Normally, he wore the pistol on his left hip butt forward, for a cross draw with his right hand, but now he placed it in the standard position, allowing him to draw both guns at the same time. He replaced the weapons in their holsters and reached out with his arm, laced his fingers into Celia's and held her hand for a moment, one final gesture of farewell in case luck was not on their side.

Then they set their mounts in motion again, riding at a slow walk. The canyon narrowed, and

Celia fell into line behind him. Once they left the thick, sandy wash, they were on solid rock again, and the steady clip of the horses' hooves marked their passage. The battle drums were beating, Roy thought as he swept the trail with his single blue eye, searching every shadow, every contour, alert for the slightest flicker of motion.

Behind a big stone, a hand poked out, flapping a white handkerchief. A second later, Dale Hunter slid into view. With a few long strides, he reached Dagur's side. Moving sideways, he looked up at Roy and spoke urgently.

"Don't slow down. Don't let the rhythm of your passage alter. They are a few hundred yards ahead. Franklin is on the left, in that tunnel that forms a cave. Longhurst is fifty paces farther out, behind a boulder on the right. Franklin is meant to shoot you. I'm supposed to kill Celia, and I expect Longhurst has orders to gun me down. Mr. Smith must suspect I've betrayed him."

Roy glanced back at Celia, to make sure she was holding her nerve. She lifted one gloved hand and nodded at Dale, a calm, ladylike greeting. Reassured, Roy turned back to his friend. Quickly, he told Dale how he had heard someone in the darkness the night before, while they had been talking by the corrals.

"Mr. Smith must have someone spying on you," Roy finished.

Dale nodded. "It's clear to me that he no longer trusts me. If I had escorted Celia out alone, I could have simply let her go, and Mr. Smith would have been none the wiser. But he sent Franklin and Longhurst along, to make sure that I'm forced to kill her."

He gestured for Roy to slip his foot out of the stirrup. "I'll get into the saddle behind you, and then you can climb down. Use the rear entrance to the tunnel. With the sound of two riders approaching, Franklin won't feel the need to watch his back. You'll enjoy the advantage of surprise."

Roy waited for Dale to swing up behind him on the horse, and then he lifted one leg over Dagur's head, slid down from the saddle and jogged a few steps alongside Dagur to reassure the horse.

"Good boy. Ride with Dale. I'll be back soon."

Roy studied his friend, now seated in the saddle. He and Dale were about the same size and their long canvas dusters were identical, bought at the same time. Dale was leaner, but the bulky coat disguised the difference in their build. Roy pulled off his battered hat, held it up to Dale. "Give me yours. The silver band glints in the sunlight. And tuck your hair under your collar, and pull the hat brim low so they can't see you don't have a patch over your left eye."

With one final look at Celia, Roy laid the flat of his palm against his heart, the way they had done on the night he made her his wife, Indian fashion. From the tremulous smile that came and went on Celia's face, he knew she had understood the meaning of the gesture.

Without another word, he darted forward, skirting the rock wall. Trying not to make a sound, he raced ahead along the narrow canyon, heading for the rear entrance of the tunnel where Franklin was waiting to kill him.

The patch that normally covered his brown eye pulled aside, Roy stared at the solid darkness inside the narrow passage in the rock wall. Originally, the tunnel had been too cramped for a man to fit through, but the outlaws had enlarged it over the years, creating a sentry post in the cave that opened up at the other end of the tunnel, overlooking the canyon. The ambition of Lom Curtis had been to get hold of a Gatling gun and station it in the cave, turning the hideout into an impregnable fortress.

Roy eased forward, his left hand trailing along the rough rock wall to guide him, his right hand holding a pistol, ready to fire. The air smelled acrid, evidence that men had used the rear section of the tunnel for a latrine. Faint light came ahead, and then the narrow passage twisted sharply to the right. Where the cave opened up into the canyon, Roy could see a man silhouetted against the light, cautiously leaning forward to peer outside.

Roy took aim with his Smith & Wesson, moved another step forward. Something clanked on the ground, tangled around his boots. He pulled the trigger, but his balance was off. The shot went wide. Franklin spun around, lifted his rifle and fired. The shot missed, ricocheted within the confines of the tunnel. Stone chips flew in the air. A sharp flash of pain pierced Roy's left eye. His vision blurred.

Agony pounded through his head. He could feel the blood running down his left cheek, a warm trail that reminded him of the scent of death. He blinked to clear his vision, took aim once more. Franklin had pulled out his pistol by now and was shooting into the tunnel without aim, unable to see into the darkness. Roy felt a bullet hit his thigh.

He threw himself against the rock wall, fired his handgun again. Two shots rang out, overlapping. He felt an impact in his shoulder, spun around with the force of the blow and lost his balance. Just before his head crashed against the jagged stone floor beneath him, he could see Franklin spread his arms wide and topple backward, falling out of the cave like an eagle launching into flight.

Dale can take out Longhurst, the last remaining killer. Celia is safe.

That was the last thought in Roy's mind.

Then there was nothing more.

In all her born days, Celia had never felt so frightened. Life had been unkind to her before, but her intellect had always allowed her to make sense of the danger. An illness could be understood, even if not conquered. Prejudice and superstition could be explained. But the evil around her now—she could not relate to it, could not comprehend the cause of such violence and find the right way to combat it.

So she chose to follow orders and rode in meek silence behind Dale Hunter. Slowly, with the time appearing to expand like a piece of elastic cord, they made their way between the two soaring walls of red rock. The air was getting warmer as the sun climbed higher into the sky, and she felt her skin grow damp inside the elegant velvet riding suit.

How important it had seemed once, to hold her head high in front of the townspeople, to ride out with her back stiff with pride! Now everything that had happened to her in Rock Springs seemed meaningless. Meaningless, compared to the basic goal of staying alive: to draw another breath, to live another day, to see Roy again, to fight for the happiness she believed they both deserved.

Gunshots shattered the quiet. Like the thunder rumbling, an echo bounced between the canyon walls. She tried to count out the shots. One… Two… Three… Then a volley of gunfire that merged together. She could tell one of the earlier shots had sounded different, the sharper retort of a rifle.

The taste of blood filled her mouth. At first, she thought it was a trick of her mind, empathy for Roy, who might be lying wounded somewhere high up within the cliffs, but then she felt the sting in her lower lip and realized she'd bitten into her own flesh, hard enough to draw blood.

Above her, she could hear a series of thuds. She tipped her head back to look up from beneath the brim of her hat. Like a rag doll, a man's body tumbled down the rock wall and fell onto the path, spooking the gray mare Celia was seated upon. She pulled at the reins, brought Baldur under control again. As the horse sidestepped the prone body, Celia craned her neck to look down at the fallen man and recognized the reptilian features and the small stature of Franklin, the man who had given her such vile, lustful looks.

Not Roy. Not Roy. Her heartbeat drummed out the words.

She forced her breathing to calm down, tried

to control her shaking limbs while she lined her mount in an orderly procession after Dale Hunter, who was making his way along the canyon, sitting easily on Dagur. Ahead on the right, peeking out from behind a jutting boulder, something flashed, the glint of metal struck by a ray of sunlight.

Dale Hunter shifted in the saddle, a quick flash of motion. Two shots rang out. Celia could see Dale flinch, could see a crimson patch spread over his shoulder, staining the canvas fabric of his fawn duster. From farther ahead came a groan of pain, and the lifeless body of another man toppled onto the path.

Dale twisted around to look back at her, a grim expression on his face. "That's all of them, for now."

"Roy?" Her voice caught in her throat. "Where is he?"

"I don't know." Dale gripped his wounded shoulder, still holding the gun in his hand. A curl of smoke rose from the tip of the barrel.

In the air around them, Celia could smell the acrid smell of gunfire, the coppery scent of blood, the ugly reek of death and violence. Another wave of terror swept over her, making her feel lost and lonely, unable to bear the uncertainty any longer. "Can I call out for him?"

Dale Hunter nodded.

"Roy!" she yelled. "Roy!"

Every constraint that had in the past curbed noisy outpourings of emotion vanished. Celia kept yelling out his name, her tone shrill with fear. Seconds passed, turned into minutes. Panic closed around her, as if the canyon walls were coming together and crushing her. Her voice grew hoarse. Tears of loss and fear and loneliness streamed down her cheeks.

"Roy!" she called out. "Roy!" She kept up shouting out his name until her throat grew too sore to release the sound and her words muffled into desolate sobs.

For there was no reply.

Only the echo of her own voice.

Celia wasn't sure how long she had argued with Dale Hunter, but one thing she knew for certain: she was not going to budge. The horses were getting restless, spooked by the bodies on the ground. Dagur tossed his mane and neighed, nostrils flaring. Dale leaned forward in the saddle and stilled the horse with a terse command.

"We've got to go," he said to Celia once more, as if talking to a recalcitrant child. "They'll have heard the gunshots at the camp. Someone will be riding out to check. There's little time."

Terror and grief flared up in Celia again, distilling into a flash of anger. "You'd leave a fallen comrade behind? To be jeered over, to be left for the buzzards to pick clean? Damn you, Dale Hunter. I thought you were a friend, a man of honor."

"I'm trying to get you to safety. That's what Roy would want."

Celia met his narrowed eyes, green and icy cold. She saw a flicker of rage in their depths, and a hint of contempt at her outburst. There was pride in the haughty set of the man's shoulders, in his finely drawn features that carried the heritage of his affluent, educated background. Understanding dawned on her, and a flush of shame heated her cheeks. Of course—he was getting her out of the way first. Then he'd come back for Roy.

She lifted her hand in a placating gesture while controlling the mare beneath her. "I'm sorry. I know you mean well, but I can't go on. Not without him. He might be alive, and if he is not, at least I'll have his body to bury. I want to get him a proper grave, with a headstone, or at least a wooden cross to mark his resting place."

When Dale hesitated, she went on, "Please... he once said that with his mismatched eyes some people claimed that God and the Devil were fighting over his soul. If I leave him here, it will seem like the Devil has won. I want him buried in a churchyard, where everyone can see he is with God."

Dale contemplated her, then cast a quick glance

back down the canyon. Celia could sense his hesitation, pushed for her advantage. "They won't be coming after us. Not yet. It is *our* bodies Mr. Smith expects to have landed sprawling in the dust. He doesn't want his men to find out he ordered the killing of a woman. He'll wait awhile. It's only when Franklin and Longhurst don't ride back to the camp to report success that he'll feel the need to send someone out to investigate."

"*Maldita sea*, you're right," Dale Hunter replied in a tone of respect. "Roy said you have more brains than all the men at the hideout put together."

Dale jumped down from Dagur, his long duster flaring wide. He jammed his fingers into his mouth and gave a piercing whistle. A moment later, with a steady clip of hooves his bay gelding trotted over from some hiding place along the path. Dale gave the horse a quick pat of reassurance and took down a coil of rawhide rope fastened to the saddle.

"Wait here," he ordered Celia. "I'll have to go back down the trail. You can't get into the cave from this end. The cliffs are too steep."

Boots crunching on gravel, he jumped over the prone bodies of the fallen outlaws and hurried back down the trail. Celia waited. The sun burned bright in the sky now but it delivered no comforting heat. A chill enveloped her, as if the world had turned into a place without light. Without warmth.

"Dear God," she prayed. "Let him live. And if you can't do that, let me be carrying his child. Let me have something of him, something to cherish, something born of our love."

A screech came from overhead. Celia tilted her head and looked up. Buzzards were already circling, high up in the air, drawn by the scent of blood... Waiting, waiting... She knew the scavenger birds could be seen from the camp, alerting the outlaws that the gunfight had left dead bodies on the ground. How long would it be before Mr. Smith started worrying? Had she brought death upon herself and Dale Hunter by insisting they mustn't leave Roy behind?

"Celia!"

The muffled call of her name cut through her fearful thoughts.

"Over here!" the voice went on. "Up, behind you!"

She swiveled her head, spotted Dale Hunter peeking out from a dark oval in the rock, a shadow she had thought to be a depression, but now realized must be the opening to the cave.

"He's alive, for now," Dale called out. "I can't carry him out through the tunnel, it's too cramped. I'll have to lower him down on a rope.

It'll probably finish him off, but if you want a body to bury, I'll get him for you."

Dale vanished from sight. Seconds later, Roy tumbled out of the cave. His limp body jerked to a stop and swung to an upright position, a rope loop circling his torso beneath his arms. Blood streamed down his face. One of his eyes was a ragged mess. The other eye was closed. Not open and staring in the final look of death.

From that tiny indication of life, Celia drew a glimmer of hope. She jumped down from Baldur, landed on her feet with a jarring thud. Clearheaded now, filled with purpose, she paused to wrap the bridle reins around a rock. If she allowed the horse to run off, the mistake might cost her the chance of staying alive. Scrambling over boulders and scrubs of thistle, she hurried to stand by the cliffs below the cave.

"Don't jolt him," she instructed Dale.

"It ain't exactly easy to haul a heavy body down."

Then Roy was there, booted feet swaying as he descended, the gun belt around his hips with one revolver missing, the long duster bunched up beneath the rope that cut into his torso beneath his arms, and finally his pale, blood-smeared face lined up with hers.

"Your eye, what happened to your eye?" Celia wailed as she studied the damage, saw the scattering of small, bleeding cuts on his forehead and on his left cheek.

The rope went slack, and Roy toppled to the ground. Celia sank to her knees, pressed her fingers to his throat. His skin was warm, warm with life. She found a pulse, measured the rhythm of it. It was weak, but even. Pausing, she smoothed back his golden hair, a tiny caress to give her strength, to give her hope. By some miracle, his thick, wavy hair was clean of blood, and she relished the cool, clean texture of it before she withdrew her hand.

Only vaguely was she aware that the rope still attached to Roy was jerking while she examined his clothing, looking for telltale holes from bullets, looking for patches of blood. One wound on his thigh. The bullet had gone right through, did not remain embedded in his flesh. Another wound in his shoulder. No entry or exit hole, merely a groove where the bullet had grazed the skin. She found no other injuries, apart from those small cuts she'd already seen on his face and the damage to his left eye.

Dale slid down, jumped aside and let go of the rope. "I reckon a rifle shot inside the cave bounced between the rock walls and sent out a shower of stone chips. Bad luck—one must have hit him in the eye."

Reaching inside his shirt, Dale pulled out Roy's

missing revolver and replaced it in the holster. "An outlaw likes to be fully armed, even in his grave." He took out a knife, reached up with his arms to cut away the rope as high as he could, and then he put the knife back into the scabbard on his belt. Bending down, he hoisted Roy's inert body onto his shoulder and straightened, grunting with the effort.

"Dagur, boy, come here," he called out. "You can carry your master."

With an eager whinny, the horse sauntered over and turned sideways, ready for the rider to mount. "Sorry, boy, it's not quite that easy." Dale gave another grunt, heaved Roy's inert body up and arranged him to dangle on his belly across the saddle, arms and legs hanging on either side. Using the loose end of the rope still tied around Roy's waist, Dale secured him in place.

"He'll die if we don't tend to his injuries," Celia protested.

"He'll die no matter what," Dale replied.

After yanking the final knot in place. Dale led Dagur to the other horses. He waited for Celia to follow, helped her to mount on Baldur and handed Dagur's reins to her.

"Ride out and never come back. Don't stop at Miss Mabel's. Follow the trail and take the right fork. It leads to a ferry crossing on the Colorado River. There's a sign, Lees Ferry. If by some miracle Roy lives that far, there's a mining town another twenty miles south. They have a doctor there."

She looked down from the saddle at him. "What about you?"

"I'll stay here, gain you some time."

"They'll kill you."

A wry smile hovered around Dale Hunter's mouth. Raven-black hair skimmed his shoulders as he jerked his chin toward the man strapped across the saddle. "Just like my *amigo* here, I'm already dead. *Adios, querida. Vaya con Dios.*"

Despite all the horror and bloodshed, Celia managed a faint smile in return. "You are no more Mexican than I am. Roy told me. You're part French Creole and part Yankee."

Dale gave a courtly bow. "*Mais oui, ma chérie. And now get your ass out of here, before you too turn into crow bait."

Chapter Fifteen

Celia strained her ears as she led the way through a cool, shady passage where the canyon walls drew close together. What a terrible choice she faced—to ride fast, causing a jolting in the saddle that would aggravate Roy's injuries, or to keep the pace easy and increase the risk that the killers might catch up with them.

It occurred to her that although she'd shouldered the responsibility of caring for her sick mother and keeping house for her ailing father, she'd never had to make decisions alone. After Papa went to prison, she had barricaded herself inside the house until Roy came along and told her what to do. For the first time in her life, she was in sole charge. Her judgment, the choices she made, might make the difference between life and death.

The canyon widened again. Two saddled horses

stood by a cluster of rocks. Celia halted, uncertain. She recognized the mounts from the hideout remuda—a dun with a dark mane and tail and a big chestnut with a blaze on its forehead. Franklin and Longhurst had ridden out on those horses and had picketed them out of the way.

Making a snap decision, Celia jumped down from the saddle, eased over to the animals. Having spare horses might come in handy, and by taking them away she would reduce the chances that they would break loose and return to the hideout without a rider, raising the alarm.

"Good horse. Good boy."

She'd spent enough time by the corrals for the horses to be familiar with her scent and her soft, female voice. Holding out one hand, she let each animal nuzzle her palm in turn, their breath moist against her skin. When she could be sure they had recognized her, she pulled out their picket pins and led the horses over to Baldur and Dagur. Arranging the animals nose to tail, she tied the bridle of each one to the saddle of the one before, creating a four-horse string.

After completing the task, Celia went to Roy, pressed her fingers to his throat and felt for the pulse. Still beating. Still alive. She longed to stop, cut away his torn and dusty clothing, clean and dress his wounds, but there was no time. It made no sense to tend to him, just to hand him over to the killers in better shape.

She remounted on Baldur, urged the horses into motion. The trail started rising now. Twice more, she paused to measure Roy's heartbeat. The cadence of it seemed unchanged—faint but steady. She drew courage from the feel of the small, regular throbbing beneath her fingertips. It seemed like a promise that he would hold on, that he would fight to stay alive, provided she did her part and got him to a doctor.

When the trail forked, every instinct pulled her toward Miss Mabel's Sunset Saloon, a familiar sanctuary with friends, with comfortable lodgings and medical care. Resisting the temptation, Celia took the right fork. She couldn't tell if it was her intellect ruling her, or if following Dale Hunter's instructions came easier than disregarding them.

Up on the plateau, the cool breeze revived her, and the open vista calmed her nerves after the oppressive closeness of the maze of canyons. Something moved in the distance, creating a cloud of dust. She squinted ahead, a hand lifted to shade her eyes.

A wagon. A wagon drawn by two horses. Quickly, Celia untied Dagur's bridle from her saddle and turned back to look at the buckskin.

"Stay, boy. Stay, Dagur. Don't move."

She knew the horse would obey. The only time

the gelding had ever ignored an order to remain still was when she'd tricked him with an offering of oats and sugar. A recollection flashed through her mind of their bet while Roy was shaving, the mirror propped against the pommel of Dagur's saddle. She could hear Roy's voice, could hear his laughter, could feel his lips against hers as they kissed.

"Please, God," she prayed in her mind. "Let him live."

She kicked Baldur into a canter and raced up to the wagon. Loaded with a mountain of goods covered with a tarpaulin, the vehicle was driven by a grizzly old man with a thick, gray-streaked beard and a wrinkled face. His skin was coppery brown, perhaps a sign of Indian blood, or merely a thick layer of the desert dust.

Celia wheeled Baldur around and rode alongside the man, leaning toward him in the saddle. "Stop!" she called out. "I want to buy your wagon."

The man burst into a cackling laughter. "Me wagon's me home, young lady. I'll sell it no more than I would sell the skin on my back."

"How much?"

The man's eyes, almost hidden by the folds of his wizened complexion, narrowed in a shrewd look. "I told you. Me wagon's not for sale."

She gestured at the tarpaulin-covered load. "What do you have in there?"

"Trade goods. Tools. Yard goods. Vittles. No rifles or guns, mind you, if you suspect I'm selling to the Injuns. A drop of whiskey, but I'll not risk a prison sentence by selling hard liquor to the natives."

"You're a trader. Fine. I'll buy everything. And then I'll buy your wagon."

The man gave another burst of wheezing laughter. "Lady, you're out of your mind. There's a thousand dollars' worth of goods in there, including me profit, of course."

"Fine. I'll give you a thousand dollars for the goods, and another thousand for the wagon. I'll throw in two fine horses with saddles and bridles. You can keep the goods I don't want. We'll unload them right here. You might be able to sell some to the settlers passing by along the trail."

They had been moving slowly northward, with Celia riding alongside the wagon. Now the old man pulled on the reins and brought the wagon to a halt. He set the brake, wrapped the reins around the handle and turned to face Celia. Shrewd blue eyes studied her while the man stroked his straggly beard with one hand.

"Eh, lass, you mean it? Let me see the color of your money."

Celia pulled a rawhide pouch rattling with gold

coins from her saddlebags. She was carrying her father's share of the robbery takings. The rest of their funds were in Roy's saddlebags. She loosened the string on top, pulled out a handful of gold coins, lifted her fist and let the coins clatter in a glittering stream back into the pouch.

"There's a thousand dollars in here, for the trade goods," she told the old man. "Start unloading."

The man hopped down, peeled away the tarpaulin. Celia ran an assessing gaze over the load. "Get rid of the tools…just leave me two of each kind… shovels and forks and picks…whatever you're carrying… What's that big thing? A plow…? Take it out… Leave all the fabrics and the foodstuffs… No, leave the whiskey…and I want to keep any household goods, pots and pans…"

She left the man to deal with the task of unloading and rode back to fetch Dagur and the two outlaw horses. When she returned, the old man halted his labors with a thoughtful look at Roy draped across the saddle. "You should have told me," he said quietly. "Had I known it's to take your man's body for burial, I could have turned back on the trail and taken you to the ferry for nothing."

Celia's mouth tightened. She wanted to acknowledge the kindness, but her mind recoiled at the man's assumption they were headed for a burial. "He's still alive," she replied, perhaps a little too sharply. "I want to travel fast. Help me lift him into the wagon."

One side of the wagon bed was empty now. Celia spread out the wool blankets and unraveled a bolt of canvas to go on top, to create a soft mattress. While she worked, she bombarded the trader with questions. She'd driven a buggy a few times, when she and her father had rented one from the livery stable. She'd not found the task complicated, but a wagon with a two-horse team might pose a greater challenge.

She learned the horses were called Ben and Nevis, after a mountain in Scotland, and the way to make them go was to say *walk* or *trot* or *canter*—the last only in a great hurry, and with a light load. *Easy* made them slow down and *whoa* brought them to a dead stop. For turning, they obeyed *left* and *right*. Repeating a command made it stronger, so for a tight turn she might say *left, left, left*, and speak firmly. It sounded simple enough, Celia thought, suppressing her misgivings.

When she was done preparing the bed, they pulled Roy from the horse and carried him to the wagon. He seemed more comfortable lying on his stomach, so Celia settled him like that, with his head turned to the side, his injured eye facing up. The bleeding appeared to have cleaned the wound and she carefully arranged a length of cotton over his head, creating a canopy that would protect him from dust.

To finish with, she untied the two outlaw horses and swapped the money pouch she had handed over to the trader against the larger one she took out of Roy's saddlebags. "I don't have the time to count the money but I'm sure there is at least two thousand dollars in there."

The trader balanced the bag of gold coins in his hands. "Perhaps I've overcharged you a mite…"

Celia was busy tying Dagur and Baldur to the rear of the wagon. She gave the horses a quick pat and a soothing word, and then she circled to the front of the wagon and climbed up to the bench.

"No, you didn't," she told the old man. "The payment is also to forget that you ever laid eyes on me. And you should get rid of those horses and saddles as soon as you can. The men that used to ride them had a bounty on their heads."

Saying no more, Celia called out *trot*, and the horses set off at a brisk pace. The team was well trained, and Celia found directing the wagon a manageable task. For a while, the old trader, Fergus McLean—*Never seen Scotland but I like to think of meself as a Highlander*—rode alongside, giving instructions. When he deemed she had mastered the skill, he returned to the pile of trade goods discarded by the trailside, with the aim of loading the most valuable items onto his spare horse and caching the rest to be retrieved later.

By the time Celia passed the sign for Lees Ferry and the trail dropped down to the river, she was confident enough to control the wagon on the steep slope. The small, fertile valley bustled with life. A large party of settlers traveling south must have just arrived, for she counted four wagons waiting to cross, with teams of oxen pulling them and milk cows and pigs and goats tied to the rear.

After almost three weeks surrounded by surly, heavily armed men, the signs of ordinary life overwhelmed Celia. Chickens clucked in their cages. Children raced about, yelling and laughing. Women stood gossiping in groups while men sought counsel from each other.

Celia parked her wagon at the end of the line, hopped down and rushed to the water's edge. The air was cool and moist, smelling of mud. The current appeared sluggish on the surface, but as she studied the whirling water, she could see the power of the river.

A man, around forty, dressed in homespun, halted beside her. "Howdy, ma'am."

She gave him a curt nod in greeting, jerked her chin toward the ferryboat about to dock on the other side. "How long does it take to get across?"

"Don't rightly know. We only just got here and haven't been watching. Maybe a quarter hour. Maybe more if the current is strong or the animals are slow to load."

"Are you all together, the four wagons?"

"All the way from Salt Lake. Headed to Phoenix."

"Who is your leader?"

"That would be Theo Hardman. Over there."

Celia strode off to where the man pointed. Half a dozen males, some of them elderly, some barely out of their teens, all dressed in homespun and wearing wide-brimmed straw hats, stood in a circle, debating. Not waiting for them to pause in their conversation, Celia boldly cut in.

"Mr. Hardman?"

"That would be me." Past fifty, sturdy as an oak, the man stood with his legs braced, his hands clutching the suspenders she could see beneath his unbuttoned coat. His face was ruddy, his hair and beard iron gray. Celia got the impression of an indomitable will and the stubbornness of a mule.

"I am in a hurry," she began. "My husband is sick and I wish to get him to a doctor as soon as possible. I'm willing to compensate your party for the delay if you let me cross first. How much do you think would be appropriate?"

"Well, now, the day is aging. Our hurry is as great as yours."

"I'll pay you twenty dollars for each wagon if I can go first."

"Listen, young lady…" Officious, the leader blustered, rocking on his heels, even though Celia could see the eager glint of acceptance in the eyes of the other men.

"What ails your husband?" a slender, clean-shaven man asked. "My cousin Sarah knows a bit of nursing. She has delivered a dozen babies and never lost one yet."

"Don't see how midwifery is much use for a man who is ailing," someone commented, drawing a chuckle from the rest of the group.

Celia used the ripple of amusement to do some quick thinking. After having cared for two dying parents, and with all her book learning, she was bound to know as much as this Sarah might know. And it would be better if no one saw Roy and could describe him, knew he had passed this way, still clinging to life.

"No," she said slowly. "I wouldn't recommend it. What ails my husband looks like some kind of a lung fever…it might be contagious…no point in taking a risk for you all to catch the disease…"

"Theo, if the man has a fever, best to let them go first, protect our children and womenfolk."

Celia listened to the murmured comments, but the leader, in thrall of his power, refused to budge. Her mouth tightening into a grim line, Celia hurried back to the wagon. She moved the tarpaulin aside, lifted out a bolt of calico, with a pattern of pink roses on a cream background. Thank heavens the load had contained a large quantity of fabrics.

"Ladies," she cried out. "My husband is sick and I am in a hurry to get across. I've offered twenty dollars for each wagon if you let me go first. Should your men agree, there is also a bolt of yard goods for each woman."

The ladies glanced in her direction. No one moved. Celia raked her gaze over them. All were dressed in brown or gray or black, plain colors. She held up the calico with pink roses. "This material would make lovely curtains. And I have thick green wool for winter suits, and white muslin for nightgowns. A full bolt for each woman. You can divide them up and each get several different kinds of fabric."

The tallest of the women moved. Not toward Celia, but toward the men huddled in debate. Another followed. Like a flock of angry geese, the women pushed their way into the circle of men. Voices rose, the sharp ring of feminine pleas that grew into indignation, cutting across the more muffled masculine arguments. With satisfaction, Celia watched the elderly leader grow sullen and the women's faces glow with triumph.

Like a victorious army marching from the battlefield, the women hurried over to Celia's wagon, and she handed out the bolts of fabric. When the ferry docked again, Celia steered her wagon past the others, onto the craft, the heavy gait of Ben and Nevis echoing on the timber planks. She gave another twenty dollars to the ferryman to take her through on her own, leaving the rest of the space unoccupied.

While the flat-bottomed vessel made its way across, fighting the whirling current, Celia climbed up to the wagon bed and tended to Roy. She washed away the matted blood, poured whiskey over the bullet wounds and dressed them with a clean strip of muslin.

His damaged eye was beyond her medical expertise, and she dared not touch it, apart from making a mild saline solution and trickling it over his eyelid, hoping it might flush out any dirt and reduce the risk of infection.

His insensate state made her ministrations easier as she did not need to worry about causing him pain. The moment the ferry reached the shore, Celia scrambled over to the driver's seat, picked up the reins and set off in the race to give Roy a chance to stay alive.

Shadows lengthened over the barren landscape. Celia's arms ached from the effort of controlling the wagon team. Her body had grown stiff from sitting on the hard bench and her muscles sore from jolting over the rutted trail. She no longer stopped every now and then to check up on Roy. Alive or not, she would get him to a doctor. Worrying about his condition would only slow her down.

When darkness fell, the horses whinnied in protest as she urged them on. Celia pulled to a halt. She searched through the pile of trade goods, found a lantern and a bottle of kerosene. She filled the reservoir, lit the lantern and climbed down.

After taking a moment to revive the tired Ben and Nevis with lumps of sugar and crooning words of praise, she set off walking in front of them. Holding the lantern high to illuminate the trail, she led the way, the kerosene vapors stinging her eyes.

By the time a glimmer of yellow squares that could only be windows broke the veil of blackness ahead, Celia was stumbling on her feet. For the last mile, her greatest fear had been that she might trip over, and the horses would pull the heavy wagon right over her.

"Trot," she yelled. "Ben, trot. Nevis, trot."

She set off running, the reins tightening in her hand as she surged ahead. Behind her, the clop of hooves grew louder as the horses picked up speed. By now, she could see the outline of buildings ahead, could hear the tinny sounds of music from a saloon.

The town was not much, just a widening in the trail with a few timber buildings on either side. Beyond them, she could see white shapes, like a herd of huge animals squatting on the ground. Closer by, she could see they were canvas tents.

A boomtown. A place so new most buildings were still temporary, timber skeletons with canvas walls. She came to a halt by the first permanent building, a small frame house that had no light in the window. There were people outside the saloon at the opposite end of the street, but she did not want to waste another second.

The pounding broke the quiet of the night as she hammered her fist on the door. "Wake up. I need a doctor."

A light came on inside. A hatch opened in the door and a shotgun barrel poked through. A raspy, gruff voice spoke. "What do you want?"

"A doctor. Emergency. I have an injured man."

"The last house on the left." The gun barrel vanished, and curious pair of hazel eyes surrounded by a wrinkled face appeared in the hatch. Like the voice, the features were strangely genderless. It could have been either a man or a woman of advanced years.

"Watch out when you pass the saloon," the person advised Celia. "If the drunken men see you, they'll drag you onto the dance floor. By the time you get them to listen, your emergency might no longer be one. The undertaker is opposite the doctor, just in case."

Not pausing to reply, Celia hurried to the horses. She surveyed the street ahead. Enough light spilled out from the saloon to illuminate the crowd milling outside. She saw a dozen men, heard their drunken voices. No women. She rearranged the reins, climbed up to the wagon bench and urged the horses into motion, her command harsh to demand one final burst of speed from the tired team.

"Ben, canter. Nevis, canter."

Obedient, the horses surged ahead and hurtled past the crowd. Celia brought the wagon to a stop by the last house on the left, a two-story building, so new the timber still smelled of pine resin. She set the brake, wrapped the reins around the handle, and then she was banging on the door.

According to her experience, doctors in remote Western towns fell into one of two categories: Older men, fallen on hard times, bitter from failure, banished from more lucrative opportunities, perhaps due to a medical error or drunkenness. Or young, newly qualified men, eager for adventure, seeking to establish their own practice, something lack of funds would not allow them to achieve in more civilized places.

When the door opened, a lean, sandy-haired man of no more than thirty appeared on the threshold. In her mind, Celia said a prayer of thanks. Shirtless, barefoot, only dressed in dark wool trousers, the man held up a light, blinking sleep from his eyes as he stared at her.

Celia took a deep breath. Relief at the competent air of the doctor fanned the spark of hope within her into a bright flame. "I have an injured man in the wagon. Two bullet wounds, and a stone chip pierced his eye. He is alive but unconscious."

Not waiting for a response, she set off toward the wagon. The doctor turned back to place the lamp on a small side table in the hallway and then he followed her. Celia climbed up first, and the bare-chested medical man vaulted into the wagon after her. She folded aside the canvas hood that had protected Roy's face and edged out of the way to let the doctor inspect him.

"I can help you carry him inside. I'm stronger than I look."

The doctor shot her a glance, his lips twisting into a wry smile. "You barely look more alive than he is. Stay out of the way." He crouched beside Roy, examined him with competent hands, talking calmly and listening to her replies.

"How long ago did this happen?... Less than twelve hours?... That's good... Nice dressings... Excellent, I can see the bullet in his leg went right through and missed the bone… Did you clean the wound?… Whiskey? That's fine… Saline solution?… I understand…"

Every time he said "good" or "fine" Celia felt her hopes ratchet up another notch. The doctor had been working his way along Roy's body and was now bent over his face. He glanced up at Celia over his shoulder. "I won't examine his eye until I've disinfected my hands. Are you sure you are strong enough to lift him? I could shout out and get men from the saloon to help."

"No…" Celia bit her lip. "He's been living on the wrong side of the law. The fewer people see him the better…" She drew a shaky breath. "It won't make a difference to how you care for him, will it? He is a good man at heart."

The young doctor spoke very quietly, not looking at her. "I believe all men are good at heart. If a man goes bad, it is because something robbed him of the chance to be good." Carefully, he rolled Roy onto his back. "You take his feet. I'll take his shoulders."

They heaved the inert body into the air, slid him down from the wagon bed and carried him into the house. When Celia fretted over jolting him, the doctor smiled.

"Don't worry so much. He's been bouncing in the wagon for hours. A little jolt now will make no difference." Inside the hallway, he lifted one bare foot and kicked open the door on his right. "Through here. The treatment room is at the back."

They passed a waiting area with chairs lined against the wall and lowered Roy onto a metal gurney. "My greatest pride," the doctor said. "A gurney that rises and falls—an examining table and hospital bed combined."

He went to a pitcher and basin in the corner of the room, poured water into the basin and began washing his hands with a cake of carbolic soap. "Now, scoot. I want to look at his eye and it won't be a pretty sight. I don't want any fainting or feminine tears."

"I can help."

The doctor contemplated Celia while he spread soap along his forearms. The corners of his mouth twitched. "All right," he said. "Why don't you go and sit in that armchair." He jerked his chin to indicate a big, overstuffed recliner in the opposite corner of the room. "It will take me a minute to get ready," he added as he turned back toward the basin.

Celia collapsed into the chair, her head slumping against the padded backrest. She could hear the doctor talking in his calm, even voice. Her eyelids fluttered down. She would rest. Just for a second. The doctor's words faded into the distance. And, just as the medical man must have intended, unable to fight the exhaustion, Celia drifted off to sleep.

Chapter Sixteen

The smells of disinfectant and coffee stirred Celia into wakefulness. The young doctor, now wearing a pale blue shirt, which was clean but lacked the touch of an iron, was holding a steaming cup in front of her face. She uncurled her legs and rubbed her eyes.

The doctor proffered the cup to her. "There's breakfast, too."

Craning past him, Celia stared at the inert shape on the gurney, which now stood raised to examination height. "Is he…"

The doctor lifted his brows. "Is he dead? You don't show much confidence in my professional abilities."

Celia scrambled to her feet, almost knocking the cup out of the doctor's hand. "He's alive?"

"His pulse is steady, his breathing even. You did a good job cleaning out the bullet wounds. I don't expect those to fester. I've cauterized the flesh and sewn up the holes. The eye... I'm unable to save his sight. He'll be permanently blinded in one eye, but with any luck, if infection doesn't set in, I don't have to take the eyeball out. It won't look too bad."

"And if you have to...?" Celia hesitated. "Is it a difficult procedure?"

"It's supposed to be."

"*Supposed* to be." She suppressed a shiver of alarm. "You never have...?"

The doctor shook his head. "Never. And I hope that I never have to."

He had been standing in her way, blocking her access to the patient. Now he laid one hand on her shoulder. His tone became grave. "He is still unconscious. There is a lump on the back of his skull. I believe he must have received a severe blow to his head. I don't feel a fracture, but his brain must be swollen inside his cranium. Unconsciousness is nature's way of forcing his brain to rest while the swelling goes down."

"Will he recover?"

"I'm not God. I can't predict life and death, but according to my medical assessment he ought to recover. However, I can't guarantee that his mental faculties will return to normal. He may have memory loss. His reasoning may be impaired. He might lack full control over his body. He could have lost the ability to speak."

Celia bit hard into her lower lip. She closed her eyes, but the tears spilled free anyway. *Dear God, just let him live*, she had prayed. Once again, her mother's warning rang through her mind. *Be careful what you wish for.* She should have wished for more.

All through that day, Celia sat by Roy's bedside and talked. The doctor—Dr. Millard, from Boston, via a short spell as a junior resident at a charity hospital in New York City—believed insensate patients might be able to hear and relate to their environment.

Celia talked about her childhood, about the books she'd read. She described the ranch they would one day have. Picturing their future home in her mind, she furnished each room, down to the details of pictures on the walls, curtains in the windows, the rugs on the floor. And, when despair made one of its frequent inroads into her optimism, she pleaded with him.

"Please get well, Roy. I need you. Even more, I deserve you. Remember? *I deserve to be happy.* I yelled it at the cliffs, and the echo called it back, proving my words to be true. I deserve to be happy, but I can't be happy without you. So, you must get well. You hear me, Roy Hagan. You must get well."

The wrinkled face Celia had seen peering through a hatch when she first arrived in town belonged to a female in her sixties, the blacksmith's spinster sister, Miss Pickering. Employed as the doctor's housekeeper, Miss Pickering came in every day to clean and cook. Getting her meals served on a tray left Celia free to spend all her time talking to a man who never opened his eyes, never gave any sign that he could hear her, never showed any sign of life except the slight rising and falling of his chest.

There was only darkness. And then the pain came. It felt like a hot poker piercing his head. He tried to fall back into the darkness, tried to embrace it, but a voice called out to him, talking softly, like the sound of a cool stream rippling over stones in a creek.

The voice curled around his mind, holding him captive. He longed for the darkness, longed to escape the pain, but somehow he knew that if he let himself sink too deep into those empty shadows the voice would go away, and he could not bear the thought of being alone again, without the comfort of that soft, gentle voice.

So he fortified himself against the pain and listened. The voice grew clearer. He started to make out words. The voice talked about a home. One by one, the rooms opened up before him. His muscles twitched as he imagined taking a step, entering the house.

"Dr. Millard! Dr. Millard!"

The sudden sharp rise of the voice jarred his brain. Pain arrowed from his eye. Too much pain. Too much pain. The voice was gone now, replaced by hurried footsteps. With a sigh, Roy sank back into unconsciousness.

Again and again, he emerged out of the shadows, drawn by the voice. *Celia.* Memories flooded through him, swept over him. The voice was Celia. She was his, but not truly his. Not his. Not by the laws of man.

He fought the pain, broke through the barrier of it. *Don't move. Keep still. Absolutely still. That's the way to do it.* He slowed his breathing, put all his effort into opening his eyes.

The room was bathed in soft light. Celia sat in a wooden chair by the bedside, her unbound hair tumbling past her shoulders. Startled, she jerked upright in the seat.

"Roy? Roy? Can you hear me?"

Don't shout. It hurts. Don't shout.

Letting the air out of his lungs, he closed his eyes again.

"Dr. Millard! Dr. Millard!"

Footsteps. A man's footsteps.

Celia's anxious voice. "Dr. Millard, he opened his eyes. I am certain of it."

"Mr. Hagan?" the doctor said.

Roy didn't care to talk to a medical man. There could be no good news except that he was alive, and the pain had already assured him of that. But he couldn't bear that anxiety in Celia's voice. With supreme effort, Roy forced his eyelids to lift once more. Celia was leaning over him, looking down at him, her expression tender. He'd forgotten how luminous her gray eyes were, how glowing her skin. How red and tempting her lips, how beautiful the curve of her breasts. His gaze drifted lower, to her belly. Maybe she carried his child...

He swallowed. His tongue felt thick and clumsy, glued to the roof of his mouth. He made a small, rasping sound, managed a single word. "Water."

The doctor moved forward past Celia, filled Roy's vision. Holding a cup in one hand, the medical man scooped water into a beaker and trickled it between Roy's lips. Roy let the cool water slide down his throat and studied the doctor. Young, with neatly clipped sandy hair, regular features and an air of competence.

"Welcome back to the land of living, Mr. Hagan," the doctor said.

He wasn't quite back, Roy thought with a touch of wry humor. Not fully. Maybe he never would be. But he wasn't ready to die just yet. Revived by the small sips of water, Roy moved his lips, spoke in a hoarse voice.

"Preacher. Get a preacher."

The young medical man's face clouded. He gave a terse nod, handed the cup and beaker to Celia. "Give him more water. I'll fetch Reverend Brown. I thought…" He shrugged his shoulders. "Perhaps I placed too much confidence in my medical abilities. If your husband wishes to unburden his conscience, he may feel the end is near."

When the doctor had walked out of the room, Roy sank deeper into the thin mattress. He wanted to explain to Celia, to wipe out the worry in her eyes, but he had to preserve his strength. The pain felt like a formidable enemy, and he was too weak to fight back. Celia kept trickling water between his lips. He longed to drink in deep, greedy gulps, but he knew that raising his head would bring too much pain.

Talk. Let me hear your voice.

It was as if Celia understood, for she spoke again. "I will not let you die. Do you hear me, Roy Hagan? You are not going to die."

She looked so fierce, her brows furrowed, fire in her eyes. He wanted to smile, but his face felt too sore for it. He gathered his strength. His arm twitched, and then he lifted his hand, his fingers grazing the folds of Celia's skirt at her waist.

"Oh… I see," she said, with a note of bittersweet understanding in her tone. "You want us to be married, in case I'm with child."

He made a sound, no more than groan, and closed his eyes.

"I think there'll be plenty of time later on," Celia told him firmly. "Once you are up on your feet, we could get married in a church. I could wear a white dress and a veil. But if you really are that worried about appearances, we can do it right now, right here."

He knew she was smiling, and he wanted to see it, wanted to see her smile. He found the strength to open his eyes again. Celia was leaning over the bed, looking down into his face.

"Your eye…" She hesitated. "Can you tell that something is different?"

Baffled, he met her gaze. And figured out what she meant. He saw the world as he was used to seeing it, with only half of his vision. But he could not feel the soft piece of cotton over his left eye, or the rawhide string holding it in place.

He was not wearing his eye patch.

And yet he could not see the left side of the room.

He swallowed hard, rasped out the word. "Blind?"

"Yes." Celia nodded, her expression grave. "You have lost the sight in your left eye. And it is no longer brown. It has a kind of milky film over it. The iris looks white, or very pale blue. It is fairly close in color to your blue eye, but opaque instead of clear."

Roy opened his eyes again. Snippets of conversation from their first meeting, from when he had bid for Celia's lunch basket at the church social, drifted through his mind.

God and the Devil are fighting over me. Which do you think will win?

Why, Miss Courtwood, the Devil has already won.

Despite the news of his physical infirmity, something made him renew his attempt at a smile. Perhaps the Devil hadn't won, after all. The loss of his brown eye didn't worry him. He was already used to a limited vision, and the injury disguised the unusual feature he'd been born with, reducing the chances that his outlaw past might catch up with him.

He could hear the front door open and close, could hear footsteps outside. "You…you tell them what I want."

Celia took his hand, squeezed it. "All right. I will."

He let his eyelids flutter down. Footsteps made a trail into the room. He could smell something sweet, like hair pomade. A new voice—the boom-ing voice of a man used to bellowing out ser-mons—drifted into his consciousness.

"Is he the patient who needs to unburden his mind?"

Roy felt that inner smile again. Too tired to move, too tired to speak, he listened while Celia explained. "Reverend, I'm afraid I haven't been quite honest about our marital status. We're mar-ried, but only in an Indian fashion. We would like you to marry us properly, in the eyes of the law as well as in the eyes of God."

Roy barely stayed awake long enough to say "I do." And although he didn't hear Celia say her vows, it didn't matter. He'd make her repeat it later, just for him, without a preacher present to intrude on the occasion.

Roy lay in bed and watched Celia carry in a tray, preparing to feed him. He was conscious the whole time now, but his memory was hazy and he found it difficult to concentrate. The physi-cal inactivity was making him edgy and restless.

He spoke in a low voice. "I'm sorry. You nursed your parents. It's not fair that you should have to nurse me, too."

"It's good for a woman to feel needed."

Roy mulled over the comment. Celia could have no idea of how much he needed her. Not

just to spoon food into his mouth or clean up after
him. To fill his days with a reason for living. To
offer him the love and acceptance he had lacked
his entire life. But when he'd dreamed of a future
with her, he'd seen himself as a protector, a pro-
vider. Not an invalid who sometimes forgot his
own name. He'd been right to think she'd be better off without him, and having broken away from
the outlaw life had not changed the truth of it.

Despite Roy's initial pessimism, his recovery
continued until he was able to stay on his feet all
day. Before discharging him, Dr. Millard gave
him one final examination.

"You will suffer from headaches and dizziness
for several weeks, but it will pass. I believe your
brain injury was moderate and caused no permanent damage."

Roy waited for the doctor to leave the room.
Sitting sideways on the gurney, he pulled on his
clothes. Celia was moving about, packing away
their belongings. She snapped the jaws of her carpetbag shut and walked over to him, holding out
his gun belt.

Roy hesitated. "A double rig is the mark of a
gunfighter."

"Not all gunfighters are outlaws. It is better to
be prepared."

He took the gun belt from her, strapped it

around his hips and felt the familiar weight of the heavy Smith & Wesson revolvers. While he'd been convalescing, he'd had plenty of time to think, and despite the haziness of his mind, he had reached a decision.

"I'll escort you to Winslow and leave you there. Without knowing what happened to Mr. Smith, it will be too dangerous for us to remain together. I can't risk someone coming after me and getting you involved in a gunfight."

Celia stood in front of him, shoulders squared, girded for battle. "You promised we'd go away together. Someplace where no one can find us. Someplace far away."

Roy had planned for the conversation, had his excuse ready. "I'm in no state to go rattling in a wagon to Montana or Oregon. It will be weeks, maybe months before my strength returns. And by then, you might be heavy with child."

"Women give birth on the trail."

"Not you. Not my child." Roy dropped to his feet, stepped up to Celia and curled his hands around her upper arms. "If we did make a baby on that last night at the hideout, I don't want our child to be shunned like I was. I want him to have a better start in life than I did. I want him to be loved and accepted. To have a home."

"We have a home. My father's house in Rock Springs." Celia looked up at him, a frown on her face. "I've been thinking…if we go to Montana or Oregon, we'll live the rest of our lives wondering if someone will track us down. I believe that we should face the dangers now. Meet our fate and be done with it. We should go home."

"*You* should go home. I should disappear."

Celia shook her head, her mouth pressed into a stubborn line. When she spoke, her tone rang with mockery. "Roy Hagan, the fierce outlaw. What a coward you are. Don't you remember anything? You promised to have courage. To have the courage to love me. Love me openly, whatever happens."

"That whatever could be someone coming after me."

"Then you'll serve your time and I'll be there when you get out of prison."

Roy hesitated. He'd known it was a futile argument. He didn't really have the determination to ride out and leave Celia behind. Perhaps he had brought up the idea in order to satisfy his conscience, rather than from any real expectation that Celia would agree.

He tightened his hold on her upper arms and studied her face. His chest constricted at what he saw there. Such courage. Such optimism. Such beauty. Such faith. Faith in him.

"Celia…" He spoke haltingly. "When you said that a woman likes to feel needed… I may no longer need you to nurse me, or help me to remember things, but I still need you." He withdrew one of his hands and laid it across his heart. "I need you here."

"I know," Celia replied softly. "Perhaps I've known since the day you bid for my lunch basket at the church social."

Roy bundled her against his chest and held her in a fierce hug. But even as they embraced, worry threaded through his mind. Celia had been thinking like an honest citizen, assuming the only danger was from the law catching up with him. She was forgetting about Mr. Smith—that the greatest danger came not from the county sheriff but from the outlaw leader who had sworn never to let any of the men in the Red Bluff Gang break away.

To Celia's amazement, everything in Rock Springs looked exactly the same. Of course, she'd barely been away for two months, although it felt like a lifetime. She craned her neck, looking left and right as Roy steered the wagon along Main Street, with the saddle horses trotting behind.

They rounded the corner. Her heart was thudding, her hands clasped into fists as she searched ahead. The house seemed intact! The shutters were closed, the boards that secured the front door firmly in place. She waited impatiently while Roy turned the wagon into the narrow driveway by the house and brought it to a halt.

He set the brake, climbed down and reached up to lift her to the ground. "I'll put Dagur and Baldur in the stable first, before I unhitch the wagon team."

"Do you mind if I run up to the mercantile and check for any news?"

"You go along. Is there a crowbar in the wood-shed?"

"There is, unless someone has stolen it."

Her feet tapping with eager steps against the dusty ground, Celia hurried back to Main Street. While Roy had been convalescing, she hadn't dared to post a letter to her father, in case the address for Yuma prison started someone asking unwelcome questions.

The mercantile door was closed to keep out the cool winter air. She pushed the door open, sent the bell jangling above. Two women were waiting at the counter. They turned around to see who had entered. Celia recognized Mrs. Haslet, a tall, thin woman of sour disposition, and Mrs. Shackleton, the rotund, good-humored widow who ran the boardinghouse.

Mrs. Haslet stared at her. "Miss Celia! Your scar, it's gone."

Celia lifted her chin. "Perhaps the Devil didn't want me, after all."

"I never…" The thin woman cleared her throat and fell into an awkward silence.

Mrs. Shackleton took over. "We didn't believe what the bishop said. Not really."

"But you were too cowardly to say so?" Celia retorted.

With a rustle of skirts, the two women scurried out, leaving their errands unfinished. Celia watched them go. Something swelled inside her, a new sense of confidence. When she had first seen Roy, she'd wondered about his secret, how he could face the world so unflinchingly. Whatever the source of his strength, she too possessed it now.

She turned toward Mr. Selden. "I apologize for my sharp tongue. It seems that I have scared away your customers."

The neatly dressed old man took down his glasses. "They'll be back. And it's their own shame that chased them out." He glanced between the aisles to make sure the store was empty. "It's not my place to gossip, but we heard the bishop has been dismissed. He was caught embezzling church funds."

"I see." Celia's lips twisted into a rueful smile.

"Everyone is ashamed of how they treated you. They are even prepared to forgive your father's involvement in the bank robbery. They reckon he was left with no choice, having to secure your future. Only don't go flouting his ill-gotten gains. That might put their backs up again."

Celia found no suitable reply and remained silent. They had sold most of the trade goods in the wagon to a storekeeper in the boomtown. With the elevated prices paid in such places, they had just over a thousand dollars left in total, even after having settled the doctor's bill.

The bell jangled again. Celia looked over her shoulder, saw Roy enter.

Mr. Selden's expression brightened. "Hello, stranger. Welcome back."

She moved to stand beside Roy. "Not a stranger. He's my husband now."

"Husband?" Mr. Selden beamed. "You'd best introduce him, then."

Celia studied Mr. Selden carefully, saw no suspicion in his manner. Her nerves tightened. Was this how they would live from now on? Watching everyone, suspicious of everything, always on guard? Without thinking, she pressed the flat of her palm against her belly, as if to protect the unborn child she hoped might be growing there.

Roy stepped forward. "We talked it through. I never knew my pa, so we've decided I'll take Celia's name, as a way of honoring her father. So it's Mr. and Mrs. Courtwood. The given name's Roy, but it's best if you call me Courtwood."

Mr. Selden replaced his glasses, peered through

them. "Son, I see you've given up your eye patch. It don't look too bad. Not like the hollow of an empty socket."

"Celia prefers it uncovered."

She tugged at his sleeve. "What did you come in for?"

"A crowbar. Couldn't find the one in the shed."

They bought a large crowbar, and a few items of food. After they had paid for their purchases and were preparing to leave, Mr. Selden ducked beneath the counter. "Almost forgot. A letter came for you a few days ago. Mrs. Dudley at the post office wrote *gone away* on it and wanted to send it back, but I claimed it and kept it for you."

He handed her a small, worn envelope. It bore an official stamp of the Yuma Territorial Prison. As Celia studied her name and address on top, a hollow sensation knotted in her stomach. For instead of her father's bold, ornate handwriting, the address was printed with the neat, regular letters that came from a typewriter.

Celia stood on the porch and waited while Roy levered away the boards at the entrance and unlocked the front door. The house smelled musty inside. She hurried through to unbolt the back door, flung it open and cast a forlorn look over the wilted flowers and the dried-up vegetable patch in the garden.

While Roy unloaded the goods in the wagon, she settled at the kitchen table and took out the letter. Carefully, she tore the flap open and scanned the text. A wail of grief caught in her throat. Her father was dead. The letter was from the prison doctor. Her eyes fell on the final paragraph and she stared at it until tears blurred the words.

Your father died with a smile on his face. In his hands he clutched the letter in which you told him that you were safely settled and married to a horse wrangler.

I have seen many men die—some from illness, some from injury, some at the end of a rope—and, Miss Courtwood, I can assure you of this: when your father passed away, he was at peace.

With a sob, Celia pressed the letter to her chest. A sense of relief flowed over her, blunting the edge of her grief. Whatever happened, she could draw comfort from the fact that by marrying Roy she had eased her father's fears for her future, had granted him his final wish.

Life became what they had always dreamed of. They shopped at the mercantile, went to church on Sundays. Neighbors greeted them in the street. Roy got a job at the livery stable, helping the elderly owner, Mr. Romney, who suffered from stiff joints. Slowly, acceptance grew around them, tentative and thin, but it was something they could build on.

As the weeks went by, Celia became certain she was pregnant, and the news gave joy to both of them. And yet, at night, when they lay in bed together, Celia clung to Roy, trying to dispel the fear that haunted her.

They had no means of knowing what had happened at the outlaw hideout. If there had been something in the newspapers, they had missed it while Roy lay unconscious. Was Dale Hunter dead? Had Mr. Smith resumed his respectable existence in Prescott? Did he know they had escaped? Was he looking for them? Did he know where to find them?

One afternoon, while Celia was cooking supper, Mr. Selden hurried over to the house. Not pausing to wipe away the smear of dust on his spectacles, he stared at Celia as she faced him on the doorstep.

"A stranger passed by the store." Mr. Selden spoke with an uncustomary mix of urgency and doubt. "He was asking questions about a man called Roy Hagan who wears a black patch over one eye. I told him… I didn't notice until after… he had a star pinned to his chest. He was a federal marshal. I hope I didn't do wrong."

Celia's mind shut down, as if her brain had suddenly ceased functioning. She could hear her own voice, dull and flat, like a machine talking. "No. Nothing wrong. Thank you for letting us know."

Slowly, she closed the door and leaned against it. For what felt like hours, she remained on that single spot, unmoving. Roy found her there when he came home from work. In the kitchen, the pot on the stove had boiled dry, the smell of burning vegetables thick in the air.

"What's wrong?" Frantic, Roy stared at her. "Are you hurt?"

"No." She found her voice. "It's not me. It's you. The law is after you."

She told him about Mr. Selden's visit, about the federal marshal.

"Fine," Roy said. His shoulders shifted in a small shrug that was exaggerated in its nonchalance. "That's what you wanted all along. For me to turn myself in, so we can one day live without listening to every sound in the night, spending each day worrying that someone might come at me with their guns drawn."

"No." She flung her arms around him, clung tight. She breathed in the scent of him, leather and hay and horses, so achingly familiar. Each evening, it marked his return from the livery stable. The prospect of him gone filled her with an aching loneliness she could not bear.

"That was before I… I can't… I can't be without you now. We'll pack up. We'll go away. Right now. Tonight. You can harness the wagon horses while I pack."

Roy eased their bodies apart. "We can't run. Not with you pregnant."

"Then you run, find some remote place to hide. I'll join you after the baby comes."

"It's not what I want, Celia. It's not what *you* want. Remember what you promised me. That you'll have the courage to love an outlaw. Love him openly, and pay the price for it. Well, it seems the bill collector is knocking on the door."

Celia swallowed. "I'm not as brave as I ought to be. I don't want to be alone. And I don't want to have to deal with the scorn of the townspeople again. They'll turn against me if they see you hauled away in iron chains."

"You won't be on your own, Celia. You'll have a baby. Our baby. Something to fight for. A creature more vulnerable than yourself to keep safe. And you're stronger than you believe. When you think it through, your only crime is to love me. If people hold that against you, against the child, they're wrong. You will face them with your head high and find some other place where you and the baby won't be shunned because of me. You'll have plenty of money, enough for a fresh start somewhere else."

Celia frowned. "I know... I know... But why allow us to be separated? Why not escape? If the outcome is that I'll have to find some other place where I can raise our child free of prejudice, why don't we both go and seek a new start?"

Roy shook his head. He spoke softly, a wistful expression on his face. "Sometimes it's good to live for the moment. But sometimes it is better to look ahead, think of the future. And do you really want a lifetime of looking over your shoulder, of never sleeping at ease, of being suspicious of every stranger, of having to lie to our child? You said it yourself when we returned to Rock Springs. Let's face it now and get it over with."

On and on, they argued, neither of them convincing the other. Twilight fell outside. They went into the kitchen, threw away the burned supper and had some bread and cheese instead.

"Go," Celia said to Roy as darkness fell outside. "Go now. Go, and write to me, and I'll join you as soon as it is safe to travel with the baby."

Roy rose from his seat, knelt beside her chair and wrapped his arms around her. "I want one more night with you. We'll decide in the morning if I should go, or stay and pay whatever price the law wants to extract for my outlaw past."

Celia awoke to a loud banging at the front door. Beside her, Roy lay with his eyes open, already in full awareness. "They are here," she whispered. "Go out through the back door while I delay them."

With a faint smile, Roy shook his head. He'd never intended to run, Celia realized. Her eyes roamed over his features as she recalled all the dangers he had warned her about. What if they pinned other crimes on him? If the judge was a cruel, unjust man? How long would he be away? Would he survive the dangers in prison?

Feeling helpless, Celia watched as Roy got out of bed, pulled his trousers on and headed down the stairs. She swung her feet down, bundled herself in a wrapper and hurried after him.

Roy had already opened the front door, and in the thin dawn light Celia could see a small man standing on the porch. Behind him, a lathered horse was puffing and heaving, evidence of how hard the man had ridden to get there.

Eyes wide, she watched as Roy closed the door again. When he turned, he was holding an envelope. Not daring to ask, she waited. He tore the flap open, pulled out a folded sheet of paper. A slow smile spread across his face.

"So that's what the president's signature looks like."

He handed the piece of paper to her. She read the words out loud. "Certificate of Pardon... For services to the United States Government and the Territory of Arizona… Chester Arthur, President of the United States… Dale Hunter, Deputy United States Marshal…"

Stunned, she looked up. "Dale Hunter lives. He did it. You're free."

"No," Roy said, still smiling. "I'll never be free again, and I don't want to be. I'm tied to a wife and child. A house that is a home. A town filled with people willing to call me a friend." He moved closer to her, drew her into his embrace. "For the first time in my life, I belong. I'm no longer alone. I love you, and I'll live with you, and when I die I'll be buried beside you. That's all a man can dream of. A place to lay down roots, to make a life. An honest life."

Epilogue

The sun was setting when Celia came home from the mercantile. In truth, her wages from the two hours she worked every afternoon made little difference to their finances, but she enjoyed being a part of the community, building up friendships.

As she rounded the corner, she spotted the post office messenger stepping down from the porch of their house. Thank heavens she no longer needed to fear every letter or telegram. However, even after three years of peaceful living, her hand instinctively settled over the bump at her waistline in a protective gesture. This time, Roy was convinced it would be a boy, but secretly Celia hoped for another girl.

At the front door, the succulent scent of roasting meat greeted her. One benefit of marrying an outlaw, Celia thought wryly. A man used to living alone knew how to take care of the necessities, including cooking.

"I'm back!" she called.

"In the kitchen!" Roy called back.

The sight that met her sent a wave of joy through Celia. Freya, dressed in a clean dress, her golden curls shining in the evening light, was sitting on the kitchen table. Roy was bent over the child, with both of them peering into a leather pouch.

As Celia stood watching them, Freya lifted one clenched fist and spread her fingers open. A cascade of gold coins fell with a tinkle back inside the pouch.

"Freya," Celia blustered. "What on earth are you doing?"

The child looked up, blue eyes shining. "Play with Papa's money."

For an instant, the surge of emotion kept Celia silent. How could happiness be so complete? Perhaps unhappy years taught a person to appreciate good fortune all the more when it finally arrived.

When Freya was born, she had blue eyes. But according to the midwife, all babies had blue eyes. Anxiously, they had watched the child grow. More than two years old now, they knew Freya had not inherited the distinctive feature that had caused Roy so much grief.

"Do we have enough?" Celia asked, indicating the money pouch on the table.

"A mite over three thousand dollars."

She pursed her mouth. The exact amount was

three thousand two hundred and seventy-one dollars, and Roy must be aware she could name the figure without counting. "But is it enough?" she pressed him.

"Jones, that newcomer from the East, is offering four thousand."

With a sigh, Celia stepped closer. Ike Romney, who owned the livery stable where Roy worked, was getting on in years and wished to sell the business. Ever since Roy received his pardon, it had been his dream to buy out Romney.

Dipping her fingers into the pouch, Celia stirred the pile of gold pieces inside. "I'm sorry," she said. "I wish I could have done better, but it is difficult to make money without access to the ticker tape. Not getting instant stock quotes means I'm missing out on the best opportunities."

The child grabbed a handful of coins and tossed them in the air with a squeal of delight.

"Freya, don't throw Papa's money around," Celia scolded.

"It's Mama's money, too," Roy commented, ruffling his daughter's hair with one hand while collecting the scattered coins with the other. "And it just might be enough."

"Enough?" Celia stared at him. "But how can it be, if Jones is offering more?"

"Ike Romney has no place to go. Jones is living at the boardinghouse, and he wants to take over the rooms at the back of the livery stable. Romney will let me have the business for three thousand, provided I employ him part-time and let him live there."

"Employ him?" Celia lifted her brows. They both knew Ike Romney suffered from arthritis so badly he could barely get around. Memories of her father's illness drifted through her mind. Just like her father, the poor man had little hope of finding any other employment. "Of course," she said with a gentle nod.

Roy spoke quietly. "In truth, it would be more like a pension. But a man has a right to feel valued. And Romney has no family. This way, he can remain part of the business and know he won't be turned out to die alone." Roy looked up, his blue eye bright, contrasting with the opaque white of his blind eye. "Romney just wants to belong. And every man has a right to that. To belong."

"I understand." Celia gave a wistful smile. "And considering I have nursed two dying parents, I can handle taking care of a cranky old man when the time comes." Her attention fell on the telegram peeking out of Roy's shirt pocket. "I saw the post office messenger. Is it not from the stock exchange?"

"It's from Dale Hunter."

"Dale Hunter!" Celia gripped the edge of the

table to steady herself. Memories of that horrible day in the canyon filled her senses—the heat and dust, the sound of gunfire, the smell of blood.

Since Roy's pardon, Dale Hunter had never contacted them, but they had heard gossip about him—a Deputy US Marshal who had been left for dead in the desert, buzzards and coyotes fighting over his carcass, tearing out pieces of him.

Roy pulled out the telegram and glanced at it. "He's leaving the Marshals Service to become a rancher. He has one final job to do, here in the Arizona Territory. He is letting us know that he plans to stop by and say hello."

Celia swallowed. "I wonder… How badly is he scarred…? I mean…" She made a small, helpless gesture with her hand. From the bleak expression on Roy's face, Celia knew he understood. They had both been ostracized because of physical flaws. Had the same fate befallen their friend?

"I don't know." Roy gave a hesitant shrug. "I've seen his name in the newspapers, but there has never been a photograph. His high-born mother expected him to move back East and marry a debutante and live off the family fortune, but it seems Dale would have none of it. I believe it caused a rift between them."

For a moment, silence fell over the kitchen, Freya, sensing the somber mood, huddled against her father's chest. Absently, Roy wrapped one arm around the girl and spoke to Celia over the child's head. "However Dale looks, it will make no difference to who he is."

"Of course it won't," Celia replied. "He is your oldest friend. We owe him our lives. He was prepared to die so we could live. And we have him to thank for your pardon." She whirled around, snatched an apron from a peg on the wall, grabbed a bucket from the counter and dashed to the back door.

"Where are you going?" Roy called out after her.

"To fetch water from the well. I want to scrub the guestroom…air the bedding…perhaps there'll be enough time to sew new curtains…" Celia hurried out into the twilight. Behind her, she could hear her husband's murmured voice, telling their child a story about a brave knight called Dale Hunter who rode a fine horse and had once upon a time saved their lives, allowing them all to live happily-ever-after. With a smile, Celia touched the gold coin in a silk pouch around her neck. Her talisman, a promise that their happiness would last.

* * * * *

MILLS & BOON

Coming next month

A KISS AWAY FROM SCANDAL
Christine Merrill

Hope turned back to the mirror, and flashed a smile that would blind a duke at twenty paces. Then, the curtsey. "Good evening, my Lord." This time, she dipped deeper and felt an embarrassing tremble in her front knee. She was nearly one and twenty, but hardly infirm. She could do better. She must do better.

She tried again. "Good evening, my Lord."

"I should think good morning would be more appropriate. It is not yet eleven."

She stumbled at the sound of a voice behind her and raised her eyes to see the reflection of the stranger who had entered the room as she practiced.

It was he.

Who else but the Earl of Comstock would be wandering around the house unintroduced, as if he owned it? In a sense, he did.

"And I have no title."

"As of yet," she said. There was no longer a need to practice her smile. When she looked at him, it came naturally. Who would not be happy in the presence of such a handsome man? Though she had never been one to dote on the male form, his was perfectly proportioned, neither too tall nor too short, with slim hips and broad shoulders on which rested the head of a Roman God. His blond hair was cut a la Brutus, curling faintly at the fringe that framed a noble brow, unmarked by signs of worry. His grey eyes were intelligent, his smile sympathetic.

Praise God, she had been delivered just the man she'd prayed would come: young, handsome, and judging by the twinkle that shone in those beautiful eyes as he looked at her, single. But not for long, if she had her way.

He tilted his head. "You are correct. I have no title, as of yet. Nor am I likely to get one. But they are sometimes awarded to men whose service merits them, and I am not yet thirty. With time and effort, anything is possible, Miss Strickland."

She steadied herself from the shock and turned to face him with as much grace as possible, struggling to maintain the expression she'd been practising in the mirror. "Then you are not my cousin from America?"

"The future Earl of Comstock?" His smile softened. "Unfortunately, no." He bowed from the waist. "Gregory Drake, at your service, Miss Strickland."

Continue reading
A KISS AWAY FROM SCANDAL
Christine Merrill

Available next month
www.millsandboon.co.uk

LET'S TALK
Romance

For exclusive extracts, competitions
and special offers, find us online:

f facebook.com/millsandboon

⊙ @millsandboonuk

𝕐 @millsandboon

Or get in touch on 0844 844 1351*

For all the latest titles coming soon, visit
millsandboon.co.uk/nextmonth